THE BROKEN CROWN

AMORY CANNON

The Broken Crown
Copyright © 2016 by Amory Cannon

Cover design ©Jennifer Zemanek/Seedlings Design Studio 2016

Printed in the United States of America

Library of Congress Cataloging-in-Publication data
Cross, Amryn.
The broken crown /Amory Cannon.
p. cm.

Summary: Emilia, an exiled princess turned warrior, must attempt to win the affection of the Imperial Prince if she hopes to restore Christianity to her pagan kingdom. She faces a choice between the life she was born for and the one God called her to. Both of which could mean death.

ISBN 978-1500736873
1. Kings, queens, rulers, etc. —Fiction. 2. Christianity —Fiction. 3. Love — Fiction. 4. War —Fiction. I. Title.

First Edition, 2016

www.AmoryCannon.com

For my sister, Salem, who read my first stories and encouraged me anyway.

Blessed be the Lord, my rock, who trains my hands for war, and my fingers for battle…

The King will desire your beauty. Because He is your Lord, bow down to Him.

From the lost Aletheia

DAUGHTERS OF ATLAS

ZEPHYROS
CASSIA- PRINCESS OF ZEPHYROS
GLORIANA- PRINCESS OF ZEPHYROS
OCTAVIA- LADY OF DUBRIS
BELLA- COUNTESS OF LEODIS
CLARISSA- COUNTESS OF VECTIS

AUSTRINA
DAVINA- PRINCESS OF AUSTRINA
AUGUSTA- LADY OF PRAETORIUM
VICTORIA- LADY OF ANAVIO

BOREALIS
EMILIA- PRINCESS OF BOREALIS

EUROS
CORDELIA- PRINCESS OF EUROS
LIVIA- PRINCESS OF EUROS
JULIANA- LADY OF CORIA
FELICIANA- LADY OF DEVA

PROLOGUE

The sky is blacker than I've seen it at noon. Normally at this time I'd be inside eating a pastry from the kitchen and looking over my lessons. But today isn't normal. It's anything but.

My father, King Alector of Borealis, stands beside me on the dais overlooking the courtyard where a large portion of our kingdom has gathered. His hand rests heavy on my shoulder, and though I want to hide my face in his thick robes, I don't dare. It's not a gesture he'd welcome.

Still, I tip my chin up to study my father. He surveys the crowd with a solemn scowl and tightens his grip on me. A squeak parts my lips before I can quell it.

"Emilia." His eyes turn to me now, and I feel as if he's surveying me, studying me for signs of the same disease that's tainted my mother. "I know this is hard for you, but it is the law."

Harsh is the law, but it is the law. I've memorized those words from the Codex—the laws set forth by the first Emperor of Atlas to protect us from the Insurgos who wait on the fringes to overthrow each of the six kingdoms. The threat of rebellion has been instilled in me since I was born. The Emperor who ruled before the current one insisted anyone showing signs of Insurgo sympathies be driven from our cities. My grandfather and the kings of the other countries burned the sacred book, the Aletheia, and slaughtered thousands in the Great Crusade. They burned the bodies on a pyre as a sacrifice to our gods.

"Please, father. Mother is no threat to you." I've waited for the right moment to appeal to him on my mother's behalf, but it never came. Now I'm out of time.

"Hush, girl." He raises his hand but doesn't strike me. There are too many people watching. Though he is king and people fear him, I am the precious princess they adore. "Your mother is queen. What better position for the Insurgos to use her to overthrow my kingdom? She made no effort to hide her prayers to their God."

It's true. I first heard my mother pray when I sat at her feet while she braided my hair. Not the sort of memorized prayers we recite in the temple, but a conversation with someone I couldn't see. The cadence of her voice, the magical quality that saturated the room—I felt light as a feather when she prayed.

Not until my father's guards burst into the room one night and pulled my mother from me did I realize there was anything strange about her prayers. It was the religion of the Insurgos, who believe in a single God and threaten the sanctity of everything this empire was built on. According to my father, their Aletheia and their philosophy revolve around conquering and ruling those who have been set above them.

The crowd below us roars, and I look away from my father to see the masses part and a small faction of the King's Guard lead their prisoner toward the small stone circle in the center of the courtyard. A large wooden stake towers over everyone except me and my father who stand above it all. My father says he feels closer to the gods up here. I could not feel further away.

My mother's head hangs low as she follows behind the guards. Still, I see her lips move, and I feel her prayers surround me. There has to be something, anything...

Fight! Screaming at her won't save her, and the bit of self-preservation I have reminds me my father probably wouldn't hesitate to burn me as well. Already I'm a problem for him. Without a queen in residence, my position as princess is precarious. If he remarries, my line of succession will be invalid.

It's rare to see my mother without her crown, and her bare, dark head looks common in comparison to her usual splendor. But my father already made show of stripping her of her crown. Now he'll execute her as a commoner.

Everything in me strains toward her, but my feet remain firmly planted on the wooden dais. There's nothing I can do. Nothing.

She doesn't resist as they lead her to the center of the stone circle and stretch her arms around the wood pillar. This is wrong. No matter what my father says, no matter what the law says, I feel it in my bones.

This God she believes in, he'll save her, won't he? But I don't know this God so I'm not sure what to expect. Perhaps he'll just receive her death as an offering like our gods do. Maybe she'll walk through the fire like in the stories she used to tell me about the three men thrown in a furnace.

A mixture of gasps and cheers rises from the masses as a guard lowers his torch to hover just above the hay and kindling surrounding my mother, all soaked in oil to consecrate the offering to our gods. Then all eyes turn to my father.

"Alexandra Aurelius, you have been found guilty of heresy against our high god Caelus and his court. Additionally, you are guilty of high treason against your husband, King of Borealis, and His Imminence Emperor Cyrus of Atlas for your collusion with the Insurgo rebels. For these crimes you have been sentenced to burn at the stake. May Caelus have mercy on you."

He recites my mother's sentence without any emotion, which only makes the tears in my eyes fall harder.

I can barely see through the blur they create, and I'm grateful for that much. Because I don't see them light the fire, but I hear the whoosh of the flames as they lick the oil anointing the altar.

By the time I clear my vision and fix my eyes on where my mother once stood, flames roar as high as the heavens. I can't stop the scream, the plea, that tears from my throat, and only my father's hands on my shoulders keep me from running toward the fire.

She's already gone. I feel it in my chest where the lightness used to live. I don't know this God she loved, but I do know he's dangerous. Maybe my mother didn't know just how dangerous. Maybe she did. But I don't want to believe that, because that means she loved him more than she loved me. Enough to die for him instead of living for me.

Why couldn't she stay with me?

As the flames from my mother's sacrifice kiss the sky, I wipe my tears away and vow I'll never bow to death as she did. I won't go down without a fight.

1

This man must die. And I must be the one to kill him.

Tension knots between my shoulders as I pace the length of my tent as if to escape the thoughts or the responsibility. Outside the sturdy canvas walls, my fellow soldiers jeer the man who sneaked into our camp last night. A man I know. If only I'd let them kill him last night, his blood would not be on my hands. Now I have no choice.

God, steady my hands and my heart.

Shoulders thrown back and chin raised, I smooth my tunic and adjust the sword on my waist. Then, with a deep breath, I lift the flap on my tent. "Bring the spy to me."

All eyes turn to me, full of irritation and expectations. They won't refuse me, even if they don't know who I really am. They respect me—or rather, they respect Nox. I gave them a new name to go along with my new identity, and since then I've proven myself here, which makes the crown I've hidden away in my pack superfluous.

Milo, the only soldier stationed here longer than my seven years, jerks the disheveled captive from his knees and shoves him toward my tent.

Tipping my chin higher, I refuse to look at the beaten man's face, at least not yet. There will be time for that in a moment. Instead, I stop Milo's forward progress with a raised hand and meet his hard stare with a steely one of my own. My pulse pounds as it always does when he looks at me like that—as if he sees me for what I really am.

"Give me a minute alone with him." It's not a request, but Milo doesn't immediately acquiesce to my demand.

"This is dangerous, Nox." His dark eyes spark like flint, ready to ignite a well-known temper. "You can't be alone with him."

"Come now." I force a sly, sweet smile to compliment my syrupy tone. For the most part, I avoid any appearance of femininity because it's dangerous in a camp full of men. However, situations like this require some finesse, and my mother taught me never to underestimate the power of a smile and female charms. "You can't possibly think I'm in danger from him."

It's ludicrous. Milo trained me from the time I arrived at this military outpost, a scrawny ten-year-old who could barely hold a sword. I've worked hard to become what I am, an elite soldier who can best anyone in the camp with the exception of Milo. This prisoner, an older man, would be no match.

"Well, no. I'm sure you're in no danger." Milo drags his eyes from me to the prisoner, then back. "But what could you possibly want with him?"

I take a deep breath and hope my lie will be convincing. "You never mastered the art of interrogation. He may have some information to relay before we dispatch him."

Not that I'm a skilled interrogator or orator. But only this prisoner knows me for who I am, what I've truly become. Though I have only a few clumsy words to offer him, I will do it in private.

Milo seems pacified with my answer and turns his back as I lift my tent flap so the prisoner can pass through. Only when satisfied the soldiers won't challenge me do I duck inside the tent.

"Levi," I whisper as I take in the slumped man before me. Though his posture speaks of the beatings he received, his green eyes remain bright. "What are we going to do?"

The first time I stumbled across him while on patrol in the nearby forest, I nearly put an arrow through him. He'd worn the mark of the Insurgos—an embroidered red cross—on his sleeve and carried a sword. But he'd knelt to pray, and instead of killing him, I listened.

When I first professed my belief in Jesus and the God of the Insurgos, a large, wide expanse opened up in my chest, filling every crevice with warmth. The warmth has since faded, but the largeness remains. Only twice have I felt as warm and safe as I did in those first days—once as I prayed on the battlefield, and then a secret moment alone in my tent as I held my crown. There's no rhyme or reason to it, and that only makes the restlessness in my chest more troubling. It's a new feeling, and I don't know what it means.

"You're going to kill me." Levi's words feel as firm and unyielding as my shield lying on my cot. Unlike my shield, they do not deflect the pain. "It's the only way."

"It can't be." I resume my pacing, mind frantic with possible escape routes. But with all the soldiers nearby, all of them hold certain death. I might escape, but Levi would slow me down, and there is no reason for me to leave if he isn't with me.

"I knew when I came to you last night that I would die. And it is an honorable death if you heed my message."

"I don't want a message," I snap. "I want to find a way to get you out of here."

"So you could be caught helping me?" Levi raises gray-tinged brows. I've always thought he had an ageless quality about him, but he looks older now, as if he decays before my eyes. "We can't both die, Princess. You have a higher calling."

The use of my title, so unfamiliar for the last seven years, stills my movements. Levi knew who I was the moment he saw me. I look too much like my mother—same ebony hair, dark eyes, tanned olive skin—who he knew well, for him to think otherwise. Now that my mother is dead, and I'm exiled until my father is assured I don't share my mother's sentiments, Levi has been a piece of home I hadn't known I missed.

And now I have to kill him.

"What's the message?" He's given me so many messages over the years, words that opened my heart to the true and living God. Words that could get us both killed in Borealis or any of the other kingdoms of Atlas where Christianity was outlawed fifty years ago.

"Don't be afraid," he whispers as he clasps his gnarled hand around my slender one. His fingers bite into my skin. "The whole of Atlas will nip at our heels soon. The Emperor won't allow us to survive. You can be the one to save us all. That is why you must embrace what's coming. You are who you are, you've been placed here, for such a time as this."

The restless wings in my chest flutter madly in response to Levi's words. For a brief moment, I feel they might actually give me flight. It's not the lightness I felt when my mother prayed, or even when I sometimes pray, but the sort of dizziness that makes me feel I'm already high above the ground. It sounds like the Aletheia, perhaps one of the few passages Levi memorized before my grandfather and the other kings burned the scrolls years before. He gives me bits of what he recalls each time we meet in secret in the forest. But what is important enough about this one to cost him his life?

"Oh, Levi." My shoulders slump, and I pull my hand from his and sink back on my cot. Moisture pools in my eyes. How could he be so misguided? "I'm no deliverer."

"You are the princess of Borealis."

"And my mother was the queen. That didn't stop her execution when they learned she was a Christian. I'm here because my father wants to break me before he makes me his heir." *If* he makes me his heir. "He'll never welcome me back to court if I demand clemency for the Insurgos. Christianity is a death sentence in Atlas."

"Then you must appeal to the higher court."

"The Emperor would never agree to see me. I'm not even sure I hold any standing in Borealis anymore." I tangle my fingers in my braid near my scalp and pull as if the pain can clear my head. "Why can't you understand this is life and death? You risked everything for this, and it means nothing."

"You will understand one day."

"Levi." My voice breaks on his name. He needs to understand. "They'll make me kill you now. You're one of them, and the king demands no leniency be given to Insurgos."

"Yes." He nods once, a confident gesture. "If I perish, I perish. And I'm ready. You must do this, Princess. If you don't, they may suspect your loyalties, and your life will be in danger as well. This will prove your strength for what's to come."

"How can you ask me to do this?" I've killed men before, but only in battle and only those who threatened my life. Here, it does not seem right I should hold life and death in my hands.

"It is the law. And the law is harsh, but it is the law." That he quotes the Codex, the very laws I—as a princess—will be sworn to uphold, infuriates me.

"Time's up." Milo throws open my tent with no warning and fists Levi's collar. He meets my eyes with a sneer. I've never had to guess how he feels about the Insurgos—the same way he feels about the men from Zephyros who relentlessly attack our borders and would take us to war. "The crowd's gathered."

Levi's eyes hold mine as Milo drags him from the tent. Every fervent prayer I've learned rushes through me, though none pass my lips. They don't feel like enough. What to do?

"For such a time as this."

Is this really part of God's plan? Will that absolve me of the blood on my hands? I have so many questions still to ask my teacher—about God, about my mother.

With trembling hands and a heaving stomach, I exit the tent with the grace of a princess I've yet to become. If executing good men is what it means to rule this country, perhaps I never want to become her.

Soldiers gather four deep around Levi, leaving barely enough space for me to walk to him. I feel their eyes on me, a sort of hushed reverence as they wait my response. I know what is expected and so do they.

I stop in front of Levi and try to think of anything but the kind words he whispered over me and the stories he told of my mother's childhood. He's right about one thing—if I refuse to kill him, I'll be branded guilty by association. Milo found the two of us speaking last night. Levi immediately surrendered and pled guilty to treason against the crown. All before I could even wonder what he'd come to tell me.

The words come to me again, unbidden. To save us all...for such a time as this.

My fingers involuntarily curl around the sword Milo places in my hand. It fits so naturally there, as if I was born for this rather than the crown. I chance one look at Levi. This is the price for that destiny.

A low murmur rises, and it takes a moment for me to realize Levi is reciting the Aletheia. "Blessed be the Lord, my rock, who trains my hands for war and my fingers for battle. He is my—"

I take a deep breath and swing the sword with frightening precision.

Levi dies with a prayer on his lips.

Hushed whispers outside my tent wake me shortly before dawn. I know because through the small tear in my tent I've yet to mend, the black sky has softened to a lighter blue. Not light enough for me to see the blood on my hands, though I still feel it caked under my nails.

I buried Levi at dusk and told my comrades it was to keep the vultures away. Over his unmarked grave, I whispered his last words.

Now I focus on the whispers rather than the guilt that sits on my chest. Two people—Milo and one of the scouts who was on duty last night. Their low, solemn tones pull me to a sitting position with my bedroll bunched around me. If something has worried them, I dare not try to sleep through it.

My muscles protest as I silently stand—a testament to how they tensed to fight off my nightmares—but I ignore the ache as I've been trained to do. Certainly my father would be glad of that. He didn't send me here to be comfortable. Whatever his given reasons, he and I both know he sent me here in hopes I'd be killed in a skirmish with the Insurgos or our constant battles with Zephyros. A tragic end to the heir he never wanted.

I slip out the back of my tent and appear next to Milo and the scout without ceremony. The younger man starts, but Milo gives me an appreciative nod.

"Nearly perfect," he whispers. "I only heard you inside your tent, but not once you left it."

This is high praise coming from Milo but well worth my hours of training.

"More than I can say for you two," I hiss. "Can't you gossip outside someone else's tent?"

"We have visitors."

Milo's words send icy daggers through me. Has someone come looking for Levi? Are we about to be attacked? The fact that Milo hasn't raised the alarm gives me a flicker of hope. At least the attack isn't imminent.

"Who?" I finally ask as I study the face of my mentor. As always, it is hard and nearly unreadable, especially in the predawn light.

"A group of five men," the scout says as his hands ring the pommel of his sword. He presses the blade to the ground as if to casually lean against it. No self-respecting soldier would treat his weapon so flippantly. "They camp a couple of miles from here. I found them while I was scouting."

Five? Five is not considered a lucky number by the citizens of Atlas. We have six of everything because there are six gods. Caelus—the patron god—is said to bless everything in multiples of six. There is even a mock sixth kingdom—the abandoned island of Solitarius—so the gods will bless the empire. So for there to be five travelers, I can only conclude they mean to add one more to their group.

"What sort of men?" I ask. Regardless of number, it's very strange to find a band of so few so far from the city—at least three days journey. If they are looking to cross into Zephyros, the country with which we share our western border, they might have done it much further south. The only things this far north are the mountains and the sea. And of course the Insurgos.

"Imperial Guard seals on their capes. Their leader wears the pendant of the Commander of the Guard," the scout tells me with the hushed awe that most use when they reference the Emperor or any of the ruling monarchs who comprise the Atlas Empire.

I don't share his enthusiasm. There is certainly no good reason for the Imperial Guard to be this far north, not when Aurora—the seat of the Empire—shares our southern border. "What do you make of it?" I ask Milo, ignoring the scout. I don't trust any soldier who leans on his sword.

"I don't like it." He spits then wipes his mouth with the back of his hand. "But if they're headed this way, I guess we'll find out soon enough what brings them here. Though I can't think of a single thing out here that would warrant a few Imperial soldiers."

I can think of exactly one. I swallow hard and picture the crown in my bag. A tiara really—a single aquamarine stone set against white gold and pearls. If I am right, I may wear it again for the first time in seven years.

"Should we prepare to welcome the Guard?" the scout asks. He looks to Milo instead of me for the answer. I don't correct him.

After yesterday, I don't care if I ever make another important decision again.

I could see no other choice, but the feeling of wrongness still weighs heavy on me. Did my father ever feel this when he signed my mother's death warrant? Probably not, because he made me watch and swear on the crown I would not fall prey to my mother's weaker nature. That I would not blaspheme the gods in favor of the religion and revolution of the Insurgos.

But an oath is only as strong as the person who makes it, and at ten, I was weak. Though he'll probably never know it, my father did me a favor by sending me to the farthest military outpost he could think of. With little action my first few years, save the occasional Insurgo raid or sailors crossing the mountains to return home, I had plenty of time to learn the ways of a warrior. And when I met Levi, I learned the Aletheia, too.

"Ready the men," Milo commands. "I expect they'll be here soon."

I start to follow the scout, to help with the preparation to welcome the visiting dignitaries—or as close to it as we get out here—but Milo stops me with a hand on my shoulder.

"Not you. You need a bath. There's still blood under your nails. I can't have the Imperial Guard thinking I'm treating the only woman in our camp poorly."

Of course. The Guard will not know I'm capable of incapacitating any man who thought of treating me poorly. But my stomach buzzes with the fear that they will know something else about me.

I retreat to my tent and gather my things into a pack to take to the river to bathe. The sun is rising higher now, so I have no trouble winding through the familiar path in the woods to the wading pool.

My fingers tangle in my hair as I unwind the braid and let the strands hang to my waist. Normally, I would hurry through my ritual, afraid someone might see me bathing. But today I have no fear, or maybe I have too much, and so I take my time.

Though the water is icy, I let it numb me as I swim around before lathering my skin with a bar that smells of lavender. I bear surprisingly few scars from battle, but I linger over each one and wash it with care. I'm proud of them. Proof that I am stronger than when I left home.

When I am clean, I pull myself on the grassy bank and reach for my clothes. I wear the same uniform as the rest of the Borealis military—a royal blue tunic with close-fitting black pants—which I've taken in so they don't hang on my small frame. I buckle my empty weapon belt around my waist and slip into my sturdy boots. Except for my hair, which I leave undone to dry, I look just like the rest of my company.

My return trip to the camp is considerably noisier than when I left. Men scurry across the camp, cleaning our one permanent building that houses most of the supplies and hoisting our colors— a blue standard with a silver bird. The anxiety that thrummed beneath the surface all morning has come to a head. I'm about to jump in and help, when one voice rises above all the others.

"Attention! Presenting Commander Felix Fidelis, Captain of the Imperial Guard." The camp herald bows low as a great white horse and its rider pass before him. The rest of the camp follows suit, but I am frozen in place.

2

The horse is the most exquisite animal I have ever seen. Its silvery-white coat gleams with the light of the morning sun. Clearly, even on the long journey from the empire's seat in Aurora, the horse has been meticulously cared for. The stallion's every move is graceful, even more so than the four that follow it. The tack and saddle on each mount are black with sparkling gold accents. I haven't seen such finery in years. Finally, I raise my eyes to the owner of the beautiful horse.

Commander Fidelis looks nothing like I expect. Though the heavy beard that masks his face makes it difficult to tell, he appears younger than most of his companions with his unlined face and few visible scars. Certainly much too young to have risen to such a high position. The Imperial Guard is the elite force in Aurora and requires physical prowess as well as mental. Their reputation is known throughout the empire, and even the weakest soldier is better than most other nations can conjure up. Other than the Commander's age, he is nearly indistinguishable from the other guards. Even from this distance, I can tell their eyes are dark and unfriendly.

His eyes find me, and I realize I am not bowing like the rest of my camp. It seems strange to me, how circumstance dictates who is worthy to be revered. In my father's court or any court in Atlas, the Commander wouldn't warrant a second glance. He is no more than a glorified soldier. But here, among men who have never laid eyes on any royalty—or so they believe—he is almost a god.

Milo is the first to rise, and he greets the Commander with a clasp of forearms. "To what do we owe this pleasure, your grace?"

Felix Fidelis still looks at me as those around me slowly rise. I can't read his eyes so I take a bold step toward him. His lips twitch, barely visible beneath his beard, but he doesn't look away.

"I'm here under order of His Imminence, Emperor Cyrus and His Majesty, King Alector to retrieve Princess Emilia Valentina Aurelius of Borealis." His voice is strong as he recites the titles, as if he's practiced them on his long journey from the empire's capital. I, however, have not practiced a response.

"Princess?" Milo laughs and rubs the back of his neck. A few of our company echo his chuckles. "My grace, there is no princess here. I'm afraid you're mistaken. Nox is the only woman, but she's no royal. Isn't that right?"

All eyes turn to me now, and I dig my short nails into the palms of my hands. This moment feels much different than I imagined it would. And though I thought I was ready, the thought of confirming the Commander's words makes me ill. I don't wish to be the sort of princess my father expects.

But, because I have no choice, I reach into my bag and pull out the crown. A collective gasp rises from the crowd as I hold it up for them to see.

Milo's jaw drops, and the men who have just risen for Felix now stumble to their knees in front of me. I want to yell for them to stand, that I am no different than I was yesterday, but it would be a lie. Levi is dead, and I am a world away from the girl who walked into their camp seven years ago. Yesterday, I might have refused whatever the Commander asks of me, but Levi's message weighs heavy on me. Is this God's way of setting his plan in motion?

Only Commander Fidelis remains on his feet, and he walks toward me with a singular purpose. When he stops just in front of me, I see his eyes are not so dark, but rather a lighter golden brown. Still, they don't hold any warmth as he drops to his knee and bows his head.

"Rise." I choke around my command because it feels foreign in my throat. He rises then studies me with his head cocked slightly.

"You look well, my lady." To his credit, his tone remains even, but for the first time, I get a glimpse beyond the hardness of his eyes. I know what he's thinking. I don't look like any princess he's ever seen. But I have the crown, and I look like the former queen of Borealis so he can't refute me. The deep golden tones of my skin, the waves of thick black hair, dark eyes—they all mark me as unusual at best and lower class at worst. But they are my mother's traits and my birthright.

This is my moment to take charge. To show everyone I am who I say I am. *God, give me wisdom.* Levi wanted me to appeal to a higher court, and there is none higher than Emperor Cyrus. But I'll have to prove I belong in the highest courts of the land.

"You will address me as Highness." My voice is stronger this time as I meet the Commander's stare with one of my own. If he has a retort, he keeps it to himself. "I am Princess of Borealis, daughter of Queen Alexandra and King Alector."

"Very well, Highness." Do I imagine irritation in his voice? "My orders are to escort you to Aurora where the Emperor has decreed all the princesses of Atlas will gather for his son, Prince Ronan, to choose a wife."

The bottom drops out of my carefully constructed façade, and I struggle to replace my blank expression before anyone notices. But Felix's lips twitch again, and I know he's seen my slip.

An arranged marriage? To a prince I've never seen let alone met? Even that is the best scenario. I don't want to think about the worst. This is my father's doing, and he's put me in a very precarious position. I haven't been good enough to be named his heir, to appear in his courts, but he will gladly marry me off to the Prince in order to strengthen the relationship with Aurora. And if I'm not chosen he will add that burden to the weight of shame I already carry.

Felix rests a hand on his sword and straightens his shoulders. I find myself admiring him despite our less than cordial meeting. He demands respect, and I can tell his guards willingly give it. The four of them remain on their horses, but they sit tall in the saddle, eyes on their commander.

"Highness," Felix emphasizes the title, "it's imperative we leave immediately. The festivities begin in a week, and we'll need at least that long to reach the palace."

So this is it. No time to process. No decision to make. I can only act. It's the type of situation I thrive on, though I can't begin to say I'm happy about it. "I'll get my things." I barely take a step when a hand encircles my arm.

"There's nothing you need here, Highness." I'm tiring of that title already, especially with the edge Felix adds to it. I look down to where he holds my arm, and he immediately relinquishes his grip. "We have supplies for you at our campsite."

It's just as well. The personal belongings in my tent are depressingly few. My crown is the only thing I've brought from home. Though I have a sword and shield, they are made of far inferior stuff than the Commander's. Perhaps, he's right. It would be better to start over.

Holding my chin up takes great effort as I follow Felix to his horse. I'm not keen on riding with him to the campsite, but he left the extra horse there. Perhaps to exert some manner of control over me. Whatever the reason, I have to swallow it down and pretend I'm in charge. This is my only choice.

There's no one to say goodbye to except Milo, who gives me a slight bow and nod of his head. Seven years summed up in a small gesture. It nearly brings tears to my eyes. I'm taking nothing with me and walking toward the unknown. If not for Levi's words and the prayers that fill me, I would be utterly empty. It reminds me too much of the journey I made years ago when I left Borealis behind.

"By your leave, Highness." Felix tips his head in a bow, then reaches for my waist, presumably to help me mount the horse. I take great pleasure in stepping away from him and vaulting into the saddle on my own. I haven't needed assistance mounting a horse since I left the palace.

The scowl beneath his beard is more noticeable now, but he says nothing as he situates himself on the stallion in front of me. There is nothing warm about him, even when my chest presses against his back and my arms reluctantly circle his waist. His body is as hard as his eyes.

I expect him to urge the horse to a gallop as we leave Milo and the others behind. Instead, he gives just enough reign for the horse to trot at an easy pace, which jars my teeth. I suspect he does it on purpose.

"You're the Captain of the Imperial Guard, are you not?" I ask as I let my hands drop from his waist and curl my fingers around the saddle instead.

"Yes, Highness." He doesn't turn around. It doesn't make sense.

Something about his answer bothers me. "And have you escorted the other princesses to Aurora?"

"I have not, Highness."

The title holds no meaning now. "You may stop calling me that. Who did you anger to be sent all the way out here for me? Should you not be protecting the Emperor?"

He doesn't answer right away. Silence spreads between us for so long that I begin to think he's ignoring me. Finally, "I'm here because the others travel with their own entourage. You have—"

No one, I finish silently as he shuts himself up. At least he thought better of finishing the sentence. My father did not think me worthy of the fanfare of an escort from Borealis. Instead, I'll travel with a group of taciturn guards and their surly captain. I'm merely chattel, a bargaining piece if I'm fortunate enough to win the heart of the Prince.

I don't let myself dwell on that thought long. The best scenario would be for me to marry the Prince and hope that, over time, I might soften his heart to my faith and the truth of the Insurgos. That won't likely happen. But if I lose, I can't come back to this outpost now that they know the truth.

The things I know about Aurora or the Prince can be counted on one hand. Not only is Aurora the seat of our empire, but it is the throne of secrets. That is, of course, how the empire was formed after the original ruling family, the Valerias, was deposed. Aurora's soldiers are rumored the be the most disciplined, well-trained men in the empire, so much so that the mere threat of their deployment is enough to quell most uprisings. And, of course, it is the golden city complete with a glittering palace. Even if that's only marginally true, it's enough for me to know that I do not belong in a place like that.

We arrive at their campsite in what feels like seconds. The faint embers of a fire still smolder inside a defined rock circle. Their tents and a few packs are placed around the ring. I'm surprised they didn't leave at least one person here to guard their things. Then again, they are the Emperor's elite soldiers. I suspect they'd have no problems replacing anything stolen from them.

I slide from the horse before the Commander can instruct me to and land lightly on my feet. He follows my lead, then reaches into his pocket and hands me a few sugar cubes.

"You want me to feed your horse?" It seems an odd request, one I'm debating on refusing when he laughs.

"No, I want you to feed your horse. Get to know her." He gestures to a horse, approaching from behind the tents on the lead of another guard.

I try not to act disappointed as the man hands me the lead. The mare before me is a beautiful sorrel chestnut with a shining coat someone must have brushed every day since they began their journey. But she is tame, docile. She has nothing of the spirit in the eyes of Felix's horse.

"Does she have a name?" I ask as the filly nudges my side.

"That's for you to decide, Highness." The Commander runs a hand over the horse's mane before returning his attention to his mount.

"And what's your horse's name?"

"Ares," he replies as he allows the stallion to nip the sugar cubes in his hand.

A fitting name. In the old language, the name Ares was associated with war and strength. The perfect name for the perfect horse. I look at my horse. She doesn't make me think or war or strength, but of peace and gentleness.

"She's a gift from the Prince of Aurora for your trouble, Highness," the Commander adds.

I hold out my hand and let the filly eat the sugar from it.

I certainly can't be disappointed now, but I file the meaning of it away for further study. The Prince has sent me a gift. Why? "Thank you, Commander, but I don't require a title every time you address me."

It's on the tip of my tongue to ask him to call me Emilia, but I'm afraid it would diminish my precarious position, make me look weak. But who am I kidding? I may be strong as warrior, but I am very weak as a princess. I don't know how to be this girl I left behind at ten. But I do know kindness goes a long way toward establishing friendships, and I could sorely use a friend. "I'm sorry I said that in front of those men."

"It's your place. You are the princess, are you not?" There's a faint hint of amusement in his words as he echoes my earlier question to him.

"I have the crown. I'm not sure that makes me the princess."

"I volunteered for this journey," he says, deep eyes looking me over with a frown. "Don't make this a waste of my time."

He doesn't mince words, and I like that about him. I'm not used to the flattery of court and—despite my earlier request—the ridiculous titles and politics. But I do wonder what would make him volunteer for such a ridiculous task, and why would the Emperor let one of the most elite protectors leave his side? Something feels wrong about this.

I hold to the hope that this is God's plan, because if it were my choice, I would not be here at all. I have no interest in ruling and no interest in a royal husband. But the images of Levi and my mother push me forward as does the warmth that rushes through me as I offer up a silent prayer.

Show me your path, God, and I will follow.
I straighten my crown and begin saddling my horse.

3

We've travelled for nearly three days when I finally speak to the Commander again. Sitting atop my mare, my voice is hoarse from lack of use. I ask him to take a wide berth around the capital of Borealis.

Though I don't like to admit I'm afraid of anything, I'm not sure I could handle facing my childhood home with the weight of everything else hanging over me. Though our natural route wouldn't have taken us near the palace anyway, the fields and forests just outside the city are swollen with memories of time spent there with my mother and, on rare occasions, my father. Reminders of happier, simpler times before royal pride and paranoia engulfed love and security.

Whether Commander Fidelis guesses the reason for my detour request or doesn't care, he doesn't ask why, but orders the guard at the front of our pack to change course. I'm grateful I don't have to explain.

Two days later, by the time we approach the lush valley where Borealis, Aurora, and Euros intersect, the sun sits low in the sky, and I can barely stay atop my horse. My eyes blur against the sting of a cool wind as the hours I've lain awake at night catch up with me. My head bobs once, twice, and then I'm slipping into the warmth of sleep.

I'm jerked awake by the sensation of falling and find my horse is no longer under me. An arm around my waist pulls me to another horse, and for the few seconds I'm suspended in midair between the horses feels like a dream. I recognize the white coat of Felix's mount, which has now come to a stop.

The Commander turns in the saddle and glares at me—dark eyes and lowered brows. I don't look away, though the heat of embarrassment tingles on the back of my neck. Yes, I dozed off and nearly fell off my horse, but that's my first misstep on this journey. He's fortunate I'm not a typical palace-bred princess. Otherwise, I would've never been able to ride for so long or manage my own tent and supplies. Without my training we'd be days behind.

For reasons I can't explain, I want him to acknowledge that. At least say something. His silence has been loud since we left camp. Perhaps he is a dullard with nothing going on in his head; or maybe he knows the less he says, the more precious each word is. My instincts insist it's the latter.

"Make camp," Felix calls to the rest of the men, whose names I've not learned. Since we began our journey, they've not sought me out to begin a conversation. Maybe they don't think it's proper. At any rate, I'm grateful because it gives me quiet time to pray without prying stares. Because without weapons—which Felix refused me—they could kill me if they suspect I've abandoned the gods in favor of the Insurgo's religion.

"Thank you," I say as I slide down from his horse. "This way we'll be refreshed for our entry into Aurora tomorrow." I'm not foolish enough to think I can enter the city without notice, though it's certainly my plan to try.

"All you need to do is ask, Princess. I'm yours to command." He dismounts with ease and starts to lead his horse and mine to a nearby tree to tie off.

"Felix." I say his first name for the first time, and he pauses. Something about his words upset me. Maybe I should get used to commanding those around me, but I liked him better when I thought he simply acted out of concern for me. But I tell myself his motives don't matter. "Send one of the men out for firewood and two others to gather berries and any game they see."

He nods, almost imperceptibly. So far we've dined on jerky and dried fruit every night, and I miss the warm meals that came with the permanence of a military base. I imagine these men, though trained to survive on much less, miss the feasts of the palace as well.

I help Felix and the remaining guard unpack our tents and bedrolls and set each up. Neither of them speak, but I feel the Commander's eyes on me, studying me, as I tie off the last of my tent poles.

The guards return with two rabbits and a variety of berries, which Felix insists on tasting before he'll let me sample them. Not until I'm in the middle of preparing a stew from the rabbits does the implication hit me.

I haven't had the luxury of a taster since I was a child, and I'm not sure what it means that Felix was willing to check for poisonous berries for me. It's foolish, because we would be lost without the Commander had he succumbed to some toxin, but I'm impressed he didn't force the task on one of the other men.

We eat our fill of stew and berries, and everyone lingers around the campfire until only embers glow against the black night. The guards draw straws for first watch, though I volunteer and am laughed at. It's still easy to forget these men don't know me as Nox or as a soldier. To them I am a princess and both easy and exceedingly difficult to dismiss. But I don't fight them on this because I did fall asleep on my horse earlier, and I don't know what I might face when we reach the palace tomorrow. Rest might be the best thing. So I bid them goodnight as the watchguard stokes the fire and the rest of us disappear into our tents.

What might be hours later, I open my eyes to a blackened tent, ears tuned to what I think is a rustle outside. When I hear it again, I'm on my feet, reaching for my sword before I remember I left it behind at the Borealis outpost.

A gurgling scream rends the night, and I dart out the rear of my tent. The sound of a slit throat. It chills me to the core. I crouch as low to the ground as possible and strain my eyes to make out the shapes creeping in the darkness.

From the tent beside me, Felix appears with his sword drawn. I try to catch his attention, but his eyes focus on what I've just seen in the center of our camp. At least seven men rifling through our things with moonlight shining off daggers at their waists. They stand near the fire now, and I can see their faces.

The Commander charges into the midst of our attackers with his sword swinging. One man falls immediately before they notice Felix's panther-like grace and form a circle around him. He disarms one man, whose sword flies in my direction. I start toward it as the bandit moves to recover it. His eyes catch mine as his fingers curl around the weapon.

I sprint for the cover of trees as shouts come from the bandits and my guards who have woken. The one who spotted me sprints behind me and manages to grab my arm.

He blocks my attempt at a punch with his forearm and throws me to the ground. The impact knocks the breath from me, and I barely have time to recover before he's on top of me.

His rank breath fans over my face before I bring my knee up into his groin. He doubles up, and it's enough that I can roll out from under him and launch to my feet.

My bare feet dig into the dirt at a run, this time toward the camp. The ring of clashing swords sets my teeth on edge. Shouts come from all around me. Felix's voice calls to me, instructs me to run, and I do, but not in a direction that pleases him.

A strange calm always comes over me right before a battle, and this time is no different. But I'm in the middle of it all before I remember I have no sword to draw or shield to hold. Though I've sparred weaponless with many men, this is different, and I regret my impulsiveness.

The man I fought off minutes ago has returned to camp, and his eyes lock on me with a sinister gleam. I can't know if he means to kill me or take me as entertainment, but I'll never allow the latter.

I dart in and out of the pairs of men, each swinging swords and fists and staffs. The bandits are large men, but they are noticeably unskilled warriors compared to the disciplined Imperial Guard. The man following me seems to be the swiftest of the group, and he mimics my every move until we stand face to face in a clearing just beside the others.

Wild desperation colors his actions as he lifts his sword high and runs toward me. Instinct takes over as I roll under his swing and kick out my leg just in time to trip him. He rolls as well and easily springs to his feet. More agile than I gave him credit for, especially for such a big man.

All I need are a few well-placed jabs and I could take him down. My muscles fatigue quickly as I strike and recoil, strike and recoil. Days of travel have left me stiff and sore. I need something else.

A good defense might be better than the weak offense I've shown. I crouch in anticipation of his next move, though the singing clash of steel on steel rings at my back.

The man lunges toward me again, and I dart backward only to crash to the ground as I trip over something. It barely registers that it's a body before my attacker is upon me, his sword raised once again. I close my eyes as he swings.

Metal meets metal, and my eyes fly open. Felix stands over me with his shield blocking the fatal blow. He uses his forearm to push the man away, then quickly dispatches him with a single swing of his own sword. His eyes are steady as he turns toward me and pulls me to my feet.

"Stay behind me," he urges as he turns to the fighting once again. And for a moment I do. I am defenseless and one of the guards is dead, so only Felix and three others fight the remaining five bandits.

The dagger in Felix's belt catches my eye. It's not ideal, but I could even the fight. I'll have to act quickly. So with stealth and speed that would have made Milo proud, I pull the dagger from the Commander's belt and charge toward the nearest attacker. I don't look back to see if Felix follows me.

Daggers have never been my specialty, but my hands know what to do as I fling dirt in the eyes of the first man I come to and plunge the knife in his chest. Blood spurts onto my face, but I have no time to clean it. For just a second before life drains from the man's eyes, I think I see Levi on the ground in front of me.

It's enough to knock me back on my heels. But I can't stay there. I must move.

I spin around to find Felix engaged with the largest bandit. He meets every blow of the man's sword with a parry, but can't get in any shots of his own. Felix gives up ground to the larger man, exhausted from our days of travelling. He won't be able to last much longer.

Do it now. I don't have much time to think.

My hand tightens around the knife as I raise my arm and then snap my wrist forward, letting the dagger fly straight and true.

It sinks into the shoulder of the attacker, who lets out a monstrous roar and turns to find the source of the pain. This is all the time Felix needs to ram his sword into center mass and finish the man.

I watch it all happen in a dizzy blur. Around me, the other guards have won their fights, and bodies litter the ground. My hands are coated in red, and I feel the same stickiness on my face.

I've killed again. And this time, even though it saved my life and Felix's, it leaves a metallic taste in my mouth. I choke on another man's blood and heave the contents of my stomach onto the ground.

Afterward, with an acid burn in my throat, I collapse to the dirt, and I blink Levi's face from my mind. Accomplishment and remorse wage a battle in me, but unbidden words trump them both.

Blessed be the Lord, my rock, who trains my hands for war and my fingers for battle.

My fingers are stained but steady. My movements on a battlefield are as natural as breathing. I've always felt this was what I was born for. Was it God's will that I be a warrior? If so, he must know that I can't be both warrior and princess. What I wouldn't give to know the rest of that passage. If only my father hadn't burned every copy of the Aletheia. If only I hadn't killed Levi before he could finish. Now I might never know.

Shock fades, and I look up into the lightening sky with sun just peeking over the horizon.

Felix towers over me, but I don't have it in me to pull myself up and look like a princess, so I duck my head and study the blood under my fingernails.

"Are you hurt, Princess?" He sits beside me in the dirt but maintains a respectable distance. And that's all I want. I don't want his pity. I just don't want to be alone, though I can hardly count on Felix for pleasant company.

"No." I look through the loose strands of my hair to find his face. "Are you?"

His eyes widen, as if I shouldn't be concerned for his well-being. Maybe no one ever has. After all, he is only a guard. Then, for the first time, his features soften toward me, and it's easy to see how young he really is. "Yes, I'm fine."

"And the others? I know… I know we lost one." I can't help but feel this is my fault, but it is the price of battle, and I've seen worse. Did word somehow get around that a princess was travelling this road? But my crown has been in my bag since we left the outpost behind. Who were these men?

"Yes, we lost Atticus." He hangs his head and digs his heels in the ground. Hesitance colors his posture, and it looks strange on him. "With your permission, I'd like to dig his grave before we break camp."

Why would he ask me? Hate for my position nearly overwhelms me. If my crown was within reach, I would pull it apart piece by piece.

"Princess, I… I wouldn't ask except I trained Atticus from the time he joined the Guard." Felix mistakes my silence for refusal.

"Of course you may." An urge hits me so strong and so sudden that I can't resist. "But only if you let me help you."

I expect his refusal, or at least a protest, but he only nods and says, "I'd be honored, Highness."

"Felix." I wait until he meets my eyes. "My name is Emilia." However inappropriate this is, I could use a friend.

"Emilia." He tries out my name. "I've never seen a woman fight like that, let alone a princess."

"I've been a warrior almost as long as I was a princess."

"But you move with such grace. I've been around soldiers for most of my life, and I know you can't teach that. It's a gift."

"One I'm likely to lose once I'm stuffed up in the palace." The thought sobers me. What else might I lose there?

Fighting, sparring, has always been natural for me, but it took training to harness my skill and hours of prayer to temper my rage. What if I'm watched so closely that I can't even pray? God has been my refuge since Levi introduced me. Loneliness creeps over me.

"Will I still see you?" I ask, though I look away when I do. "Will you still be my personal escort?"

It's not a fair thing to ask from the Commander of the Emperor's Guard. Of course he can't be my escort, and that's not what I'm really asking. I want an ally, a friend.

Years in the military and being the daughter of a warring king have taught me the importance of alliances. My agenda demands them. It would help to enter the palace with one person on my side, and the Commander of the Guard is a strategic pawn.

I still can't guess his age, though older than me, but to be in such a position when he can't be over twenty-five indicates he is valuable. But how to ask without informing him of my plans? I don't want to be seen as asking for favors in the competition for Prince Ronan, but that's exactly what I'm doing.

He rubs his beard and considers my offer. There's not much to consider. I have nothing to offer him. Our alliance is only beneficial to him if I marry the Prince and become Empress. Only then would I have even a semblance of power. Even then, what would Felix want from me? After years at the same military camp, it feels strange to have just fought beside a man I know nothing about.

"I won't see you when you get to the palace, at least not often. I've seen the things Ronan has planned for the princesses—the parties, the outings—and you won't be needing the company of a guard."

It feels like rejection, but he's probably right. Soon I'll be surrounded by dozens of girls with more frills and lace than I've seen in years. A prince I've never met who could be my husband. I can't imagine a moment to breathe, let alone a social hour with a guard I do not know.

"But, perhaps," Felix continues, "you would have time for dagger lessons with a member of the guard. Ronan will be very interested in you learning self-defense."

Despite everything, the corner of my mouth turns up. His humor surprises me. "I believe my self-defense is more than adequate."

"As is your use of daggers. I can attest to that."

We both glance at the body lying facedown with the handle of the dagger protruding from his back. Delirious laughter bubbles in my throat, but I swallow it. "I was aiming for his leg. I only wanted to slow him down."

"In that case, maybe you could use a little work." His smile is hidden behind his beard, but I hear it in his voice. "Prince Ronan is my friend. We grew up together. And I hate the idea of the whole competition because I've seen the girls who've arrived at the palace. But you're different, and you could be just what he needs."

Until this moment, I've only thought of Ronan as the means to an end. He is what I need to help the Insurgos. What he needs hasn't entered my mind.

"I hope so." But I can't imagine how I'll ever rule if I marry him. I'd always be subject to him as my husband and as the Crown Prince.

There are so many things I don't know, chief of which is if I could even love someone. I loved Levi in a way and, of course, I loved my mother. But the sort of love that exists between a man and a woman is a mystery to me. And I don't think the kind of man that holds a competition for his bride is the one who will love me either.

I study Felix, and he looks right back, as if in that moment we are equals. I was wrong about him. He isn't as unkind as he appeared, just hardened and quiet.

He stands and holds out his hand. I take it and rise to my feet and to the occasion. I hope he's not the only thing I'm wrong about.

4

My muscles ache from a morning of grave digging as we ride into Aurora that afternoon. Felix shows no ill effects from the exercise except he is quieter than usual. The mood is solemn but not as heavy as I expected it might be. To my knowledge the Imperial Guard has seldom entered into battle, largely because a short demonstration of their skills is usually enough to deter most opposition. They are intimidators as much as they are warriors. But this intimidation doesn't prepare one for losing a friend in battle. Perhaps it is their training, but Felix has shown something more akin to true grief at Atticus's untimely demise by asking to dig a grave than the other three.

No one speaks until we stop just outside Aurora proper. Until then they've communicated when necessary by body language and, in Felix's case, a stern look. Now Felix looks at me with sharp eyes and seems to hesitate over something. Not for the first time, I wonder what he's thinking.

Whatever has passed through his mind, all he finally does is instruct me to put on my crown so we can make an official entrance. Though much less grand than the other princesses, I'm sure. I won't dwell on that. My meager parade through the city will hardly be the end of my differences from the others. I'm all too aware of that.

Everyone waits, the air fully of expectation, as I reach for the saddle bag I have strapped to my docile horse. The smooth leather of the bag is more familiar to my hands than the contents of it. Though I've held the crown a few times over the years, I haven't placed it upon my head since I was ten.

I take it out for the third time in too few days and look it over once again. Felix sighs, impatiently I assume, and I don't have time for nostalgia. No time to remember much more than my mother weaving my dark hair around this tiara when I was a child and it was nearly too big for my head. So I force it on my head, metal stabbing my scalp even through my thick hair.

It feels smaller since I've grown, but impossibly heavier.

I consider leaving it askew on my brow, to show how little respect I have for what my birthright has given me, but I think of Levi and I think of the task handed to me. And I know I must be something different. Something more. And so I busy my hands with a task I've never undertaken on my own. My fingers are clumsy and awkward, and it takes too long to straighten under the stares of my companions. I nudge my horse with my knees, and she turns so our backs face the soldier. It's an inadequate moment of privacy, but all I can afford.

When I finally get the crown situated, I turn my horse, and my travel companions freeze with their eyes fixed on me. It's clear that, until this moment, they—with the exception of Felix—haven't thought of me as a princess. I've been their cook, their fellow warrior, and maybe even something pretty to look at along our journey, but not royalty. Even Felix seems stunned. His eyes search my face.

Desire to see myself pulses through me, punctuated by the puzzling look on his face. Amusement? Disappointment? Maybe I still don't look like a princess.

What do I look like with a crown on my head? More than that, what do I look like at all? Mirrors were a luxury the military couldn't afford. When I did catch a glimpse of myself in the blade of my sword or some other reflective surface, the image was always distorted.

Until now I've liked that. I learned who I was apart from what I look like, but I remember enough of court life to know appearances are valued above all else. Will Prince Ronan take one look at me and send me home? No matter how secure I pretend to be, that thought is devastating. That not only will I be at a loss for how to fulfill Levi's task, but maybe after all this time and all this penance for a crime I did not commit, maybe I will still not be loved.

So, I ask Felix, "Do I look ridiculous?"

He clears his throat and whips his horse around as if I've caught him breaking some law. "It looks fine," he calls over his shoulder.

Another guard, Antony, falls in beside me and offers a wide smile. "Forgive my liberties, but you look beautiful, Highness." He inclines his head, then nudges his mount even with Felix's.

Beautiful. I mull the word over as we approach the city gates. My mother was beautiful, and Levi said I look like her. But in the end it wasn't enough. Will it be enough for me? How can I possibly make the Prince love me? Because even if I am beautiful, I will certainly not be the only princess to be so.

My heart tattoos a staccato rhythm against my chest as we pass through the Aurora gates and enter the chaos. Felix immediately circles around to ride beside me, and just his presence is enough to turn most people's curious stares away.

The scents of a market—overripe fruit, livestock, and body odor—assault me as we form a single-file line to pass through the masses. My horse balks as a chicken flies directly in front of us, and I pull up short to keep control. Vendors hawking their wares pull my attention from one side of the congested street to the other.

A table of embroidery, a stand of shining apples, a booth for basket weaving. Customers with packages piled so high they can't possibly see over them. My eyes follow one such woman, not much older than me, who stumbles as she tries to follow a man through the crowd with her arms full of eggs and produce.

She tumbles forward almost in slow motion, and I reach out a hand as if I could help her. When she hits the ground with packages splaying out before her, almost no one notices, and they are content to step on or around her to get to their next destination.

But the man the girl followed has noticed. I pull my horse to a stop as he storms, red-faced, toward her. She stays on her knees before him, and though I can't make out her words, she is clearly pleading with him.

His hand across her face resounds with a smack I feel in my gut. But he doesn't stop there, and I flinch with every strike.

How can these people just keep walking? Don't they see this poor girl? Hear her screams?

"Stop," I whisper. Only Felix, who is just behind me, seems to hear. So I raise my voice. "You there, stop!"

The man's eyes flicker up to me, and he pauses. It's enough for me to gesture for Antony to intervene. My young guard does just that, and steps between the man and the girl as I dismount my horse. Felix dismounts as well and catches my arm.

"Highness, we shouldn't stop here. I can't protect you in a crowd this size."

"If he hits her again, I won't be the one in need of your protection." I jerk my arm from him and face the man in question. "What right do you have to harm this girl?"

"She's my slave, and she just ruined the eggs I bought. Clumsy, stupid girl." He starts for her again, but Antony restrains him.

I stare into the man's eyes as I stand safely on Antony's other side. Felix lingers near me, but says nothing. "She is a woman, and slave or no slave, you have no right to treat her that way."

Despite being restrained, the man snarls at me. "She's mine to do with what I will. Her family owed me a debt, and the Emperor gave her to me as payment. I don't know who you are, but you can't tell me how to treat my property. I'm not breaking any laws."

Behind me, the girl is still on the ground whimpering, and her fingertips just brush the edge of my cloak. "Girl, what's your name?" I adopt a tone I've heard my father use, one that conveys authority and leaves no room for arguments.

"Hannah, my lady." Her voice is soft and shaken with tears, and she will not lift her head to look at me.

By now the people in the market have slowed to look at the spectacle I've created. Ironic that beating a girl in public doesn't garner a second look, but stopping the violence stirs whispers among the vendors and patrons. I feel each set of eyes on me as I kneel before the girl and lift her chin with my finger.

Watery blue eyes flick to mine, then back to the ground. "It's all right, Hannah. Look at me, please." She does, and I take her hand as we stand. "Now, Hannah, can you tell me how large is the debt you owe to this man?"

"A merchant's yearly wage," the man shouts, then spits at the ground near my feet.

Behind me I hear the whistle that can only be Felix drawing his sword, metal sliding against metal. I throw my hand back and my fingers collide with his forearm, stilling his movement. I don't want anyone to get hurt here, but I will prove a point.

"Then I'll pay it." My voice remains even, though the steadiness is a façade. This girl I've become in this moment is someone I don't know, and as such, I don't know what will come out of her mouth next. "I'll pay the debt, and you'll let her go."

All around us, gasps and murmurs replace the shouts and chatter of the market. The man looks from me to Hannah then back.

"I want to see the money," he demands.

I feel the tension radiating from Felix and know he's dying to put this man in his place. But though my crown marks me as royalty, I am not this man's princess. If my unfamiliar face were not enough to mark me as an outsider, my sun-darkened skin and black hair certainly are. He reminds me once again that I have no power here, and I feel as though I'm only playing a part.

"You will address the lady as Her Highness, Princess of Borealis," Felix insists.

"I don't care what she's princess of." The man spits again, and this time he hits my face.

I blink once, twice, trying to reconcile the slimy feeling on my cheek with the crass man in front of me. My fingers twitch, but the satisfaction that I could disable him with a single blow calms me. This is not the time.

Felix disagrees. I don't even feel him brush past me, but there he is, jerking the man forward and pushing him to his knees in front of me. The Commander rests the pommel of his sword on the back of the man's head and forces him to stare at the ground.

I don't know what to do now, but people are staring, whispering, and I must do something. Perhaps I should demand the man let Hannah go free, but I've already offered to pay and there are witnesses. But pay with what? The coffers in Borealis are likely full, but my father will certainly not send me coin to free a slave girl. Besides, I need a show of good faith now, and a down payment will not do.

My crown slips with the sweat on my brow, and I raise a hand to stead it. As my fingers curl around the precious metal, I know what I must do.

The crown pulls some of my hair from my braid as I remove it, slowly and deliberately so the people can see. I hold it up so the single stone catches the light. Then I nod to Felix who reluctantly removes his sword from the man's head.

When the slave owner looks up, his eyes sparkle at the gift I offer him. And it is a gift because it's worth at least five times the debt the girl owes.

For the first time, a hushed silence falls over the crowd. Spittle still drips from the man's lips, and I resist the urge to wipe it from my face. Instead, I lower the crown to him.

"My crown for the girl's freedom." I raise my voice to make sure the onlookers can hear. I don't want any misconceptions about our deal. "If you accept, you can never have her back, and you must leave her and her family alone. I've paid their debt."

He takes the crown in his dirty hands and pulls it forcefully from mine, as if he thinks he deserves such a gift. "Agreed, Your Highness."

The sneer of my title is all the motive Felix needs to backhand the man across the face, sending him and the crown sprawling into the street.

I turn my back on the sight and survey the girl before me. Hannah is almost my height, but you'd never know it with the way her shoulders slump. Even now that I've freed her, she cowers within herself, eyes still on the ground.

"Hannah," I say softly. "Do you have anywhere to go?" It occurs to me, now that I have made a show of her freedom, Hannah's life might not be that much easier when she has to fend for herself. Despite it all, I might have made things worse.

"I am your humble servant, Highness." She bows in a deep curtsy.

"Stand up," I hiss. She's nearly undone everything I just did. Now the whole of the market will be talking about how the Princess of Borealis stormed in and began confiscating slaves for her chambers.

Hannah rises slowly and finally raises her eyes to mine. Her face holds a softness, and though somewhat plain, the gentleness in her eyes more than makes up for the lack of striking features.

"I didn't buy you for myself. You are free now." Her eyes light up at the word. "I have no expectations for your service."

"But I would choose to serve you, Highness. Please." Her voice breaks. "My family is dead, and I have no place to live. I'll be a good servant. I can cook and sew and braid hair." She looks at my braid and bites her lip. "Though I suppose you already have a lady for those things."

A lump forms in my throat, and I glance at Felix for his approval. I don't know why I think he might read my mind, because his face is an unreadable mask. There is no one to make this decision but me.

"As a matter of fact, I have no ladies at the moment, and I would be honored if you would accompany me to the palace."

"Yes, Highness." Hannah takes my hand and kisses my knuckles, a show of fealty that makes me weak. Who am I that people should swear to me?

I gesture to Antony to help Hannah on his horse, then turn to Felix. "What did I just do?" I whisper.

"I don't know." He shakes his head and makes a way for me to step through the crowd back to my horse.

"How am I supposed to walk into the palace with no crown?" The ramifications of my decision hit me hard. I'm already at a disadvantage with my lack of entourage and court manners. How can I think to enter court without the one symbol of my position?

Felix stops beside my horse, and rubs a hand across my saddle without meeting my eyes. "The crown doesn't make the princess."

I said something similar to him when we first met, but I meant the opposite. Having the crown didn't make me a princess anymore than not having keeps me from being one. Or so he says. It remains to be seen if I can pull any of this off. But I think of Levi, of the rest of the Insurgos I've yet to meet, and know I have to try.

"Wipe your face." He steps away from me but offers the hem of his cloak. I wave it off and wipe the spit from my cheek with my own garment. Felix shakes his head, but I think I see a smile as he returns to his own horse.

I've surprised him, and I've surprised myself. As my horse dances beneath me and I nudge her to a trot behind Antony and Hannah, I allow myself a smile and a quick prayer.

Thank you, God for bringing me this far. Guide me as you guide my fingers in battle. And, please, let the Prince love me.

5

The palace walls in the heart of Aurora rise high into the sky, as if the first Emperor who built this place could reach into the heavens. Maybe he meant it as a symbol of the conduit of his power with the gods. Whatever the reason, it feels like a beautiful lie. The gods those around me serve are as fictitious as the stories of dragons we were all told as children and as much of a sham as the court magicians who practice a devilish sort of magic.

The shadow of the structure washes over me as our little caravan passes through the gates. People here seem unimpressed with our entrance and continue about their business.

I can hardly blame them. With my crown gone, the most remarkable thing about our group is that we are led by the captain of the guard. Felix does garner a few respectful bows from the soldiers patrolling the grounds, but Hannah and I are barely given a second glance.

When we reach the royal stables, I dismount my mare and pass the reins to a stable boy who leads her into a stall. Felix joins me, a silent and steady presence, as I watch the animal go.

"She disappoints you." As usual, he is direct.

When I turn to look at him, he's studying me with a flash of interest in his eyes. And I remember he's supposed to be my ally.

"She's beautiful," I insist, but what I don't say carries more weight. My eyes drift beyond the stable doors to a small corral where a flash of black darts back and forth. "There," I point to the horse, "who does that horse belong to?"

Felix scoffs but falls in step beside me as I approach the pen. "No one. Beautiful as she is, no one has been able to break her yet."

As exquisite as Felix's white stallion is, this black filly before me may be its equal. Though her coat is dull from lack of brushing and her mane is tangled, her well-muscled body and lively eyes speak of the incredible potential in her. She slows long enough to look me in the eyes, and I'm taken aback by the depth of intelligence in them.

"Would Ronan let me have her instead?" I can't help but ask. I should be grateful for anything the Prince gives me, but I can't explain my draw to this horse.

"He'd think you crazy for asking. This horse is dangerous, Emilia. She hasn't let anyone near her."

I hold out my hand, and the horse approaches. She sniffs me—hot, moist air prickling my skin—then dances away with a whinny. A smile finds its way to my lips, and from the corner of my eye, I see Felix shaking his head.

"I suppose you have a name for her?" There's resignation in his voice, as if he already knows better than to try to stand in the way of something I want. A wise choice.

"Athena." It's an old name. I don't know the precise origin, but the name was always associated with battle and strategy. Precisely what I'll need to win over the horse and the Prince.

"Of course." He shrugs and moves to guide me away from the pen. "You may play with your new pet later. For now, you must get settled in your rooms. There's a masquerade ball tonight where you'll meet Ronan."

My brief moment of respite crashes down around me. I'm not here to play a game. I have a job to do, and I won't be letting only myself down if I can't do it. Failing to gain the Prince's trust means sentencing the Insurgos to more of the same—war and persecution. It means never being able to speak to anyone about the truth that burns in me—truth that yearns for the real God who inhabits the heavens above those soaring towers.

I've known for some time this day was coming, though I hadn't known what it might look like. The military camp couldn't last forever, and my restless heart has nearly driven me to run and join the Insurgos more times than I could count. Perhaps this is the reason why I couldn't bring myself to do it. Because this is my purpose.

As I follow Felix from the stables through the palace's winding passages, I pray. Though it calms me, it still feels like my words go no further than the space above my head. I've had glimpses of the heavy rush that comes with communicating with God, but they've been few and far between. Levi said this would happen. And so I do as he says and keep praying though my emotional connection has waned.

We've reached an innocuous wooden door when Felix stops suddenly in front of me, and I nearly crash into his back. He turns to me with the same blank expression that antagonizes me.

"These will be your quarters for the remainder of your stay in the palace. I had Antony bring Hannah to your rooms where she'll join the rest of your ladies."

Hannah. How could I have already forgotten about her when just a while before, her beating seemed so seared on my mind? I'll make it up to her somehow. I hope she's been treated kindly since she and Antony left the stables.

"Thank you." I give Felix a little nod because I'm still not sure the proper way to express my gratitude to someone of his rank. When I was little, I remember seeing my mother hold out her hand for a person to kiss. That gesture seems too much for this situation, and it never made sense to me. And if Felix deems my reaction inappropriate, he doesn't show it.

He inclines his head toward me as well, then steps forward to push open the door. I take a step, too, then stop in my tracks.

Four women, dressed in plain blue robes of the servants, huddle together in the center of the room. One appears to be crying. Hannah stands near the large bed, which occupies a good portion of this room, fiddling with the sheets.

"Ladies." Felix announces our presence, and the women just apart with hurried curtsies in my general direction. His eyes lock on the woman in tears. "Cecily, what's the trouble?"

"Your grace, Your Highness." The blond woman with tears in her eyes curtsies to us once more. "I'm afraid I have terrible news. Two of Her Highness's ladies have taken ill, and we haven't had time to replace them. Even with the new girl," she nods toward Hannah, "there are only five of us!"

She wails and immediately the other ladies, minus Hannah, rush in to console her again. I'm at a loss for words. How can she possibly think five ladies won't be enough for me? And to think, I was reluctant to take on Hannah when I assumed she'd be my only maid.

"Cecily," I say softly. "I'm not used to having ladies. I'm able to do most things for myself. You won't have to do extra work to make up for the other two."

"Forgive me, Highness, but we don't mind the work," Cecily sniffs. "But you can't have only five servants. It's an unholy number. Each of the princesses is assigned six ladies."

"She's right," Felix speaks up beside me.

I don't look at him because I'm too busy considering my options. I don't want six maids. Five is already too many. But if I don't seem concerned about maintaining the holy number of six, will I arouse suspicion? I'm certain the other princesses have embraced their six ladies. Some may have even asked for more.

"Five will be sufficient for now." I speak with confidence I don't feel. "I will work as my own sixth lady. That's the custom in Borealis."

It's a lie, but I don't imagine any of them have ever travelled to my home country to know the difference.

"Are you certain?" Felix asks. He offers me a peculiar look, as if there's something more on his tongue that he's not at liberty to say. But, as usual, I can't read it in his expression.

"Yes," I insist. "Besides, I am sure I have the finest ladies Aurora has to offer. The gods will bless us because of our purity and overlook our numbers."

"Thank you, Highness. Thank you," Cecily clamors.

I do hold out my hand this time and brace myself as, one by one, my ladies step forward to bow and kiss my hand. Hannah is last, and she lifts her eyes to mine as she bows. In them, I see a kindred spirit, and I know she knows my secret. Have I been so transparent?

My eyes flick to Felix, who quickly looks away as if he doesn't want me to see his eyes or what's behind them. Does he know, too? If so, my mission could be over before it even started.

"By your leave, Highness." He bows and abruptly exits my room, leaving me alone with five woman who stare at me expectantly.

"So... what happens now?" I don't want to look stupid, but I'd rather ask than not know.

"I'll show you your quarters while the others draw your bath and prepare your dress for the ball tonight," Cecily pipes up. Her devotion to her job is apparent on her tear-streaked face. Though she likely didn't choose her lot, she's made up her mind to serve whole-heartedly. I like that about her.

She leads me through more rooms than I've seen in years. In addition to the bedroom we first entered, there is a small servants' room off my main quarters, equipped with small beds for each of my ladies. I have a bathing room with an iron tub, a small dining area with room enough for me and a guest, and a parlor area where I suppose I'm to entertain my guests. It all feels like a waste to me, but I remind myself this is part of the person I used to be. The same one I must become again.

6

This ball gown might be the most uncomfortable thing I've ever worn, and not just because the material scratches the delicate skin beneath my arms or because the stays jab my ribs when I move.

Cecily and Hannah still fuss around me, making adjustments to my hair, then working on the mask they'll place over my eyes as soon as I allow it. They have turned me into someone else entirely, and my lips drift up in a small smile because they have employed their own strategy to make me look my best. I wonder if there's something in it for the ladies of the princess who wins Ronan's heart.

My eyes travel the length of my reflection in the full length mirror of my bedroom. I don't know what to look at first. My protests when I first saw the dress were met with rebuttals from all my ladies. The last time I was in court, it was considered scandalous to wear a dress with no sleeves and no straps, but they assure me fashion has changed. As a result, my arms—made strong from days of wielding a sword—are on display, and they're not the only things.

As a ten year old among military men, I didn't have to work hard to fit in with regard to our look. But as I grew and developed my curves, I had to take great pains to hide them. I bound myself and adjusted the seams on my uniform to camouflage the things that made me so distinctly a woman. Now, as I study myself in the mirror, my curves are on full display.

I don't know what to make of the hour glass shape of my body, how they have drawn the corset tight to emphasize my waist. I feel exposed. Everything I've tried so hard to hide is now on full display.

"You look beautiful, Highness." Hannah smooths the curls of my hair cascading down my back and gives a small curtsy. She has taken to this role as effortlessly as anything I've ever seen, and I could only wish my transition was as easy.

"I don't know what to think. I didn't know I could look like this. Are you sure it's okay?" I'm not fishing for compliments, though I'm vaguely aware that it sounds that way. What I need is reassurance that I'm not about to make a fool of myself.

Cecily seems to sense that. "This is a battle for the Prince's heart, Highness. You'd be foolish not to utilize your weapons, both here," she touches my bare shoulder, "and here." Her fingertips rest lightly against the crown of my head, and it takes me a moment to realize she means my mind.

I don't know how much my ladies were told about my past, but they seem to have realize the best way to appeal to me is to approach this whole thing as a battle. It works. Though I won't be swinging any swords, I know I'll have to fight for Ronan's hand. To do that, I'll have to pretend I'm at ease in court, even though I feel anything but.

"Thank you, ladies." I turn my back to the mirror and dip my head to allow one of them to place the mask over my face. After some adjustments, they all step back with a sigh, and I turn to the mirror once again.

I've been transformed into an elegant peacock. This time, I look past my exposed skin to the miles of dark blue fabric with the gold pin tucks in the skirt. From each pin hangs a long peacock feather, which echoes the arrangement on my gold mask. I spin and find that the bustle of my dress is adorned with a glorious fan of the same feathers.

I look to each of my ladies, then to the fingers of the original four. They bear the marks of callouses and pinpricks, and somehow I know they've spent hours sewing this dress for me, even before they knew me. The thought brings the threat of tears which I must blink back.

"Thank you," I say again, this time meeting each one of them with a gentle gaze. "I couldn't have asked for better ladies."

There's more to be said, but it might be foolish to become so familiar with them so soon. As Cecily said, this is a battle, and I must choose my allies carefully.

Felix comes to mind, and I wonder where he is right now. Will he be at the ball? When will he come to me to begin our dagger lessons? Maybe he wasn't serious about that, but I hope he was. Even in this exquisite dress, my fingers itch to hold a weapon.

A sharp knock on the door startles us all. I take a step toward the door, but Cecily stops me with an apologetic nod and answers it herself. I suppose I'll have to get used to letting people do things for me, though it goes completely against my nature.

Cecily steps aside to allow Antony to enter. He cuts a sharp figure in his military uniform—black trousers and tunic with a rich red cape attached to his shoulders with the gold emblem of the sun, the symbol of Aurora. His eyes flicker briefly to Hannah, then he bows deeply before me.

"Rise." The command comes a little easier to me now, and Antony obeys with a smile.

"I didn't think it was possible for you to look more beautiful, Highness, but you are extraordinary."

I fight the heat creeping up my neck and hope my embarrassment doesn't show. "Thank you. Are you here to escort me to the ball?" I had hoped for Felix, but at least Antony is a familiar face. I suppose I shouldn't expect the Commander to be at my beck and call.

"Yes, Highness." He offers his arm, and I take it.

It feels strange to be on someone's arm when I am used to protecting myself. But I saw Antony fight alongside me when the bandits attacked, and I know he would die protecting me.

We wind through the palace hallways in silence as I try to calm the nerves in my stomach. Though it's risky to pray, even silently, in Antony's presence, I chance it.

God, Levi said this was your plan for me and your people. Please give me light to see the next step. I don't know how to make someone love me, and without Ronan, this cannot work.

Music from the ballroom reaches us as we round a corner, and I tighten my grip on Antony's arm. So much of the rest of my life hands on these next few hours, and I haven't the slightest clue what to expect. All my training will not help me here. Cecily may have been right about this being a battle, but it's one I'm not sure how to fight.

I tug on Antony's arm to stop him just outside the ballroom doors. I inhale deeply and look to him for some sort of confirmation. He takes pity on me.

"Normally, you would be announced as you enter," he explains. "But the Prince has specifically requested that everyone remain anonymous until the end of the night when the command is given to remove masks."

It's a smart move. Ronan must be almost as nervous as I am—as all the princesses are—and this masquerade will give him a chance to observe each of us without any preconceived notions. But how will I recognize him in order to impress him?

"So I just walk in?" It seems anticlimactic after the prelude of dressing and the nerves in my stomach.

"Yes. There's already a crowd. All the nobles of court were invited as well as the entourages and guards brought by each princess. I would say you'll have no trouble blending in, but..."

He grins, and though it's probably an inappropriate response to a princess, I'm grateful for his candor. Perhaps I don't want to blend in. I need to catch Ronan's eye. I just hope I don't make a fool of myself doing it.

I leave Antony behind and take my first step into the ballroom. Breath catches in my throat, and I nearly shield my eyes against bright spectacle. Music soars high above the crowd, reaching to the cathedral ceilings which are somehow adorned with banners of gold and crystal. Even inch of the room seems to glisten with jewels and almost gaudy displays of wealth. My father's castle could not hope to compare with this one.

All around me, people dance and laugh and sway with glasses of sparkling liquid. Despite this, my hope sinks. The room is impossibly large. I can't begin to hope to find Ronan in this, especially since I have no idea what he looks like.

At least in that matter we are all equal. No one outside of Aurora knows what the Crown Prince looks like. It's no accident. He doesn't travel the empire with his father so that the Emperor and his heir will never present an easy target. No one outside of the capital has seen him since he was a boy.

On the opposite side of the room, on a dais lifted above the crowd, sits the Emperor and Empress. I can't look away. They are magnificent in their crown jewels and simple masks. Even from this distance, their presence commands respect. I can't tell much about the Emperor from here except that he has a head full of dark hair and a strong chin. But the Empress is a beauty from any vantage point. Her long dark hair spills over her shoulders onto her emerald dress. Delicate features on skin pale and smooth as ice. As I move closer, I'm struck by the glowing blue eyes behind her dark mask. Her beauty would outshine everyone in the room if she let it. Instead, she sits, subdued, by her husband's side. I'm torn between admiration and pity.

The crowd swallows me up as I make my way toward a table lined with refreshments. It's disorienting amid the heat and press of swaying couples and raucous laughter. This isn't where I want to be.

My training suggests I find a perch along the wall and survey my surroundings, and I intend to do just that. But just as I exit the throng of dancers, a tall young man steps in front of me and bows low.

"My lady." He takes my hand and kisses it, and I'm too shocked to stop him. "I would be honored if you would dance with me."

Could this be Ronan? I study his face, but nothing in it reminds me of the Emperor or Empress I've just seen. And his hair seems too light to belong to them. Still, it would be rude to refuse a dance.

However, after several turns we both regret my compliance. I am a terrible dancer, and my partner's limp testifies to the fact. I move with the music, the rise and falls, and the choreographed steps feel counterintuitive to me. Still, he bows with a forced smile as he leaves me for another partner.

I feel several sets of eyes on me, but no one immediately approaches so I make my way to the closest wall to set up watch. Once I feel nothing but cool marble at my back, I begin to search the room.

It's not hard to find Ronan, and I'm a little disappointed in this. He stands a head taller than the women that circle him near the refreshments. His mask is glittering pale gold, and I can just make out the sun emblem between his eyes. Dark hair in slick waves blends with his black ensemble. Only his cape, boasts any decoration—twinkling crystals against black velvet. He is the midnight sun. An obvious reference to his father as the Sun King, Emperor of Aurora.

He takes his time, dancing with each of the ladies and exchanging conversation. I don't approach. The time must be exactly right, and I'll have to distinguish myself from the scores of women clamoring for his attention. Obviously, this won't be by dancing. That's a distinction I'd prefer not to have.

I make small talk with the men who approach me, but no one asks me to dance. Perhaps they saw the spectacle I made earlier, or maybe they can see how preoccupied I am. Either way, they compliment my dress, my hair, anything else they can think of, then move away.

Across the room, I spot a guard slinking around the perimeter of the room with a familiar grace. His eyes seem to study the crowd as if he's looking for someone. Felix. I've seen him move with that same easy gate, been the subject of that intense stare for the past week. Even if I can't get to Ronan, perhaps I can enjoy what's left of my evening by conversing with the Commander.

I'm only two steps away from my wall when a figure steps in front of me, blocking my way. Brows furrowed behind my mask, I look up at Prince Ronan.

"I don't believe we've met." His voice is light, as if a laugh always lies in his throat. So different from the stilted greetings I've received all night.

"Perhaps not," I say, because something seems familiar about him. But behind his large mask, it's impossible to make out his features except for the deep brown of his eyes and the gentle curve of his lips, neither of which seem to resemble the features I noted on the Emperor and his queen.

"Would you like to dance?" He extends a hand, and I can only stare at it. I think I know that hand.

"Surely you've seen that I'm a poor dancer."

"I can't imagine that, since you move with such grace." The affectation he gave to his voice moments before is gone, and I instantly recognize him.

"Felix," I whisper, and his eyes widen beneath the mask. "What are you doing? Impersonating the Prince is high treason."

"Not if he asks you to."

With the pretense gone, I can see the Commander clearly beneath the costume. I'm surprised I recognized him at all. The beard which he'd worn on our journey is gone, replaced by smooth skin that takes years off his face. He's even younger than I thought, making his position that much more impressive.

"So the guard I was walking toward when you stopped me, that's the Prince?" I guess. My voice is low, but I still look around to make certain no one is listening to our conversation. Several feet away, the women who had earlier commanded Felix's attention now shoot daggers at me with their eyes, but they are gossiping amongst themselves.

Nothing is as it seems. We all wear a mask, and our secrets are the dark things that unite us under the glittering lights.

"You are too perceptive for your own good. Ronan wanted to watch the ball from an objective view. He knew women would try to impress him, and he wanted to see them for who they were. Switching places with me allows him to do that."

"And you've let those poor girls think they were dancing with a prince all night long." I place my hands on my hips and tilt my chin defiantly. I don't like deception, even if I am secretly impressed with Ronan's plan.

"They all believed I could be a prince, except you. To have been absent from court for so long, you can certainly spot the pauper in royal robes."

Though his tone remains even and his dark eyes don't soften, his words sting. Does he mean this as a slight against me or himself?

"Your eyes give you away." I'm reaching now, hoping to soften whatever damage my words might have done. But I tell the truth. "The Empress's eyes are bright blue. I can't tell about the Emperor except to say his eyes are a light color. Yours are brown." And they are surprisingly familiar to me. I hadn't realized just how closely I'd studied Felix until now. "And your hand, when you held it out to me, I noticed fresh callouses from where we dug the grave outside the city. A prince wouldn't have such rough hands." Certainly I could show him my marks, my scars, which have no business on the body of a princess.

He clenches his fingers into a fist to hide the markings as if he is ashamed of them. "We've stood here too long. Would you like to dance with me, or should I leave you to revel in your victory over all the less observant women?"

"I wasn't joking when I said I'm a poor dancer."

"I would've thought you'd be amazing. Your movements in battle are so fluid, so lithe. How can you possibly be a bad dancer?"

"It's not the same." When I fight, I move with my impulses, my instincts. "It's too regimented, too strict. Those steps don't feel natural to me."

He opens his mouth to respond, but we're interrupted by the guard I spotted before Felix interrupted me. Ronan himself.

"Is everything okay, Your Majesty?" he asks.

"Fine." Felix and I answer in unison. Then the three of us—me, the Commander, and the real Prince Ronan—exchange smiles, and it feels like the first genuine thing I've experience since I entered this room.

I look at Ronan and wonder how anyone could have been fooled by Felix. His eyes glow blue like his mother's, accentuated by his simple dark mask. Side by side, he and Felix have similar builds, and I know from their previous movements that they share the same gate. Ronan's hair is darker than the Commander's, and he has his mother's icy beauty. He is unmistakably Prince of Aurora.

"She knows," Felix tells him, and they both look at me.

"You said she would figure it out," Ronan agrees with a small nod.

This surprises me. Felix seemed upset I saw through his disguise, but he had warned Ronan it would happen. What else did he warn the Prince about me?

"Ro, this is Princess Emilia of Borealis. She arrived just this afternoon." Felix introduces me quietly, and I incline my head to show respect without drawing attention.

"And caused quite a stir in the marketplace if rumors are to be believed." Ronan smiles and his icy features melt as if the sun shines directly on him. Try as I might, I can't help the way my heart pounds when he directs that smile at me.

I've never has this sort of attention from a man, and I don't know what to make of it. Before tonight, I hadn't given much thought to what Ronan might look like. No matter his appearance, I needed him to love me. How could I have dared hope he would be so devastatingly handsome?

"Felix, I believe there are some ladies waiting to speak the Prince. Would you be so kind as to appease them?" Ronan doesn't look away from me as he dismisses Felix. I feel the Commander leave us, but I can't look away from Ronan either. "Emilia, is it?"

"Yes, Majesty."

"Ronan, please." He extends his arm, and I take it. He is solid, though not as obviously muscled as Antony or Felix. "Though don't let my father hear you being so familiar. I'm afraid you'll have to address me with the title whenever he's around."

No one pays us any attention as he escorts me to a side door leading to an empty balcony. The air is crisp as the wind blows over the mountains I travelled recently. We look for all the world like a guard and a courtier exchanging words on the fringes of the biggest celebration the empire may have ever seen. I suspect it will be rivaled only by Ronan's actual wedding.

A strong breeze courses over my bare shoulders, and I can't contain the shiver that races through me.

"You must be freezing," he says as he unfastens his cape and drapes it over my shoulders. The heavy red fabric smells like Felix, which makes sense if Ronan traded his costume for Felix's uniform. "I won't keep you out here long, but I wanted just a minute with you before we all unmask and the insanity of all this officially begins."

I swallow hard as he and I lean against the balcony rails. The cape cuts the wind, and I pull it tighter around me.

"Felix says you are smart," he continues, alternating glances between me and the garden down below. "He also says you saved his life, and I have only once known my commander to need saving."

"I was in the right place at the right time, and I've been trained for battle. It wasn't skill, Majesty, just instinct."

"I was serious about you calling me Ronan." He pauses, and something in his thoughts sobers him. "But you should know it's not a special favor."

He turns his full attention to me now, and his blue eyes are piercing. "Choosing a wife is not something I relish. I've always known I would marry for political reasons, but I didn't want it to be like this. You know that you'll be competing against all the princesses of the realm as well as some noblewomen, right?"

"Yes," I whisper. I don't want to be reminded of how slim my chance is.

"So you know that my time with you will be short, and I'll sometimes have to leave you for the company of other women."

Is he trying to hurt me? His words sting. I nod slowly.

"Then you should also know, that if the choice was solely mine, out of all the women I've seen tonight, I would choose to spend my time with you." He smiles again, and my heart leaps in my chest. "Smart, strategic, and beautiful. Felix didn't exaggerate you at all."

His hand brushes mine, resting on the railing, and then he closes his fingers around it. I want to be wary of his actions because I know that as soon as his identity is revealed, he will be the highest prize. But I feel at ease with him. Is this God's way of telling me I'm on the right path?

"There's a touch of destiny about you," he whispers into my hair. "I felt it as soon as you walked through the door." His mouth is so close to my cheek that if I turned my head, our lips would brush.

All my sense are on high alert. What would it be like to kiss a man? A prince? My only kiss was a quick peck from a young soldier who died in battle the next day. I can't begin to know how to please Ronan with a kiss or any sort of affection. I can only do what comes naturally to me, and if my display on the dance floor is any indication, that may be disastrous.

"There you are." Felix's voice drifts across the night air as he exits the ballroom to the balcony. When he sees Ronan and I, hands still clasped and faces inches apart, he stops. His posture is no longer that of a relaxed and confident prince, but that of a solider awaiting his orders.

"I was just telling Emilia about the glowing praise you gave her." Ronan pulls his hand from mine, and I let him go. No good comes from holding too tightly. It's a lesson I've learned well.

"She fought well," Felix admits, still standing straight as a ramrod.

"We should discuss the men who attacked you." Ronan leans back against the balcony's rail and crosses his arms. He looks relaxed and at ease, as if he's discussing a tea party rather than mine and Felix's near deaths.

"It's more of the same." Felix begins pacing the stone in front of Ronan and me. "The displaced villagers who are just trying to take what they can to survive. They're desperate."

That's the last thing I expected him to say about our attackers. But I don't speak up, not yet. I want to know more, and the men seem to have forgotten I'm here.

"As is my father. He only needs the book then he'll leave them alone." Though Ronan's posture suggests nonchalance, his voice is tight and his eyes are focused on the Commander.

"They don't have the book," Felix insists, with more force than I expect him to use with the Crown Prince. For not the first time in the last few minutes, I wonder about their friendship. "We've burned countless villages, and I've attended more than my share of senseless executions. When will this stop? Your father is creating monsters. Can't you reason with him?"

Though Ronan has every right to reprimand Felix for his cavalier words, he doesn't. Instead, he sighs and shakes his head as he seems to fold in on himself. "You know I can't. There's no reasoning with the man. I would leave them be, but he's intent on the Gate of Life. We both know it's an Insurgo myth, and my father is foolish to waste the empire's resources to look for it. There's no gate, no ancient gatekeeper, and no one is meant to live forever."

My heart leaps at his mention of Insurgos. Somehow, hearing of them even in the empire's capital, makes my commitment to their God more real. He's my God now. But I'm ashamed I don't know this story of the Gate of Life. Did Levi know? Perhaps he would have told me one day. I dig my fingernail into my palms and bite down on my frustration. Now I'll never know the stories of the people I'm fighting to save. I've never felt more alone, not even when I left the palace at seven years old.

Felix's eyes drift to me, and he shakes his head. Ronan follows his gaze.

"What is this gate?" I hope I sound innocent enough, but some curiosity is to be expected.

"Too dangerous for a lady like you." Ronan brushes his fingers lightly across my cheek then pushes himself from the railing. Conversation ended.

"Your father wants to do the reveal soon." Felix is back to business now as he gives Ronan the message I'm sure he was sent to deliver in the first place.

The Prince sighs and steps away from me. He removes his mask and gestures for Felix to do the same.

I study the two men, their full faces now exposed. Ronan looks like the marble statues of the gods chiseled into the facades of the temples. With nothing to obscure his features, his beauty is breathtaking. Felix, on the other hand, seems different than I remember, and it's not only because his beard is gone. I see lines of faint scars on his cheek, the hardened glint in his eyes. He looks fiercer than ever.

They trade masks, and Felix removes his cape for Ronan. The Prince makes the glittering adornments on the cape and mask look dull because he outshines them. Felix places the simple black mask over his own eyes.

"Escort her in please," Ronan instructs Felix with a nod to me. He disappears into the ballroom throng, and I'm left alone with the Commander.

"This is your cape." I can't think of anything better to say. My fingers fiddle with the ties until a larger hand covers my own and stills them. My eyes drift up to find Felix standing before me.

"Keep it," he insists softly then offers me his arm. I take it, but he doesn't walk immediately. "You impressed Ronan. It's not an easy thing to do."

"He seems impressed with you, too," I counter. Impressed is not the right word. There's a bond between the two men that I can't describe. Not quite brothers, but certainly more than a prince and his guard.

"Ronan and I have a long history," he admits. "It took me years to get to this point. You had only a few minutes."

"Perhaps after our dagger lessons, I can give you charm lessons," I offer and am surprised when he smiles. Not as blinding as Ronan's, nor as brilliantly handsome, but somehow more valuable.

"I wasn't sure you were serious about that."

We walk toward the ballroom where the crowd seems to push inward, toward the throne. Over the heads of the people, I can just make out Ronan's masked figure standing atop the dais with his parents. He's going to pretend as if he wore that costume the whole night, and no one will be the wiser. I smile at our secret. Will the women notice that his eye color has changed? I giggle over their possible confusion.

"What? Is the idea of lessons with me so humorous?"

I'd forgotten Felix still stood by my side. "Of course not. I'm just laughing at how confused all those women you charmed will be when they realize the Prince has blue eyes instead of brown."

"Is that the only difference?" He raises an eyebrow at me, and I can't tell if he's joking or actually curious.

"No," I admit. But the others are less physical. The men are similar enough in looks that masks hid their differences. What it couldn't hide was Felix's soldier's posture or Ronan's princely swagger. I find myself admiring both. "Perhaps we can begin lessons tomorrow? Maybe after dinner."

"You should see how your first day goes. Send word to me through Hannah or Antony if you still want to practice after tomorrow."

I don't know what he means. Does he think I won't want lessons because I'll be too tired or because my thoughts will be so full of Ronan I won't have time for anything else? Either way. I'm determined to prove him wrong.

7.

Felix releases my arm once he's pushed our way through the crowd. We stand in the front now with the other princesses and their escorts. I count twelve of them, and I make thirteen. Perhaps some are sisters or cousins since there are only five countries they could have come from. No one is from Borealis except me. I've known from the start my father only sent me because he had no one else.

Ronan makes great show of balancing his father's glass on his forehead, then juggling pieces of fruit someone handed him from the refreshment table. The crowd cheers and applauds, but I don't join in.

I feel eyes on me, and glance to Felix first, but he's watching the Prince's circus tricks. When I look toward the dais again, my gaze slams into the Emperor's. Up close, he is handsome, but it is lessened by the hard lines of his mouth and the coolness in his light eyes. Not that I expected to be welcomed warmly, but his scrutinizing stare seems to be reserved only for me.

After what feels like ages, he looks away and bangs his scepter on the marble floor. The pounding echoes throughout the hall.

Emperor Cyrus rises, and we all kneel in response. With my head bowed, I look from side to side for the cue to rise, but Felix's hand against my elbow is all the indication I need.

"Welcome," Ronan nearly shouts as he steps in front of his father.

I hold my breath. In Borealis, I would have been publicly reprimanded for such a show of disrespect. But Emperor Cyrus acquiesces his son and returns to his seat beside the Empress. He seems content to let Ronan run the show. For now. It's difficult to reconcile that behavior with the Ronan's response to Felix's plea to speak to his father about the raids. He'd seemed timid then.

"Tonight we've enjoyed mystery and merriment, and now it's time for the great unveiling." Ronan captivates everyone, including me, with the rise and fall of his voice. It's theatrical, yes, but no one questions him. He's a born leader. It makes me feel as if I'm only playing dress-up and someone will soon discover I'm not really a princess.

"Remove your masks," he commands with a wave of his hand, "and behold the truth behind the facade."

Music swells and torches flare as the crowd removes their masks with gasps and laughter. My mask feels heavy in my hands, but I relish the fresh air across my cheeks. I look to the other girls who stand in line with me. It was foolish of me to hope they would not be beautiful, and they each are. Most are blond with rays of sunlight in their yellow hair, but a few have rich brown locks that I envy. Their skin is pale and fair. None as dark as mine. My mother's heritage is unknown to me, but I did inherit her exotic look. It sets me apart from the rest, but I'm unsure if that's a good thing.

"Among these lovely ladies is my bride and the future Empress of Atlas." Ronan looks to each of us as the crowd roars its anticipation. "Over the next several weeks, I will observe them in a series of tests to determine their worthiness and their devotion to me. Those found wanting will be returned to their home kingdom."

I swallow hard as sweat moistens my palms. I resist the urge to wipe them on my dress. Even battle doesn't make me this nervous. The other girls remain stoic, their eyes locked reverently on the Prince.

Emperor Cyrus rises again and joins his son at the front of the dais. Ronan flinches as his father clamps a hand on his shoulder, but recovers so quickly I'm not sure if I really saw it at all. But it's not my imagination that Felix tenses beside me.

"To begin this competition, we must ask for the gods blessing upon the Crown Prince and each of these fair ladies in our presence," Cyrus booms. "I would ask Princess Emilia of Borealis, because of her position in the holy city, to incant the blessing."

The whole room spins as hundreds of eyes focus on me. Beside me, Felix is still quietly holding my elbow beneath his cape. I don't remember the words of the blessing because I haven't heard them since I was a small child. But I don't want to admit that. If I had grown up in Borealis, I would have served my time as a temple priestess before ascending to the throne. My city is the seat of worship for the entire empire, and I cannot tell them I don't know how to pray to their fake gods. To do so would be treason and an embarrassment to my country.

Silence fills the stuffy ballroom as Felix leads me to the stairs at the side of the dais. With all eyes on us, he leans close to undo the ties to the cape I still wear.

"Can you read lips?" he whispers as he pulls the tie loose.

"Yes." I breathe the word without moving my lips. An important skill to have when silently communicating with my fellow soldiers before a raid.

"Then keep your eyes on me." He pulls the cape from my shoulders with a flourish that frays my nerves. Then, he takes my hand and leads me up two stairs before passing me to Ronan.

The Prince's hand closes around mine for the second time tonight. I should feel fortunate for his attention, but dread courses through me instead. Cyrus smiles coldly at me as Ronan places me between him and his father. I recognize the cunning in his eyes. He's meant to set me up to fail. How much does he know about me?

I face the crowd and relinquish Ronan's hand. As is the custom, I lift my hands in the air, reaching toward the gods. Around the room, heads bow in revered silence. Only the royal family and the guards on the perimeter don't mirror the action. I frantically search the crowd for Felix, and find him standing with another guard at a nearby pillar. With my chin lifted toward the heavens, it's difficult to see him, but not impossible.

His lips move, and I begin the blessing.

"Most High Caelus, god of all gods, Sol Invictus, we ask your blessing and good fortune on our endeavor. Guide us by your blazing sun in the good path. Our payment to you, a sacrifice, shall fill the heavens with smoke and ash for your righteous wrath against those who are against us. Send us signs and wonders that your chosen one shall rule by the celebration of Natalis Solis."

"Sol omnia regit." The crowd intones the response in the old language. The sun rules over everything.

And they truly believe that. Everything I just uttered felt like a lie, and it is nothing like praying to my God. I feel dirty for even pretending that Caelus could hear me, for leading these people in their deception. But I look at Felix and hope he reads my thanks in my eyes. How did he know I would need help?

I don't have time for questions right now because the Emperor has dismissed the guests for the night, and amid the chaos, the girls in front of the dais are shooting daggers at me with their eyes. Though I survived the prayer, I've made enemies. A glance over my shoulder at Cyrus tells me this was his plan.

"Many thanks, Princess." He extends a hand to me, and I curtsy and kiss his knuckles, nearly losing my balance.

Ronan steadies me with a hand on my back, and I rise with him next to me. Though he means well, his presence won't help me make any friends either. "It was an honor, Majesty."

Beside me, Ronan groans softly, and before I can ask why, Cyrus has grabbed my arm and pulled me to him. Though his moves probably look harmless to our audience, his fingers bite into my arm so hard that I know I'll have bruises.

"You will address me as Imminence," he growls, his breath hot on my cheek. "I know who you are, and I will not let you disrespect this crown as your mother did with your father."

He releases me, and I step back into Ronan, determined not to let tears fall. I glance to the dispersing crowd, but no one seems to have noticed anything unusual about our exchange. Without a look in my direction, Emperor Cyrus spins on his heel and exits behind his throne.

I wilt a little, forgetting the Prince still stands next to me. But as he trails his fingers down my arm, I turn toward his handsome face.

"I'm sorry," he says. "My father is quite unforgiving about titles."

I wonder if Ronan heard all that his father said to me, if I am tainted for him because of my mother. "It was a grave error on my part," I concede. The other girls wouldn't have made that mistake.

"You must be tired since you haven't rested from your journey." He looks over his shoulder and summons Felix with a subtle twitch of his finger. "I'll have Felix take you to your rooms. Besides, I must see to the other ladies."

Of course he must. He told me as much earlier, but I deflate even more. Not even my connection with the Prince can be counted on to bolster my spirits. While I'm resting, he'll be making these same connections with the girls who looked as if they wanted to rip my eyes out moments ago.

Ronan passes me to Felix as if I'm a toy he's finished playing with and bounds down the steps to catch one of the blond girls before she exits the ballroom.

Even with a familiar presence by my side, I can't relax. There are too many questions in my head for the Commander, but I don't know how to ask them. We walk the path to my room in silence until we've left the crowd far behind.

It's Felix who speaks first. "Ronan is a good man."

I don't answer immediately because I don't know what to say. Disagreeing would be treason, and I'm not sure I do disagree. If I had been betrothed to Ronan as a child, I would be happy to marry him. I still think I might be happy to marry him, but I wonder how shallow it makes me. The things that draw me to him are superficial—he is handsome and he has the power to one day allow me to worship as I choose. But I know nothing of him as a person.

"How did you know I needed help with the blessing?" I ask my first question with a low voice in case someone lurks in the many shadows of the palace.

"I don't imagine it's a prayer you had much occasion to use on a military base." He doesn't look at me as he speaks, and we both keep walking. "It's difficult to remember the words to something you never say."

Or something you never meant. The words of the blessing resound in my head. *A sacrifice shall fill the heavens with smoke and ash for your righteous wrath against those who are against us.* Images of my mother tied to that wooden post, the faint scent of the oil coating the wood, the *whoosh* of the flames...

I double over and catch myself against the wall. Pain rips me from the inside out as hot tears well up in my eyes. This time, I can't stop them from spilling over.

"Emilia." Felix's hand is on my back, and concern colors his voice. "Are you all right?"

Words fail me, though I nod my head as the pain begins to dull. *God, forgive me. I know you are the only true God, and you never demand that kind of sacrifice. But why didn't you save my mother?*

The Commander's arms circle my waist then slide under my knees as he lifts me and cradles my body against his chest. I don't fight him, though I should feel ridiculous. But he lets me sniffle against him as he walks toward my room. All I know is I can't let Ronan see me this way, and I'm grateful for a moment with someone who has seen my strength before he saw my weakness.

I don't remember climbing into bed, but when I wake in the middle of the night, I'm alone. Beside me, tangled in the sheets as if I've clutched it tightly, is a red cape tinged with the scent of leather and smoky spice.

Years have passed since I woke up in a bed like this one. Before I open my eyes, I allow myself a moment to relish the memory of waking to my mother stroking my hair before I open my eyes and it all dissipates. My bedroom is empty, but the smell of lavender and the soft hum of a melody from the bathing room tells me I'm not alone.

A yawn parts my lips as I lift my arms over my head and stretch. I pause in mid-motion when the stays from my ball gown poke my ribs. Did I really sleep in my dress? Hard to believe Cecily didn't insist on me changing.

I'm on my feet and nearly in the bathing room when I remember how my night ended—doubled over with tears soaking my hands. The dull ache of that pain is still there, as if I ripped the scab off and it'll need time to heal again. Felix saw it all.

I spin back toward the bed, looking for the red cape I fell asleep beside, but it's nowhere to be found. Could I have dreamed it? He must think me a fool, a weak child, who cries at ghosts and holds tight to a piece of fabric that isn't even hers. Part of me is glad I don't remember anything after he picked me up last night.

I don't want to know how fragile I looked in his eyes. Or anyone else's for that matter.

At least it wasn't Ronan. I tell myself that as I give up my search for the cape and follow the humming to the bathing room.

Hannah stands over my steaming tub, generously pouring scented oil into the hot water. My entrance startles her, and she jumps as little as she ceases singing and offers a curtsy. Purple and yellow bruises mar her face, and my heart clenches for her. If her former master did these things to her in public, what else might he have done in private?

"Good morning, Highness. Are you ready for your bath?" If she's surprised to see I still wear my ball gown, she doesn't comment on it.

"Yes, but where are the other ladies?" Her face falls, and I know I've said the wrong thing. "I just want to know if I can speak frankly with you," I hurriedly add.

"They are preparing your breakfast tray and adding some last minute adornments to your dress for today. We did not expect you up so soon, Highness."

"Please, call me Emilia. There's no need for formality." Maybe because I feel sorry for her, or because I'm feeling sorry for myself, I want to cultivate this friendship. And I still need allies. Felix is good, but he isn't enough.

"But it's not proper." She looks as if I've asked her to grab a hot coal. "The punishment—"

"There is no punishment with me," I assure her. "Now, will you help me with my dress so I can enjoy this bath?"

"Of course, Hi—Emilia." Her hands make quick work of the fastenings on the dress, and I hold my breath as it slides to the floor.

I slide into the tub just as easily. Hot water soothes the tension in my muscles, and the lavender calms my restless spirit.

"Hannah, would you braid my hair?" I don't want her to leave me just yet, though I'm certainly capable of bathing myself. But I have questions for her.

She arranges my hair over the side of the tub and positions herself on a low stool behind me. I can no longer see her, but her finger work magic on my tangles.

"I would have done this last night, but the Commander told me not to wake you." She twists the dark strands together as I mull over this information.

How could I have fallen asleep in the time it took Felix to carry me to my room? What must my ladies think of me, being carried to bed after my first ball? "Did he stay long?"

"No, just long enough to settle you in. He did return early this morning to retrieve his cape, but didn't want you woken for that either."

"Oh." So I didn't dream it. And of course he would need it back for his uniform. When Ronan draped it over me last night, it wasn't really his to give.

"He asked me to tell you to name the horse, although I'm not sure what he meant by it. I—oh!" She brushes the last strand of hair from over my upper arm, and I know what she's uncovered. "Are you all right, Highness?"

I don't correct her. "Yes," I say as I picture the hand-shaped bruise on my arm. It probably doesn't look as bad as Hannah's face, but I'll never say that. "Just an unfortunate accident."

"I am familiar with those sorts of accidents," she says softly. "It wasn't Commander Fidelis, was it?"

Water splashes over the side of the tub, as I try to turn and face her. She must know it wasn't him. I won't have his reputation soiled. "No, not Felix. He's been kind to me." More than kind, though not overly friendly. I think of how he saved me from the bandit and wasn't ashamed to say I saved him as well.

"Hannah," I begin slowly. "Do you know of the bandits who attack travelers just outside the city?" This is the only safe way to approach the subject with her, because if I'm wrong about her allegiance, I could sign my own death warrant.

"Yes. Many in my village joined them when our homes were raided and burned. We lost everything and had no money to rebuild or pay our debts."

The prospect of raids sounded bad enough when Felix and Ronan discussed it last night, but hearing Hannah's story makes it real. Anger bubbles up inside me. "And who ordered these raids?" I think I already know.

"The Emperor." Her voice is low, as if she suspects someone will overhear. "It's the same on all sides of the city, even further into the mountains. He searches for the book or anyone harboring Insurgos."

Now that she's said the word, some of my anger morphs into excitement. Perhaps I'm on the right track after all. "And are there Insurgos out there? What book does he want?"

"The Aletheia," she whispers, and something ignites inside me. The restless beat of wings that have accompanied me for months finally still. This is what I am here for, and I know it with a certainty I can't explain. "And there are hardly any Insurgos here anymore. Most have gone into hiding. Some blend in within the city, others take to the high mountains."

"And others travel north to the gathering in Borealis," I supply. When I stand, my legs are shaky, and Hannah helps me from the tub before wrapping me in a large cloth. "That's where I met them."

"And where you met our God."

Neither of us speak for a moment as I decide how to answer. I've never told anyone but Levi that I believe in this God. "Yes," I finally say.

A smile unlike any I've ever seen slips across her bruised face. Her arms crush me against her in a hug unlike any I have ever known, and though I can't breathe, I also can't push her away. All ceremony and formality between us is strangled by the strange spirit that dances between us. I've heard Levi speak of it before.

Hannah seems to suddenly remember herself, and she steps back with her head bowed. I grab her hand, and she looks up with tears in her eyes.

"This is why you are here, to change our world."

"I hope so," I whisper. "But there's much I don't know. If only I had the Aletheia to read."

"We all wish that." She squeezes my hand. "But we have what we know in here," she places a hand over her heart, "and we share it."

"I don't have any words to share." If I had known Levi wouldn't be with me forever, I might have tried harder to memorize his words. I couldn't write them down, for fear of being found out, but I could have hidden them in my heart. I have nothing to exchange in this currency.

"The word of the Lord is right and true, and he is faithful."

The cadence of her voice is so familiar, words suddenly spring to my lips. "Blessed be the Lord, my rock, who trains my hands for war and my fingers for battle." It seems I did remember something after all, though I don't know what it says about me, that the only Holy Aletheia verse I have memorized has to do with war. The hunger for more grows inside me. "Will you teach me?"

"I don't know much," she confesses. "But I will give you everything I have."

Of course she will. Because it's a reflection of the God we believe in. The very reason I agreed to listen to Levi instead of kill him. This is a God who, rather than demand a sacrifice of the people, became the sacrifice. I don't completely understand it, haven't reconciled it with why my mother had to die, but I believe it.

Our conversation ends as Cecily returns from the kitchen with my breakfast tray, and the other maids follow with a new dress shortly after.

Though I'm encouraged by my talk with Hannah, I put it from my mind and focus on the court gossip surrounding the ball last night and the first outing with the Prince today. My ladies can't wait to hear my thoughts on Ronan, especially since one of them heard from a guard that I spent time alone the Prince on the balcony.

A pleasant flush warms my cheeks as I think of those too brief moments. "He is everything you've heard him to be," I tell them.

Then I recount the switch Ronan and Felix pulled that allowed me the private time. They sigh and smile, and I find myself doing the same. It feels good to be among friends. Hannah and I exchange knowing smiles. In a few short minutes, my ladies have managed to make me forget the terrible end to last night's adventures. Today is a new day, and when Antony arrives to escort me, I've made up my mind to seize it.

I am the second girl to arrive at the stables, and I find that someone has already saddled my mare for me. Not the beautiful black filly I saw yesterday, but the docile creature Ronan picked out just for me. But he didn't know me then, and though it's a suitable horse for a princess, she's too tame for me. Still, I rub my hand across her chestnut coat and let her nudge my hand while thinking of the message Hannah passed to me from Felix—name the horse. I know he means the wild thing is now mine and I smile.

The other girl stands next to a gray horse, her pale hand hovering over its coat as if she's afraid to touch the animal. She gives up, crushing her fingers into a fist and returning the hand to her side.

"It's all right," I call to her before I can stop myself.

She whips around, her blond hair falling over her shoulder, to face me. I remember her from last night, but today, without the mask and the makeup, she looks much younger.

"I'm terrified of them," she admits. Her teeth sink into her full lip and she ducks her head. "I didn't realize until they brought me here that the Prince intends to take us on a riding tour of the countryside."

That's news to me, but I repress my smile because this girl doesn't seem happy about it. If I was afraid of horses, perhaps I wouldn't be either. "What's your name?" I approach her slowly, as if she's a snake who might strike at any moment.

"Davina, Princess of Austrina." She bows slightly to me, as if she is subject to my authority. So I return the favor.

"Emilia, Princess of Borealis."

We both rise from our bows, and she offers the first tremulous smile. She is petite and fine-featured, with a cute nose I envy. Reminiscent of a pixie, which makes me feel like an awkward giant.

"How old are you?" I ask, because her stature makes it hard to guess.

"Fifteen. I believe I'm the youngest here. My ladies say most are seventeen or eighteen."

"We're all so close in age then? How convenient."

"No, not convenience at all." She raises her delicate brow, as if shocked I don't know. If only she knew how ignorant I am of this whole thing. "When Ronan was born twenty years ago, every king in the realm planned to conceive a daughter. They saw this opportunity for what it was, a chance for a stronger alliance with the capital."

So all of us were born for this moment. It leaves a sour taste in my mouth. I am no more special than any of the others, and we are all merely a bargaining chip for our fathers.

"Lucky us," I mutter, but Davina doesn't seem to notice.

"I saw you at the ball last night. You looked lovely."

Yes, everyone saw me at the ball, delivering the blessing, but I don't point that out to her. "Thank you. As did you. It was wonderful to start this event off with such a fine affair."

"Yes, I'm glad I got to enjoy it, since I don't imagine I'll be staying here long." She says this as though it's a foregone conclusion, but it takes me off guard.

"What? Why will you be leaving?"

"I know I don't have much of a chance with Prince Ronan. I'm the youngest girl here, and my family doesn't have much to offer the Emperor or Aurora."

"But if Ronan wants you here, you'll stay."

"I doubt very much what Ronan wants will factor in to the decision." She sighs heavily. "We are pawns, all of us, in our fathers' games."

Her words hit me like icy water. I've been a fool to assume this would be as simple as making a man fall in love with me— which I never really thought simple at all. After last night, I may be sent home before Davina.

Other girls approach the stables with their escorts, so we end our conversation. I do offer to switch horses with Davina since mine is so gentle, and she graciously accepts. The gray mare dances nervously beside me as I lead her away from the others.

As I whisper words to calm my horse, I study my competition. All around me, girls mount their horses, some with the aid of a mounting block, others with the aid of the groom or their escort. They all ride sidesaddle. Admittedly, it's the best choice given these ridiculous dresses we're all wearing. But I haven't done it since I was a small child, and I can't even remember how to mount it properly.

I watch Antony take a moment to help Davina and her escort, because her nerves have made even the gentle horse I loaned her prance with anxiety. Her pretty face is pinched as Antony finally climbs atop the block and plops her down on the saddle. She freezes and squeezes her eyes shut until her escort gently hands her the reins.

"Ready to try it for yourself?" Ronan and Felix have appeared behind me, both on their mounts, and the Prince smiles as if he has a secret.

Should I tell him I have no idea what I'm doing? I'm afraid to look inadequate even in these little matters, but it would it be a breach of etiquette to ride astride my horse instead.

"Or perhaps the lady needs some help." Ronan climbs off his horse and presses into my personal space. His hands grab me loosely around the waist, and there's something about the intimacy of touch, even through layers of fabric, that brings a smile to Ronan's face and heat to mine. His striking blue eyes look into mine, and though I've resolved not to read too much into his actions, my stomach flip-flops.

He lifts me easily into the saddle, and I instinctively swing one leg over each side. From the murmurs that rise around us, I know I've broken some unwritten rule. To his credit, Ronan says nothing, but remounts his horse as I smooth my skirts. The girls behind me are not so considerate.

"I can't believe they let the stable girl play dress up," one whispers loudly.

"Not even a proper lady," the other agrees. "She rides like a man, I've heard her hands are as coarse as a man's.... At least we know she'll be sent away first."

With a nudge of my heels, my horse walks forward, away from the girls. All the things they said are true, and truth is sharper than any lie and cuts twice as deep. Why did I think I belonged here? Ronan may have admired me from the stories Felix told, but he doesn't need another guard. He wants a lady, a wife, and I don't know how to be that.

But I have to learn. Unless there is another way to end the persecution of the Insurgos and allow them to worship freely, I must marry Ronan. My differences are my advantage. He will remember me when all the others blend together. So I lift my chin and direct my horse to the front of the pack.

"Good morning, ladies." Ronan has positioned himself in front of the group and paces his horse before us. "I trust you all slept well."

I hear giggles behind me, but I ignore them.

"Today we're visiting my favorite spot in the forest where we'll have a picnic. I want to take this time to talk with each of you individually, and I hope you'll get to know each other. Though my father has announced this as a competition, we should remember the unity we celebrate in our great realm."

Moments later, our caravan leaves the city's walls and moves toward the forest. Our pace feels like a crawl since some of the girls have complained about their horse's gait jostling them too much. I can't help but roll my eyes. At least from my position in the back, no one can see me.

I allow myself to fall behind, then urge my horse into a short gallop because it's the only way I can feel the wind on my face. After the second time, Felix leaves Ronan's side to circle back to me.

"You traded your horse, I see." He keeps his eyes on the group in front of us so I do the same.

"Davina needed a gentler horse." The blond girl holds tightly to her saddle, but the horse plods along. "She's terrified of them, you know."

"Do you?" he counters.

I can't help but look at him now. He's squinting in the sun's early light, dressed in a uniform much like Ronan wore at the ball last night. Behind him, waving lightly in the wind, is the red cape. "Do I know she's afraid of horses?" His question makes no sense.

"No. Do you know what it's like to be afraid of anything?"

Has he forgotten last night so quickly? Or is he making fun of me? "If you mean last night—"

"I don't. I mean now." His eyes flicker briefly to me. Could God have made a more confusing man? "You can't keep drawing attention to yourself. I've been listening to those girls' conversations, and they are capable of more than you realize."

"You've done nothing but point him in my direction."

"And you're the one who pretended to need help mounting her horse when we both know you probably ride better than Ronan. You're not that girl, and you won't win any friends by being her."

"I'm not here for friends." My voice is low and harsh as my fingers choke on the reins and pull my horse to a halt. I wait for

Felix to follow suit. "I don't have the luxury. Either I win or I face my father who exiled me as a child. I don't care if these girls like me."

"You can't be a lone wolf." He rakes a hand through his dark hair and sighs. "Apologies, my lady. I want you to win, Highness, but there is a cost. I would be remiss in my duty if I didn't give you the message."

I like his formality even less than his warning. "Am I in real danger?" Ignoring warnings, especially from the Commander, isn't an option for me. Not when the Emperor's handprint is still outlined in a bruise on my arm.

"Not yet. But you should be careful."

Antony calls to us, and I realize how far behind we've fallen. Digging my heels into my horse, I gallop forward, leaving Felix behind.

I make an effort to speak to all the girls once we settle into a clearing for the picnic. This is difficult to do since the majority won't look away from Ronan long enough to make conversation with anyone. Very few have kind words for me, but then I don't offer any of my own in return. Two girls—Livia and Cordelia— are almost pleasant, and I cross them off my list of the people who want to harm me. They are too confident in their own abilities to be concerned with mine.

Cassia and Gloriana—the two brunettes from Zephyros—make small talk with me, and I know from their voices, they are the ones who hurled insults after I mounted my horse. Felix's words echo in my mind as I consider the battles I've fought against men from Zephyros. They are cunning and wily, and we almost never took prisoners for fear they would somehow kill us in the middle of the night. I'll have to keep my eyes on these two.

True to his word, Ronan makes time for each of us. When he finds me, I'm standing on the bank of a small stream, watching the water meander toward an unseen destination.

"I saved you for last." He picks up a rock and tosses it in the water with a weak splash. Silence stretches between us. Then, without warning, he laughs.

"Have I done something funny?" Perhaps the earlier events have made me oversensitive, but no one else is nearby for him to be laughing at.

"No, no. Forgive me. It's just that, each lady has been dying to tell me everything about herself—and I do mean everything—and you keep silent." His sideways look twists me in knots. "You are quite the mystery, Princess. Will you walk with me?"

I shouldn't accept special treatment here in the open, but I'm not sure how to turn him down. "Perhaps we should sit here. You would be vulnerable walking alone with me should someone choose to attack."

It's a weak argument, and not necessarily true, but I can't think of anything better.

"You sound like my mother, always worried about the Insurgos assassinating me or my father."

Ronan stretches out on the grass and reclines on his elbows. I spread out my dress and sit beside him. Again, neither of us speaks for several minutes.

"You really have nothing to say to me?" he asks.

Of course I do, but nothing on my mind is safe to discuss, especially after he has just mentioned Insurgos and assassination in the same breath. "Perhaps another time," I say. "Besides, your head is so full of information about all of us that you wouldn't remember if I preferred pink or blue or whatever other nonsense I'm supposed to be telling you right now."

"You wore blue last night, so I might guess you prefer it. And you came as a peacock. Some say it's a symbol for immortality, but I assume you didn't know that or how it would anger my father."

His smile fades into a serious frown, and I almost prefer this look because it's authentic. The impulse to touch my fingers to his face and smooth his brow nearly bowls me over, and I look away to keep from acting on it.

"Why would it anger your father?" I keep staring at my dress as I ask. "Does it have something to do with that gate you mentioned last night?"

"Yes. The Gate is said to give immortality to those who pass through it, and my father is bent on finding it. Your costume was a reminder of all the times he's failed and what it means for the kingdom."

"What's that?"

"Revolution." His answer is cold and ominous. "The Insurgos have a leader, the Ancient, who guards this gate. The book my father searches for tells of how the Ancient will sit upon the throne. He thinks it's only a matter of time before the Insurgos rise up and try to overthrow us. That they have gathered in a secret place to plan their attack."

Dozens of questions roll through my mind, but I swallow them all. Seeming eager could get me killed. Besides, the bitterness in Ronan's voice intrigues me almost as much as the gate or this Ancient.

"You don't agree?" I allow myself a look in his direction. For the first time, I see the weight on his shoulders. He does a fine job of hiding it, but without the crowds to entertain, he's really just a boy forced to follow in his father's footsteps whether he likes it or not.

"I don't know what to think. If the Insurgos do have the key to immortality, it must be through something other than our gods. You know better than most that Caelus only grants immortality to those who have kept his will, which might change on a whim. And even then, it is only an afterlife and not more years on earth."

It takes a moment before I realize why he assumes I know so much about Caelus—because I come from Borealis. I have to choose my next words carefully. "Perhaps it concerns the God they worship."

The truth is a mystery to me as well, because I know nothing of this gate. Though I know I will go to Heaven with God after my death, I'm not sure this is the immortality he speaks of. There's so much I didn't have time to learn from Levi. Could this just be one of many things he didn't tell me?

"Your mother believed in this God, didn't she?"

His words fan the flame of the pain that incapacitated me last night. This time there is no one to catch me. "Yes."

"And she was not immortal."

It's not a question, but I feel as if I should answer. "No. She wasn't. At least not here. But she believed in the afterlife where she would live forever."

"It would be nice to be assured of such a thing." Wistfulness colors his words, and I can't keep myself from reaching for his hand. Our fingers twist together until my palm presses against his. My rough one against his smoother skin. "Thank you, Emilia."

"For what?" I can't imagine what I've done that would warrant his gratitude.

"I have listened to everyone today, but you're the first that's listened to me."

Warmth crawls through me. *Thank you, God. You gave me words when I had none.* "Being in your position must be very lonely, and I know the value of a listening ear, especially when you have a hard choice ahead of you."

"Maybe not that hard."

If the choice was solely his, his words might comfort me. But I think of my bruise and know someone else pulls Ronan's strings.

10

My message to Felix lies on the small table beside my bed. Words marked through and scribbled out speak of my indecisiveness. Though I began the note three times, I can't bring myself to finish it. My resolve to train with him wavers.

But my hesitance isn't about the training—which I don't really need—as much as it is about Felix himself. His behavior at the picnic a few days ago was odd. First his warning, then his apparent indifference toward me. I can't understand what he wants from me or why I should even care. And I have too many other things to worry about without fretting over what a guard thinks of me or this competition.

Instead I'll worry about the news we received at dinner tonight—the dinner where no one but Davina spoke to me. Ronan sent home girls, whose names I couldn't remember, and it sent the rest of us into a sort of quiet frenzy. One thing is abundantly clear, no one is guaranteed much time. Despite Felix's suggestion, I might not have the time to be subtle in my interactions with the Prince. I'm more worried about being sent away than I am a few jealous girls.

As if that wasn't enough, Ronan informed us all that our individual time with him would be dictated by this father, at least until his birthday in three weeks, at which time he would be officially considered an adult. I know I didn't imagine that he looked at me when he said this. Though neither of us seems willing to say it, we both know Emperor Cyrus doesn't like me. Whether it's my mother's history or something else entirely, I don't think he would shed a tear to see me go.

And where would I go? I pace the length of my bed as Hannah watches from a chair near the door. She's waited patiently to take my note to Felix, and if she thinks me mad, she keeps it to herself. Wherever I went, I'd take her with me. There's nothing for her here.

"Would you like me to fetch Commander Fidelis?" she offers.

"That won't be necessary." The darkness outside my window beckons to me, and I stop pacing to rest my forearms on the sill. I've never been good at sitting still, and my room feels more like a prison than royal accommodations.

"Perhaps some tea then? You've been restless since you returned from dinner."

Restless. Yes, I am. The only time my caginess has subsided was when Hannah and I spoke of the Aletheia. But I don't know any more to comfort me. I can only meditate on the verses I do know.

"It's only nerves." I turn and offer her what I hope is a convincing smile. Lying isn't my intention, but I'm not sure what to tell her. "It's very hard to sit still when I'm wondering what Ronan is doing at the moment, or who he's with."

There's more truth to those words than I want to admit. Everything about this process is tedious. Rather than spending my days training with a new weapon or polishing my old ones, I've been forced to attend teas with my competition and learn silly new dances. I miss the military where the sort of tension that exists between all the girls would've been settled with a sparring match on the first day, and then everyone would have laughed about it afterward.

I've been here a week and no one's laughing.

We're all expected to be perfect ladies with the reward of time spent with Ronan dangling over our heads. Except I've spent no time with him since the picnic. A few meaningful glances across a room—the sort that make my pulse race, my stomach turn somersaults—are all that keep me going.

"I don't know why he doesn't just send me home if his father forbids him to spend the time with me."

"Don't worry. He will choose you. It's God's will."

Hannah seems so certain of this, but I don't share in her assurance. I also don't like that phrase because it sounds so similar to the standard "if Caelus wills it so" that is tossed around so flippantly. My God's will is written his Aletheia, which no longer exist in written form, but it makes me feel better knowing that there was once a record of it. If something is written, it is difficult to change. I like the thought of a constant God. Ronan would, too.

But Levi, whose word is the only one I have, didn't tell me that I would marry a prince. He said I would save the people— the Insurgos. Becoming Empress seems the most logical way to achieve that, though it would still involve convincing Ronan. But what if there was another way?

How much truth was in Ronan's words? My father and the other kings of the realm have always been afraid of the Insurgos—a name the government chose to classify them as rebels—but I never imagined how deep that fear ran. The Emperor fears revolution. While I can't imagine Levi overthrowing the throne, I acknowledge that my experience with the Insurgos has been limited to my interactions with him and my mother. And now Hannah. All seemed peace-loving, but the idea of a true rebellion sparks something in me.

What if it were true? Maybe Levi's last words were a code I was meant to decipher—God has trained me for war and battle. Perhaps he means for me to use those skills to liberate his people.

My fingers tingle in anticipation. This I could do. But I don't know where to start. I know there are small Insurgos camps in the northern corners of Borealis, but they can't be the sum of their forces. Where would they gather to assemble their army, to plan their attack? And if I could somehow find them, how can I convince them to let me join?

"Hannah," I say softly as I continued to gaze out the window into velvet darkness. "Do the Insurgos have a home or a place that is sacred to them?"

"None that I'm aware of. My grandmother used to say that when she was a small child, the Insurgos were everywhere, in every country of the realm. Only when Emperor Cyrus's father came to power and began the Crusade did our people disperse into small villages and camps."

My ignorance both concerning the Insurgos and my competition for Ronan's hand works against me. I must remedy that. In a palace this size, there must be a grand library with volumes of history of our kingdoms. Perhaps I'll find clues there about my people. At least it's a first step.

The second will be to glean what information I can from the other girls. Are there Insurgo camps in their countries? If I can find the base, at least I may have somewhere to go if Ronan sends me home.

That thought pains me more than it should. Though I don't really know him and he was supposed to be a means to an end, our conversation by the stream softened my heart toward him. Did anyone else see what I saw when he let his guard down? Even if he doesn't choose me, I'm not sure I'll be able to abandon him without the hope in God I hold so dear. If only those words weren't punishable by death.

"You should get some rest," Hannah suggests as she pats my braid. Over my shoulder, I hear her rustling the sheets, no doubt turning them down.

"Wake me early," I tell her as I turn away from the window. "I want to explore at dawn."

She doesn't question my request, but gives me a small bow, then leaves me alone with my thoughts.

❈

Though I spent the last several years without the luxury of royal accommodations, I'm not a stranger to them. I certainly can't erase the first decade of my life. But the yawning stretch of halls and labyrinths in this palace dwarf those of my childhood. Somewhere there must be maps, perhaps in a library, but I've no idea how to find it.

Instead, the first hours of my morning are spent wandering the stone hallways, far from the fuss and bustle of court. My mind drifts between the events of the past few days as I put one foot in front of another without a destination in mind.

That I should not be here is true in every sense of the word. Not walking the halls unsupervised or even in this palace at all. Given time, I've no doubt the other girls will reiterate this in their less than subtle ways. If Felix is right, they may remove me altogether. No one is blind to the pointed looks Ronan gives me, even if he never approaches. Despite all the marks against me, I've somehow found favor with the crown prince. At least part of that must ride on the recommendation the Commander gave me.

It's a puzzle for sure. Why is Felix so keen on me winning? Why would he go out of his way to put me in Ronan's good graces and then gravely warn me of the dangers of being there?

I turn a corner to a hallway that looks nearly identical to the three before it. Stone walls decorated with gilded art and well-polished weapons and not a soul in sight. As I pass the occasional door, I sometimes hear muffled voices or the clatter of pots and pans. Perhaps I've found my way to the servants' quarters or at least the service area.

I leave the doors untried because no good can come of me announcing my presence down here. At best, they'd chastise me for wandering off alone and sent to my rooms, then probably call Felix or another guard to escort me back. But I file the location away for reference. Though my ladies have been a wonderful source for palace gossip thus far, they may not always suffice. The eave at end of the hallway would be a perfect place to eavesdrop if I ever require additional information.

Information. That's why I sought the library in the first place. It's the currency of secrecy. Being a soldier taught me that much. If the hope of controlling my own destiny is ever to be within my grasp, I need to stockpile all I can about the palace and about the Insurgos.

"No. No, this is not acceptable!" A shrill voice echoes around another turn in the hall, followed by the ridiculous heels most of the other girls insist on wearing.

I duck into the tapestry-covered eave I just passed and press my back against the cool stone. The faded cloth hides me, but I hold my breath and listen to the sounds growing nearer.

"Yes, my lady, of course. But we cannot make apple tarts if apples are not in season." A man this time, probably a servant judging by his tone, and clearly an exasperated one.

"'My lady'?" The girl scoffs and I finally recognize her. Only one person could make a single sound that condescending. Gloriana. "You will address me as Your Majesty, you fool."

The slap of skin on skin resounds in the empty hall, and my muscles recoil at the sound.

"Of-of course, Majesty."

"Now, where are my apple tarts? You must have apples somewhere in this miserable place. Everyone knows they are Ronan's favorite."

"Yes, Majesty, they are certainly a favorite of the Prince, but he understands that the apples will not be ripe for picking for a fortnight."

"Then give me something to impress him." Exasperation is anything but subtle in her tone. "I can't show up to a picnic with the Prince without something."

A flick of jealousy stings me, but only for a moment. It's to be expected in this competition. As much as I might wish to deny it, Ronan must spend time with the other girls. He might even *choose* to spend time with them. But Gloriana? It hurts more than I imagined it would.

I linger in my hiding place until Gloriana's rant and her clicking footsteps have long faded. Once I'm sure no one else haunts the halls, I slip from behind the curtain and around the corner to dart out the first door I come to.

The monochromatic gray walls give way to a lush canopy of green, and I realize I've stumbled into some sort of garden. And for the first time in what feels like a lifetime, relaxation begins to work its way into my muscles.

The air is thick with humidity, and birds flutter their wings overhead. Around me, flowers of all colors bloom with a cheery brightness I've yet to see in Aurora. In fact, I've never seen plants like this, maybe because I don't think anywhere in our realm could sustain the sweltering heat and humidity this greenhouse simulates.

"Hello? Is someone there?" A timid voice calls out from a wall of lush green.

"Davina?" Brushing aside the foliage leaves drops of moisture on my hand and forearm as I reveal the petite princess between the flowers. "What are you doing out here?"

"It's lovely, isn't it?" She pats the wooden bench she sits on for me to join her. "I found it by accident last night, but it's even more beautiful in the daylight."

"I've never seen plants like these." I join her but position myself on the edge of the bench. "We don't have anything like this in Borealis."

"Nor do we in Austrina." Her thin fingers stroke a brilliant purple flower with a sort of gentleness I don't think I ever possessed. "These come from Solitarius."

The name shocks me from the hypnotizing hum of the garden. "Solitarius? But why would someone go there for plants?"

A soft tittering laugh parts her lips, and Davina smiles shyly at me. "It's not just for the plants. Surely you must know that the realm imports sugarcane from the island. The sailors also bring back plants and exotic fruits. Have you ever had a coconut?"

"No," I admit, trying to imagine an island full of bright colors and sugar and fruit. "I thought Austrina supplied the sugar for the realm."

"At one time we did, but the cane doesn't grow as well in my country as it does on the island. And it's not as if anyone lives in Solitarius to mind us taking it. Austrina's major industry is shipbuilding. We supply the vessels for the empire's sailors. It's big business. Before the first run of the year, the Emperor himself comes to the ports to bless the ships' journeys and then stays with my family until the ships return."

"Oh. But you told me your family had little to offer the Emperor." It seems to me that Davina would fair well in this competition, or at least be in Cyrus's good graces.

"We could be easily replaced. It's true that the most convenient place for the ships to launch is from Austrina, but they could also launch from southern Zephyros. Of course they'd have to clear that area of those Insurgo refugees that no one wants to acknowledge."

"Insurgos?" I nearly choke on the word. Davina eyes me as I try to regain my composure. "Sorry, I just never knew they were a problem anywhere but the mountains of Borealis."

"Every country has them, but no one speaks of them. My father says after the Crusade they dispersed and migrated to the edges of every country."

My heart leaps with hope. That there are many Insurgo groups around Atlas might suggest strategic planning. Might Cyrus have been right about a revolution? I don't want to dare to hope it. "What are they doing there?"

"Existing, I suppose. I've heard raids happen periodically just to keep them in line, but—"

"Princess Emilia? Highness?" Antony's frantic call interrupts Davina and sends me to my feet.

Something is wrong. I would know it even if the tone of his voice didn't suggest as much. The air has changed, and the pleasant heaviness of the greenhouse now feels suffocating. I grab Davina around the wrist and pull her after me as I plunge through the green wall of leaves. We emerge in front of the doorway I entered and nearly collide with Antony dressed in his full uniform, cheeks flushed and slightly out of breath.

He steps back in surprise as he surveys the two of us. "Apologies, Highness," he says as he bows slightly, "but I've been looking all over for you. There's been an urgent meeting called, and I am to escort you at once to the Empress's drawing room. You too, Princess Davina."

"Yes, of course." I shoot him an inquisitive look though I know he can't say more, not in front of Davina. But his eyes darken, and despite the temperature of the room, goosebumps break out along my arms.

We follow him in silence through the hallways I traversed earlier, Davina clinging to my arm as if my proximity will protect her against whatever we're walking in to. I wish I was alone, or at least alone with Antony. Walking into the unknown is not a new feeling for me, but preparation is always preferable.

He stops in front of an ornately carved wooden door and bows to us once again. "This is where I leave you, ladies. I'll return to escort you back to your rooms."

"What's going on?" Davina whispers as Antony takes his leave and we stare at the door.

"I don't know, but we might as well find out."

As we step through the doors, a herald announces our entrance and all eyes turn our way. My fellow competitors fill the room, and guards stand watch at the four corners and at either side of the door. Davina leaves my side and heads for the table of refreshments they've provided for us while I scan the room.

Most girls give me only a cursory glance before returning to their conversations, but Cassia and Gloriana, who huddle together near the window, stare with narrowed eyes and perfect pouts.

Though I should ignore them, take up my position with the rest of the wallflowers, my feet carry me in their direction. Pretense builds a wall of tension between us as they greet me with icy smiles.

"Oh, I'm so relieved you're unharmed." Gloriana tosses a lock of her brown hair over her shoulder.

"Yes, especially when we saw that guard leave your room this morning," Cassia adds. "And then they called this horrible meeting…"

I debate asking them what exactly this meeting is about, but decide to play along.

"Yes, I'm quite well, thank you. And I'm afraid you're mistaken about a guard in my room. I've been alone with my ladies all morning." This lie is a gamble, but I'm confident that Gloriana at least, didn't witness anyone entering my room. "And you, Gloriana, I'm sorry that your outing with the Prince had to be cancelled because of this meeting."

The shock on her face is worth the jab and the risk of giving my spying away. Let her wonder how I know this information.

"Oh, Emilia, did you hear?" Davina appears at my side again, oblivious to the tension between me and the Zephyros princesses. "This meeting, it's about Livia. Something happened to her last night."

"Yes, quite tragic," Cassia insists. "Poor girl tripped down a flight of stairs or something. Complete accident, I'm sure. Which is why it's a waste of time to hold us here and question us like common criminals."

In my experience, criminals would never have been herded into a room and allowed to discuss their knowledge before giving a formal inquiry to those in charge. And if Cassia is certain that Livia's fall was an accident, I'm confident it wasn't.

The response I'm conjuring is forgotten as the air in the room shifts, and we all instinctively turn toward the door. Felix stands in the doorway, posture rigid and eyes hard. He scans the room, but his eyes linger on me a fraction of a second too long.

"Oh, your guard has come to see you again. Very brazen of him, though, don't you think? Especially after he was seen leaving your room."

Gloriana's words knock me back, and I look around to see if anyone else heard. But no one pays us any mind since they're all focused on Felix. "I told you I've been alone with my ladies all morning."

"The perhaps the guard was there for one of them?" Cassia suggests before she sips her tea. "Though it would be such a waste. He's very handsome."

Disgust slithers through me as she ogles the Commander. But somehow this is all his fault. As always, he gives me more questions than answers. What business would he have in my room? Surely he must know how it would look.

"Ladies." His smooth voice booms over the quiet conversations in the room, and everyone that wasn't already staring at him, looks his way. "As you may have heard, Princess Livia was injured last night. We have reason to believe it wasn't an accident as first thought. Upon orders of Emperor Cyrus, you will all submit to questioning about your knowledge of the events. You will remain in this room until you've spoken to me and I've released you." He pauses and levels his eyes in my direction once again. "Princess Cassia, will you step this way please?"

One by one, the girls file in front of the Commander, speaking in soft tones, some even shedding tears. Cassia and Gloriana appear bored, even going so far as to yawn, but I can't tell if it's because they know more than they're letting on or they simply don't care for anyone but themselves. As Gloriana walks away, Felix rolls his eyes, and I have to stifle a giggle. But it's too late because he's already set his sights on me.

I'm the last one, so there's no use waiting for him to call my name. Still, I take my time crossing the room, weaving through the crowd since no one has left the room as Felix indicated they could.

"Princess." He stands and holds out a hand in gesture for me to sit opposite him. I do so without meeting his eyes. "Can you tell me your activities from last night until you were retrieved by Antony this morning?"

"I returned to my quarters after dinner and remained there with my ladies until this morning when I visited the greenhouse and met Davina." Not enough detail to satisfy him, but enough that he can't ask more questions without prying.

"You must have left very early for the greenhouse. I came by your rooms, hoping to escort you to this meeting and you weren't there."

Oh. I'd nearly forgotten his ill-advised visit. "That's a subject I suggest you tread lightly on, Commander. You know how it might look to have you sneaking around my rooms at all hours."

His eyes darken before he glances over his shoulder and then leans in to speak lowly to me. "We didn't know if anyone else had been attacked. I organized the guards to check in on each of the girls, but Ronan insisted I look after you myself. When I realized you weren't there and no one had seen you for hours... Don't do that again."

"I'm not one of your soldiers you can order around."

"So we're back to that, are we? Highness." His emphasis of my title is hissed through his clenched teeth.

I'm about to respond, to tell him that he's done nothing but confuse me and, perhaps if he'd be completely honest with me, we could come to some sort of compromise about my safety. But I'm saved having to say any of this by the arrival of an imposing figure.

Empress Valentina stands still as a statue in the doorway, pale eyes dancing across each of our faces. Her gaze freezes me with a cool indifference more intimidating than any of the military officers I trained with. She takes a step into the room, and one by one we curtsy low as if we are a wave bowing to the force of the moon.

"Rise," she says once she takes her seat near a window.

The girls instantly line up to personally greet her, but I retreat to my corner, surprised to find Felix has taken this opportunity to take his leave of me. I take note of what the Empress appears to like—a soft word, strong posture—and what she doesn't like—magnanimous gushing or a bowed head. Most of the girls fall into the latter category, though a few manage to put on a brave front.

I wait until I can ignore her no longer. Then I square my shoulders, lengthen my neck and approach her as I would my commanding officer, though I hope with a little more grace.

"Your Imminence." I bow low and wait for the Empress to release me. She does with the clearing of her throat and a flick of her wrist. When I rise, she fixes a critical eye on me. "It's such an honor to finally meet you."

"You're not what I expected." Her voice is light and high, but still commands the sort of respect her position demands. Years of practice, I suppose. "I met your mother once. You may have surpassed her beauty."

"But not yours, Imminence." I wait for her to mention something else about my mother, the thing that's on everyone's mind, but she doesn't. Instead, she motions for me to take the seat beside her.

Though the other girls have been tittering softly in the background, pretending not to pay attention, they all fall silent as I perch on the arm of the chair, ready to take flight at the first sign of trouble.

"You'll join me today at each of my appointments." Her tone remains cool as if she's undecided how she feels about her own decision. Or perhaps it wasn't hers at all. "To see what it really means to be Empress of Aurora and Atlas."

"Yes, your Imminence." Refusing isn't an option, though I know spending the day with her means losing out on precious time with Ronan both at dinner and whatever social activity is planned for us this evening. Perhaps the Empress knows this as well.

"Each of you will have this same opportunity if you can manage to prove to me that you possess something worthy of being a queen." The rest of the girls squirm under her gaze, and I try desperately to keep my chin from dropping.

What could I possibly have done to display any sort of regal aptitude? From the moment I arrived, I've been a bumbling mess, save from the moments when I've been alone with Ronan. I'm the girl her husband hates, whose mother could have brought revolution to the realm, and who has handsome guards sneaking in and out her quarters at all hours. What does she want with me?

"Well go on, girl. Drink your tea. A queen doesn't go anywhere until she's had her tea." She flicks her long fingers toward the saucers full of steaming liquid on a nearby table.

Everyone moves toward the refreshments then as if the Empress has released us all from some sort of spell. I follow suit, but when I raised my cup to my lips, my hands shake.

"I know what you did with that servant girl of yours."

I pull my hand from the curtains blocking the carriage window and peer at the Empress through my lashes. "I'm sure I don't know what you mean, Imminence."

"Where is your crown, my dear?" She studies me with an unreadable expression. The years it must have taken her to perfect this mask have certainly paid off.

"I thought it might be presumptuous of me to wear my own crown in your presence. I am, after all, only a princess of a foreign land."

"Do you know why you are here? With me, I mean?" Her eyes drift to the parted curtain, then she looks back to me with a small smile. "You sold your crown for that girl. Oh, don't look so surprised. I have eyes and ears everywhere in the court and in the city."

My mouth is dry as the desert. Certainly she will send me home now. For all I know, this carriage could be carrying me to the edge of the city where she'll put me out and leave me stranded.

"I... I did what I thought right, Imminence. If I'd had my purse I would have offered the man gold instead, but—" I don't want to tell her that I came straight from my military service. That though my father rules a country, I have no money of my own.

"I know your story, Emilia." The facade melts a bit as a hint of kindness warms her tone. "I know you are exceptional to have survived those years in the outer provinces. To show the sort of kindness you showed that servant despite never having received any yourself is a mark of greatness. One that I may recognize while my husband, and maybe even my son, will not."

"Thank you, but I don't understand why I'm here."

"The Emperor sees this competition as a means to incite loyalty among the countries. Ronan sees this as a chance to find his wife. I'm not sure either truly realize that the girl who wins will be the Empress. She will rule alongside my son. I look at those silly little girls sitting around my drawing room, draping themselves over who they thought was my son at the masquerade... and then I see you."

She straightens her own crown, almost absently.

"Did you know that you are the only one of those girls who stands to inherit a country on their own? Each one has either an older sibling or a brother that will outrank them in the line of succession. They are desperate for a crown of their own. But you, you give yours away without another thought. I find that intriguing, and I want to help you. You were born to rule, Emilia. Whether here or in Borealis, you will sit on a throne."

"Why would you want to help me? His Imminence is not fond of me. Ronan has confirmed it." It's bold to speak this way to a woman I don't know, to the Empress, but her candor has given me a confidence I haven't known since I arrived.

"Because when I married, I had no one. It's a lonely road to travel, and I would have given anything for someone to do what I'm offering to do for you. I cannot guarantee you the crown of Aurora—in fact it's highly unlikely—but as a future queen of your own country, I'd like you to be my son's strongest ally."

I consider her offer. It doesn't take long. Though being queen is not what I want, it feels inevitable. But I can't lie to myself and pretend her acknowledgement of my lack of chance doesn't hurt. Why would God put me in a place where success is impossible? Frustration tightens a noose around my neck.

"I'd be honored, Imminence." Because what else can I say?

She smiles, slight but beautiful, and I can't help but wonder what it would be like to see her truly happy. Is that my lot as well?

"First lesson, when we're in private, you may call me ma'am. No need to be quite so formal."

"Yes, ma'am."

"And as for the guard caught leaving your room this morning... I'll speak to Commander Fidelis about being more discreet. Felix may be Ronan's best friend, and he may have asserted himself as your unofficial guard, but rumors tend to swirl around a man that handsome."

Rumors have travelled faster than I anticipated if she already knows of them. "I assure you nothing is between us."

"I know, my dear. But best to avoid the appearance of impropriety. However, I would suggest you discreetly keep Felix close. I've raised him alongside my son since we found him as a child. He's a good man, and you'd be a fool to think your position doesn't need protection of the highest order."

Found him? The question is on the tip of my tongue before I realize how inappropriate it would be to ask. That was hardly the point of her speech. So instead I say, "Security must be a nightmare with representatives from every country gathered here."

"It's the duty of a queen to pretend to be blissfully ignorant of those concerns while at the same time noticing everything that could possibly go wrong."

Finally. Something I'm already good at.

11

I skip dinner that night, though the Empress and I return from our outing in time for me to dress. But there's too much on my mind to bide the mindless company of the other girls. Though I'm grateful for the queen's attention, she's only served to further alienate me. That I am different than the rest is clearer to me now than ever.

Instead of immediately returning to my room where I'm sure to face questions from my ladies, I wander the grounds until I reach the stables. It's quiet here, with only the occasional stable boy grooming each of the dozens of horses nickering in their stalls. The sweet scent of fresh hay drifts from the mucked stable. It's oddly comforting.

An evening ride sounds appealing, but I don't want to disturb the stable hands. So I settle for the next best thing. The black horse I admired just a few days ago trots around her pen as I walk toward her.

Elbows propped against the fence, my eyes follow the black filly's smooth gate. Her hooves just skim the ground, and only the little puff of dust indicates that she doesn't glide mere inches above it. It's the sort of exquisite beauty the empire hasn't touched. Unspoiled, uninhibited. This fence I'm leaning on seems crude by comparison.

The horse reaches the end of her pen and kicks up her heels with a snort. Then, for some unexplainable reason, she trots in my direction and stops with her nose just inches from me.

There's a sort of keen intelligence in her dark eyes and an understanding that speaks to me. Felix is wrong. She doesn't need to be broken, only trained. To break her spirit would be a shame, but to guide her would keep her independence intact.

Slowly, I reach out a hand, half expecting her to snap. But she doesn't. My fingers lightly brush her coat, and the muscles twitch under my touch, but she lets me pet her.

We stand that way for so long that I lose track, my hand making small circles on her neck, and she looking me in the eyes. It's the first time I've felt understood in a long time, especially without words. As if she can sense the wildness in me and I in her.

She dances away as I move to sit on the fence, but I don't follow her. A few moments later, she has made her way back to me and nudges at my knee. Holding still is difficult when I'm eager to mount her and dig my fingers into her mane, but I want it to be her idea, not mine.

"Beautiful girl," I say. "You understand me, don't you?"

Patience has never been my strong suit, but I lock my body down and wait. My mother used to tell me that good things came to those who waited.

I don't know how much time passes with the horse nipping at the grass but still with her side pressed against me. When she raises her head with a wicker and a snort, I decide to make my move. The possibility of being thrown is at the front of my mind, but it's not enough to deter me.

"Easy, easy." I make small circles on her neck as I raise a leg and lift it over her girth. I can only hold that position so long before my muscles ache, and I have to lower myself to her back.

Her raw power beneath me makes my blood sing. I don't dare move yet, but I'd love to jump this fence and ride hard until we leave Aurora behind. I'm not sure where I'd go, but it would be better than here. If only I could figure out where the Insurgos gather, I could meet with them, maybe live out the remainder of my days in their protection even if we never bothered to fight back.

"Athena," I coo as she paws at the ground and shakes her mane. But she doesn't seem bothered by my presence or the name I've given her. Only curious.

Finally, she moves, just a few tentative steps forward until she begins to prance nervously. I reluctantly dismount as I continue to pat her neck. It's not much, but it's progress.

When she loses interest in me and trots to the other side of her pen, I hop the fence with my spirits lifted. It's peaceful under the starry sky with the scent of the stables floating on the breeze. I could almost pretend I was still camping under the stars with my regiment.

I allow myself a small smile, but it's startled off my face when I hear hushed voices from behind the stables. I dive into a nearby pile of hay and tune my ears for clues to who the voices belong to.

"Well, I don't like it." A scratchy whisper. Decidedly male but unfamiliar. Though I've clearly stumbled into the middle of a conversation, I instinctively don't like it either. Something ominous and heavy seeps into the space around me.

"I'm quite sure the Emperor and his advisers didn't ask your opinion." Another male, but icy and controlled. Nothing unusual there. He speaks as most courtiers do.

"Well, they should've. They haven't been out there amongst the lot of rabble. Miserable creatures. I've made enough to journeys to the mountains to have seen my fair share. If his Imminence wants a job done, I'd be happy to take it on myself." And an accent that suggests this man isn't a noble, though the man he's speaking to mostly likely is.

"Not this one. Trust me when I say you won't want the backlash. The Emperor asked for the most desperate men you could find. If they're Insurgos refugees, then that's even better."

My ears perk up at the mention of the Insurgos. Has conversation about them always been so common? I don't remember hearing them mentioned except on rare occasions when I was a child. And anyway, what could Emperor Cyrus want with them?

"And what am I to promise them in exchange for their blind commitment if you won't even tell me what they're needed for?"

"Freedom." The other man makes a grunt in response to the single word. "Yes, you heard me. They'll be given enough money and food to take care of their families, for a new start. They'll be free to choose their futures. It's something they've never had."

"When should I tell 'em?"

"See what interest you can stir up first. Then send a message to me, and I'll arrange for a new place for us to meet. And if I find your tongue's been wagging, I'll cut it out myself."

Long after their footsteps have crunched away under the rocky ground, I sit in the hay, my hands shaking. Processing what I've just heard seems impossible, but I know it's significant. The Emperor wants to hire desperate men—Insurgos even—to do a job, to keep his hands clean. But what? Nothing good, I'm sure of that.

I should tell someone…but what would I say? And who would I tell. Though my gut tells me that conversation will lead to high stakes consequences, I know nothing specific. Besides, who would I tell that would share my concern for the Insurgos? Who would dare to consider that Emperor Cyrus, our mighty Sun King, is plotting something devious that he must hide it rather than just will it with a sovereign decree?

My head is still spinning as I turn the last corner to retreat to my rooms for the night. All I can think about is collapsing into my bed and leaving the events of today far behind. So when I see Felix standing guard at my door, my shoulders slump and my pace slows.

"Emilia." No pretense with my title this time. He's at my side, hand on my elbow as he tugs me to a stop. "You really can't keep running off without letting someone know where you're at."

Frown lines crease his brow as his eyes scan my face, but I do nothing but stare back at him. I don't want to fight. I simply don't have the energy for it tonight.

"Is something wrong?" His voice softens as his frown deepens.

"I just want to go to bed." Or turn my back and leave Aurora for good. It's suddenly too much—the attack on Livia, the lessons with the Empress, the Emperor's secret plots. But I can't let my knees buckle in front of him again, so I raise my chin and stare him down. This may be a gesture of queens, but they've adapted it from the soldier. As I am both, I possess intimidation in spades.

It seems to work, and Felix releases his hold on my elbow. "I can tell the Prince you're well then?"

"Quite well, thank you." It doesn't sound convincing even to my own ears, but it's the quickest way to get some time alone. Time to think.

He doesn't believe me, and his eyes give him away. But to his credit, he backs away slowly, offering me a shallow bow. "Very well. I'll report back to him that you are quite well. He asks me to send his regrets as well that he didn't see you at dinner."

The idea of sitting around a table to watch Ronan make small talk with everyone else while he must ignore me in front of his father sounds even less appealing now than it did earlier. Him communicating his remorse through Felix doesn't make me happy either. "You can tell him that when he wishes to see me, he knows where to find me."

I don't look back as I turn on my heel to walk toward my room. But from somewhere behind me, I think Felix might be smiling.

My ladies twitter with large smiles as I walk through the door. Cecily practically thrusts a folded paper at me as they all exchange knowing looks.

"What's this?" I ask even as I unfold it.

"From the Prince," Cecily blurts with a giggle. "The Commander delivered it himself."

So that was Felix's purpose at my door. Despite the exhaustion that weighed me moments before, the small neat writing on the paper makes me feel almost as light as my prayers.

Dearest,

It is a new kind of torture to see your beautiful face and be unable to come to you. I think about our moment by the stream often and wish for only a moment of your time free from prying eyes. You know my restrictions and the game we must play for a while. Discretion, my dear, but not forgetfulness. I dream of the day when it can be like the first night—when for a brief moment, the world was only you and I.

Words fail me as a new feeling takes hold inside me. Warmth rushes through me, thick and sweet, like honey dripping from the combs. Like I've been a starving person who's just taken their first bite of food. His words go a long way toward assuring me that I haven't imagined the heat in our few interactions and that distance has not cooled it. He will come to me as soon as he can do so without arousing his father's suspicion. Those words are not explicit, but I know they're what he means.

I clutch the letter tight to my chest as I fall asleep that night. Determined to hold onto something tangible to remind me what love feels like.

12

In the week that follows, I find myself longing for the routine of military life. Though solitary, at least I knew my place and what was expected of me. The fleeting glimpse of affection Ronan showed me in our first few encounters feels like something I imagined. Perhaps believing in the sort of warmth fondness brings is a childish dream I should let go. I thought I had until I met him. But as I spend bits of my afternoons with the Empress, she is good to remind me that as a future queen, my love is only for my country and that Ronan's heart is much the same. For the hundredth time, I consider hopping on Athena's back and riding away from all this.

As often as she reminds me of what I can't have, Empress Valentina also proves a patient teacher as she shows me the things expected of a queen. We visit the slums of the city and pass out food, spend time with the children who can only dream of growing up to become a princess or a knight. It's hard to watch them, knowing their lot has been cast, their destiny chosen by their birth. It makes my misery about my own birthright seem childish and petty.

On our last outing, before we reached the slums, I summoned the courage to ask the Empress about the refugees outside the city, specifically those who came to the front gate to beg or dig through the garbage for every scrap they could get. Even the lowest Aurora residents chased them away on sight. She instructed the driver to change course, and I got my first look at the refugees.

I can still see their faces when I close my eyes. Mostly women and children, though two men had stood at the back of the group. They've filled every spare corner of my thoughts. How many of them were Insurgos? Might I find a way to communicate without drawing undo attention?

Formulating a plan is harder than I thought it would be. Though my time is largely my own, most of it is spent feeling ignored by Ronan, drawing bits of information from Davina, or avoiding Felix. The latter is especially difficult since I wish very much to wrap my fingers around a weapon. Gloriana's boasts of time spent with Ronan only intensify that desire.

The one bright spot to my week of dreary listlessness is that Hannah found the palace library. I could barely contain my excitement when she reported the location to me last night, and if it hadn't been for increased guard patrols since Livia's attack, I might have visited then. Instead, I dress in the simplest garment available to me, a plain emerald gown with excellent tailoring but little else, and leave my room just before dawn.

Many years as a soldier have taught me to tread lightly, and I do just that as I wind around the hallways of the restricted area of the palace. I haven't been here in my previous explorations, but

I'm glad Hannah took the chance for me, though I'm not sure how she managed.

These halls are unmatched by any others in the palace. Not the gray stone of the lower levels where the servants live and work. Not even the subtle whites and golds of the wing where each of the contestants stay. As I drift further and further into the royal living quarters, the décor blends from elegant to extravagant—rich purples and blues accented in the brightest gold I've ever seen. Images of the sun are visible everywhere, from the door handles to the weaving designs of the papered walls.

So this is how the ruler of our empire lives. It takes less than a minute to realize it isn't what I want, even if it means having Ronan choose me. More than ever, I don't belong here.

Still, which room is Ronan's? It doesn't matter. He's probably away with one of the other girls, but I'm curious to see how it would be decorated.

"Everything's in place."

A whisper echoes off the empty halls, and I chide myself for not having a hiding place should I encounter someone. The hushed conversation continues in a room just ahead of me. These are not the tones of royals, who generally belt out orders because they have no one to question them. So I creep forward and stop a short distance away from the slightly ajar door. Two men continue their conversation as if they haven't noticed me.

"I've had Commander Fidelis double the training regimen for the guards. We'll draft as many of them as possible into the army when the war begins." The man's words are quick and low as tension seeps past the door. What war? And what does Felix have to do with this? Does he know?

"You really think this will work?" Another man, perhaps the same I heard outside the stables a week before, isn't as certain as his counterpart.

"Why wouldn't it? The Insurgos will have dispatched every king in the realm. The people will beg the Emperor for justice. The second crusade will begin."

Surely these are the ramblings of mad men. I tiptoe away, shaking my head. Rumors of wars? Insurgos killing kings? Even if they wanted to, which I don't believe, it would be nearly impossible to oppose each country's royal guard.

Still, I can't dismiss the conversation as easily as I would like, and when I reach the library doors, I'm considering turning around to find Felix. But I don't for a variety of reasons. Not the least of which is that he would probably think me mad to believe such nonsense. The other is that, once I stand before the library's door, something invisible will not let me walk away.

As a child, my palace's library seemed a dusty place of boring school lessons and not much more. Hours spent at those tables drug by as I wistfully eyed the window and envied the sound of children playing in the courtyards.

So much has changed since then, and when I push open the heavy double doors that guard Aurora's royal library, my first reaction is not one of boredom, but of awe. Shelves that span at least three stories line the walls, and more fill the floor space in between. Though it's nearly the size of the grand ballroom, the library boasts none of its overt splendor. In fact, it looks very much like a room forgotten by time. Stillness fills every crevice and cobwebs catch the light from a high window.

Empty sconces jut out from the wall where torches may have once been. Though it's not much, the sun will provide some light for me to begin my search. It topples through the window like a waterfall, spilling its pale light across a small portion of the tiled floor. A thin layer of dust covers the dark surface, interrupted occasionally by a void in the shape of a large foot.

Curious. So someone has been in here recently. Because I haven't a clue where to begin, I take careful steps behind the footprints, which lead toward the back corner of the library where little light reaches.

The footprints vanish, but I keep moving forward, pulled by something inside me. All around me, muted volumes fill the shelves, more books than one person could ever hope to read in a lifetime. Some with titles so faded, I have to page through the book to get a sense of the subject matter. It seems I've left the fiction behind and ventured into the palace records. Everything from supply receipts to trade and treaty agreements with our various nations line these pages. All organized by year dating back several centuries. No wonder these are dusty. If I ever have trouble sleeping, I know where to look for my bedtime story.

Light trails frail fingers along the base of the last shelf. How those little slivers of sunlight reach this corner, I don't know, but it seems to point me toward something so I follow. My dress pools around me as I sink to the floor to reach the books on the lowest shelf. Light doesn't touch them, so I have to reach blindly and heft the largest one into my arms. I shift it until I can read the cover.

The Annals of the Unholy Crusade. It seems too coincidental that I just heard those men mention another crusade. Suddenly, it's pressing on my mind again.

But Unholy Crusade? I've heard it called many things—Great, Glorious—but never unholy. The word alone is treacherous. This certainly wasn't penned by the court historian. The pages are stiff, and the binding creaks when I open it.

In the third year of the reign of Emperor Julius, an unholy darkness came across the land.

I slam the book shut and look around as if someone might have seen me. Even alone in this forsaken room, the words feel dangerous. My heart pounds and sweat dampens my palms. How could Emperor Cyrus allow this book to exist when he so systematically finished the destruction of the Aletheia? He must not know of it. That makes it all the more valuable to me.

"Highness?" A familiar voice echoes through the room, startling me.

I shove the book back on its shelf and resolve to return for it later. Perhaps under the cover of darkness. There's no way for me to hide a volume that large under my dress, and I don't want to be caught with it in the hallway.

"Princess Emilia?" Cecily sounds almost frantic.

"I'm coming," I call back to my lady. The path to the door seems more convoluted than it did on my way in, but I finally emerge from the shelves to the open foyer near the entrance.

"Thank goodness you're all right." Relief spills over her pretty face until she sees the dust clinging to my skirt. "What have you been doing?"

"Reading." Brushing my skirt with my clammy hands only creates balls of gray dust from the thin layer that covers the material. I offer Cecily a sheepish look because I know how hard she works on all my dresses.

"Come here." She pulls a small brush from a hidden pocket in her skirt and begins cleaning my soiled clothes. "You have only a few minutes before you are to meet with the Prince."

"The Prince?" I start in surprise and Cecily nearly rips my dress from the grip she has on it. No one informed me of a meeting with Ronan. We were to have today at our leisure until dinner tonight.

"Yes, my lady. I was returning from the laundry when I overheard the Commander shouting at two guards. I know it's rude to eavesdrop, but I heard your name, and I couldn't help it." Her hazel eyes are wide, as though she expects a reprimand for breaking palace etiquette. But this is one rule almost no one follows, otherwise there would be no gossip.

"It's all right. What did he say?"

"I can't recall exactly, but he sounded terribly worried. He gave those men a good tongue lashing for not being able to find you."

Felix upset because I'm missing, Ronan calling a special assembly…a heavy foreboding settles on me. Something is wrong.

"Here, let me fix your hair before you go." Cecily's fingers aren't as skilled with my hair as Hannah's are, but she makes quick work of smoothing my locks and tucking a few stray ones into place.

I follow her out of the library and leave the royal hallway behind with a shudder.

13

One by one, we assemble in the courtyard—some in their finery, others in their day dresses made for lounging around their rooms.

Ronan has just appeared looking pale and grave. On either side of him stands nearly a dozen guards, Felix included. Neither of them will look at me. In fact, Ronan seems to go to great lengths to avoid looking at any of us for too long. The Commander, though, watches everyone else with his sharp eyes.

"I suppose we can begin." Ronan looks to Felix for confirmation, then pulls his shoulders back to look more like a prince should.

Murmurs skitter through the crowd of girls gathered around me, and I know we've all realized there is one less than there should be. Only nine. Is all this to tell us that he's sent another home? I don't think so. Something much heavier weighs on him.

"In the early hours this morning, it was reported to me that one of the ladies had been gravely attacked." A gasp rises around me, and one girl immediately bursts into tears. My eyes scan the lot of us to determine who's missing, and my heart sinks when I can't find Davina.

"She was poisoned," Ronan tells us as several more girls begin to cry—some audibly, some with silent tears. "I'm sorry to say that she succumbed to the drug not more than an hour ago."

I swallow my emotions down because I've been trained to, but it's not an easy task. Davina was the only friend I'd made among my competitors, and a niggling thought in the back of my mind wonders if it was the reason she was targeted. The girl posed no real threat, nor, from my limited understanding, did she or her country have many enemies. Austrina is known for being the benevolent force in our ever-changing realm. The only country less likely to be involved in a war is Solitarius, and that's because no one lives there.

"By order of my father, King of Aurora and Emperor of Atlas, the guard presence will be doubled." Ronan pauses to let us absorb this bit of information. Weariness rolls over him like the foothills of my beloved mountains. What must that conversation with his father have cost him? More guards for us means less to raid the surrounding villages to search for the Aletheia, and if those men I overheard are to be believed, the guards have already doubled their training schedule for this mysterious war. "But I think we can do more to keep you safe. Beginning now, each of you will be required to train in the art of self-defense with one of the guards. You will continue this training at least twice a week until you are sent home. The future Empress of Atlas must be able to defend herself."

Maybe I'm the only one who realizes that self-defense would not have saved Davina from poison. The undercurrent of the murmurs has changed, and I find Cassia and Gloriana—their tears suddenly gone—rolling their eyes as they take care to hide their faces from Ronan. Certainly they think this is beneath them. Of course, I imagine it's hard to see the need for such an exercise when they need not fear this invisible threat. Cassia's eyes meet mine through the crowd of girls, and a sneer compliments her narrowed eyes.

That's all it takes for my bubbling anger to rise to the surface. I dart past two girls and their escorts as I move toward the princesses from Zephyros. They did this. I know it with a certainty I can't explain. But they don't know who they've awakened, and this beast in me will not be subdued any longer.

I'm so focused on my targets—who exchange nervous whispers as I draw closer—that I don't see Felix step in front of me. I collide with him, and he has to catch my arm to keep me from falling backward. Around us, the guards have begun to intermingle with the royalty, each introducing themselves to their sparring partner. It's not much of a leap to guess why the Commander stands before me.

"Are you out of your mind?" he hisses with a fake smile still plastered on his face. He makes great show of bowing to me then leading me toward the sparring rings I've seen the guards use for training. When we're alone, he releases my arm but remains standing between me and my goal.

"You know it was them." I don't make the same show of a fake smile or royal graces, but I do keep my voice low. "This has Cassia and Gloriana's hand all over it."

"Be that as it may, you can't be the hand of justice. They mean to rattle you. You shouldn't show them that they've succeeded."

He's right, but the pent up anger burns me from the inside out. I didn't know Davina well, and in many ways she was my pawn as much as Cassia and Gloriana's. But as I pumped her for information about her kingdom, about the Insurgos, an ember of friendship had kindled between us. Given time is might have become a real flame. Now I'll never know.

Judging from the demeanor of those around us, Davina's absence means very little. That upsets me most. To my right and left, girls giggle and officers flirt harmlessly as if they've already forgotten the reason for our training. Felix remains in front of me, waiting on my response.

"I suppose you're my partner in all this then?" At least I have that much to be thankful for.

"Yes. I would have thought you'd be happy about it, though. You did ask for dagger lessons."

Despite myself, I brighten up. I'd assumed self-defense would be nothing more than a series of hold-breaking moves or evasion tactics. The idea of tossing daggers or crossing swords cools the rage inside me. Cassia and Gloriana have unknowingly given me a way to spend time with Felix at Ronan's direction. I plan to make the most of it, but I also vow to not let Davina be forgotten. I will honor her in my own way.

"Shouldn't you be teaching me how to escape my captors and scream for help?" I try my weak attempt at teasing because the girls all around us seem to be doing this exact thing.

His arms are around me before his movement registers, twisting me until he has an arm around my throat and my back is pressed into his chest. I can't believe I let him surprise me like that, but I'm not too shocked to know what to do. All thoughts of Davina, of the Zephyros princesses, and of Ronan vanish as my training takes over.

I cross my foot behind him until I've changed my leverage against him. My hips are behind his, though his arm still circles my neck. But with a quick jab of my elbow, I strike his chest and force him backward, and he falls over my leg as he releases his hold.

The eyes of everyone in the courtyard are on us as I stand over the Commander who lies in the dirt. Everyone, including me, waits for his response. Finally, he smiles, and I offer him a hand up.

"I think you've just demonstrated that whoever tried to grab you would end up with the worst end of that deal," he announces, loud enough that those nearby can hear. "That's how it's done, ladies."

Applause from the other guards greets us, and it brings a reluctant smile to my own lips. For all the things I can't do in court, here is something I excel at, and now everyone knows it.

Felix holds up a hand to silence the applause, and everyone goes on with their business. "What do you say to a bit of fun now?"

"You mean that wasn't fun? I rather enjoyed it." My spirits are lifted by the exercise, though I feel a thread of guilt about it.

"I'm sure you did." But he doesn't seem angry as he gestures to a rack near the stone wall bordering the training area, which holds several gleaming weapons. "Just as much as I'm going to enjoy beating you at daggers."

"In case you've forgotten, my dagger did save your life."

He sobers, and I wonder what I've said wrong. "No, I don't imagine I'll ever forget that."

I won't either. Just as I'll never forget wiping the sweat from my brow as we shared a canteen and dug the grave for the fallen guard. The experience bonded us in a way battle often does. But I needed to be reminded of that.

"To be fair, you saved mine as well." I want him to know I haven't forgotten either. That no matter how suffocating he is, whether on Ronan's orders or his own volition, I appreciate him. "We're even."

He's not smiling anymore, but his demeanor isn't quite as solemn as a few seconds ago. "Even is something I don't think we can ever be, Highness."

I puzzle over those words as he points out the different types of daggers to me. Some I know, others I don't. But my focus is on him and not the weapons. Why do I know nothing of this man who seems to be a constant presence in my life now? The way he lovingly caresses the daggers and how his sword shines with a daily polish speak of his attention to detail and discipline, but where do those things come from?

When he has finished demonstrating the techniques for throwing knives and promises me I can try them out when we next meet, my heart is a little lighter.

I didn't really know Davina, but I'll allow myself a moment a grief for her tonight when I'm alone. And I'll offer a prayer of thanks for the Commander who stopped me from killing Cassia and Gloriana, and, in doing so, may have saved my life again. And I think maybe he was right. We can never be even.

14

"Princess, princess!"

The refugee children's cries announce my presence before I dismount my horse. Even in the Empress's absence, wearing the shabby cloak I borrowed from a stable boy, they've recognized me. Fear and excitement threaten to paralyze me, but determination pushes me through. Answers do not come to those afraid to act.

"Hello." My hushed greeting subdues them some, but still the five children gather around me, pressing into the rough fabric of my cloak and making my horse behind me prance with uneasiness. "Steady," I instruct the horse as I stroke his nose and then look down into the wide eyes of the children.

"Have you brought food?" a boy asks, and my heart breaks at the hopeful faces that echo his question.

"Some bread." It's not much, but sneaking it out of the palace without notice was no easy feat. Perhaps next time I should just tell the kitchen I'm planning a picnic for the Prince, and they'll give me more food than I can carry.

The boy takes the two loaves and eagerly tears off a piece of one before passing it around the circle. Here in the shadow of the city gates, these children are hungry. I imagine they mostly subsist on whatever meat their fathers can hunt or vegetables their mothers grow. In the winter, it's probably not much.

"Will you tell us a story, princess?" A little girl tugs at my hand until I sink to the ground to sit with them. "Tell us the one about the dragon again."

It pleases me that she remembers my story from last time, but it's not what I came here for. "I was very much hoping you would tell me a story."

Her eyes light up. "I know one. Mama tells me all the time. About the Ancient and—"

"Be quiet, girl." A man's gruff command narrowly precedes his hand jerking the girl to her feet. She whimpers under his grip, and I'm on my feet before I remember telling my body to react.

The children scatter, presumably headed for their foothill homes. We stare each other down, the man and I. I remember him from my last visit—hardened dark eyes, a crooked nose, and a slight tremor in his left hand. A glance confirms the tremor has made its appearance again, though he's trying to crush his fingers into a fist to control it. It's too late to hide what I see in his eyes though. Fear.

"You're Insurgo."

My words aren't a question, but he snarls a response.

"No, not part of them." He lets the girl go with a shove backward. She stumbles, then runs off, away from the city. "But the children are, and though I don't agree with those ridiculous fools, I need them alive to trade with. Whatever I have to do to feed my family."

"I don't want to harm her. You needn't have been so rough."

He laughs bitterly. "You haven't seen rough, Princess. We live in filth—freezing and starving—and our only crime was coexisting with those rebels. Your Emperor burned our villages for information. Don't think he won't torture a story out of a child who casually mentions the Ancient."

Even hearing the name sends a chill through me, one I can't discern the reason behind it. Who is this Ancient?

"Highness?"

I don't need to turn around to recognize Felix's voice, dripping with thinly veiled annoyance. The soft stirring of metal tack announces his dismount from his horse, and he's by my side before a response comes to my mind.

"Is there a problem?" His words are tight, like he speaks them through clenched teeth, as he shifts a sharp eye between me and the bedraggled man before us.

"No, Commander, there's no problem." I should have this man brought in, force him to tell me everything he knows about the Insurgo families living in the mountains and their foothills. But that would make me no better than the Emperor, and I've promised myself I won't become that. "Would you escort me back to the palace?"

It's the sort of question I ask just to seem like I'm the one in control. He'll escort me whether I want him to or not.

"Of course, Highness." His response comes with an edge, but it's directed at the man. Felix will want him to bow to me, and perhaps he should, but I don't care.

Instead, I turn my back and mount my horse with ease. It's not Athena, but I could hardly risk freeing her from her pen, and she would have never let me put a saddle on her.

Moments later, Felix is mounted and we trot through the gates, into the city. The markets are busy as usual, but he keeps his horse directly beside mine. Unlike when we first entered the city weeks ago, no one gives me a second glance. The Commander is a different story. I feel his eyes on me while I watch several young women in the crowd do a double take to get a better look at him. His obliviousness makes me smile.

He waits until we've left most of the crowd behind to ask about it. "What's so amusing?"

"You had quite the crowd of admirers back there." I push aside any annoyance I've felt with him and instead revel in the familiarity and comfort I have with at least one person in this city.

"I…I didn't notice." He won't meet my eyes, and it's hard to tell if he's blushing under his sun-darkened skin.

"Well, maybe you should. You can't work all the time. Even the Commander of the Guard must have some fun."

"I do."

His reticence only makes me want to push that much more. "Oh. So you've already got a girl, do you?"

"Emilia." Exasperation colors his tone, but his mouth tugs up in a reluctant smile. "Keeping an eye on you is a full time job. When would I possibly have time for someone?"

Maybe it's the rare levity in his voice, but I think I hear an unspoken word at the end of his sentence. Else. When would he have time for someone *else*? I don't begin to know what that means.

"Surely Ronan would allow you some time off if you locked me in a tower where I couldn't get into trouble."

"I imagine you could find trouble anywhere. Even in a library perhaps?"

So he knows about my ill-advised exploration of the palace's royal wing. I'm saved an immediate answer by our arrival at the stables. We each dismount, and I pass my horse to the stable boy whose cloak I borrowed. Then I focus my attention on untying the cloak's cord rather than the questions in Felix's eyes.

"Did you learn anything?"

There's a clandestine feeling in his hushed tone, and I'm unsure if he means in the library or on my journey today, so I answer noncommittally.

"Not enough."

"What is it you seek?" He's close enough to me now that I feel his body heat against my side, and his voice has fallen to a whisper. Though a dangerous undercurrent ripples between us, I feel alive, though it's foolish to believe he might have some bit of truth to share with me.

"The truth," I finally whisper back. Let him take it as he will. I want to believe the Commander shares my sentiments, but it might be unwise to trust the Emperor's most elite soldier before I've proven where his loyalties lie.

He steps away from me, and at first I think I've offended him. Then I raise my eyes to find Ronan and Cassia strolling toward us arm in arm. Something dull and bitter nudges inside me.

"Princess Cassia. Your Majesty." Felix addresses each of them with a slight bow, but I remain still.

I allow myself one look at my competition, not surprised to find Cassia looking between me and the Commander with a disapproving sneer. She'll continue to spread rumors about us, I'm certain.

With a glance, I notice a flash of something dance across Ronan's blue eyes, and I wonder if he'll believe the rumors as well. Telling him otherwise isn't an option since I've not been allowed to speak to him in private in nearly two weeks. Still, some of the heat from our only encounters sizzles from his gaze and prickles my skin.

Cassia must notice the way he looks at me—it's quite impossible not to notice—because she presses her side tightly against his and lays her head on his shoulder. "And where have you two been? Sneaking around like you have something to hide."

She gives a light laugh as if she means it for a joke, but I know what she insinuates. I do look rather suspicious in my worn cloak and dusty skirts. Felix, however, looks as stoic as ever.

"A training session," I say quickly. They needn't know about my visit outside the city. "I asked the Commander for extra training sessions. After all, isn't that what the Emperor wished?"

"Indeed." Ronan finally speaks as his eyes trail up to question Felix. In the short silence that follows, I know the Prince knows we're lying. "I'm pleased to see you've found something you're enthusiastic about."

"It passes the time."

He must catch the longing in my words because his brow softens, and I think for a minute he might come to me. But Cassia holds on tight, so I let him go. For now.

Felix and I are left alone as Cassia and Ronan go on their way. I busy myself removing the cloak so I don't have to watch the Prince leave. It seems silly to feel so upset by this, but the flicker of whatever he's making me feel isn't easily ignored. This form of torture is often used by the military—placing a prisoner close to the water but just out of reach—with mixed results. Sometimes they talk, sometimes they go mad.

"Emilia." Felix says my name like an apology, though I'm not sure for what. He doesn't elaborate either. Sometimes I think he just likes to say my name for as often as he utters it with no words to follow.

"Will you tell him? Tell him that—" I stop myself from saying *"that there's nothing between us"*. Because that's not entirely true. Felix is my one true friend here. Outside of Hannah, I have no one else.

He nods. "Perhaps we shouldn't be seen together anymore."

"No," I say firmly. "I don't care what anyone else thinks. Just make Ronan see reason. If he knows the truth, that's all that matters."

Felix swallows hard then gives me a slight bow. "Yes, Highness."

Then he's gone.

I return the cloak to the stable boy and find my way back to my rooms. I've a couple hours before I must make an appearance at dinner, so I instruct Hannah to draw me a hot bath.

As I sift the hot water through my fingers, I think of the tortured prisoner, the one who could never reach the water. A touch would never be enough for him. He could not hold onto it. More importantly, he couldn't be filled by it. The best he could hope for would be rain.

So I close my eyes, and I pray for rain.

Dinner is more of the same tedious motions that characterize the time I've spent here. There are nine of us left, and the threat of being sent home seems enough to keep everyone in check. Except me, of course.

Though I dress the part and have learned the nuances of the manners expected of me, they all fear and sneer at my wildness. It's hard enough to remember all their silly rules without the whispers passed around the table about my extracurricular activities.

"Are you all right? You've barely touched your food." Cordelia, whose sister Livia was the first girl attacked, leans into me.

"I'm well, thank you."

She hesitates, as if she expects more from me, then returns to her own meal. I suspect she's lonely since Livia was sent home to recover. There was a time I would have pitied her for that, but I've been alone long enough to know it won't kill you. And I have no use for friends here, not after what happened to Davina.

As soon as the servants clear the plates, I excuse myself from the dining room. Antony takes a step from his post against the wall as if to escort me, but I stall him with a raise of my hand. Company would only distract me. I need to be alone to think.

I return to my rooms and take a seat in front of the crackling fire in my sitting room. Flames dance, slow and enchanting, and I watch them until my eyes feel heavy. Hannah brings me a cup of tea, which only furthers my catatonic state.

My eyes have just fluttered closed when a sharp knock at the main door jolts me awake. Seconds later, Hannah appears in the sitting room with her hands clasped in front of her.

"Princess, the Commander is here. He says you left something behind." Hesitance colors her words, and it's enough that I'm immediately put on guard. There shouldn't be any reason to fear Felix's visit, but there must be something unusual about this one.

"Show him in," I instruct without rising from my chair. With a nod toward Cecily, she ushers the other ladies into their chambers to give me some privacy. A moment later, Felix appears in the doorway with a familiar red cloak folded in his large hands. "Commander."

"Highness." He bows low, clutching the cloak to his chest. "You must have forgotten that I promised you this cloak. You left it behind after our lesson today." His tone's so even that no one would suspect anything suspicious about our time spent together earlier in the day.

"Why yes," I say as I reach to accept the fabric from him. It's heavier than I expect, but I try not to frown as I place it in my lap.

Felix never does anything without a reason, including giving me something we never agreed upon. "I had forgotten about your gift, but I'm very grateful. It's a nice memento of my first night here."

"Yes, of course." And then I'm sure we're both remembering how he put me to bed after that masquerade where I fell apart in his arms. He stands awkwardly before me, as if unsure if he should go or stay. "I hope you find it satisfactory."

I don't understand why he's being so cryptic, but there are some things I won't question Felix on, and discretion is one of them. If he thinks there's a need for secrecy, there probably is.

"Won't you stay for some tea?" I gesture to the tea set next to me, and the steam coming from my cup warms my hand.

"No, my lady. I can see that you are preparing for bed, and I wouldn't want to disturb your nightly reading."

As much as I'd like him to stay, I'm eager to see what he's brought me. Something to read, I imagine, since I've never told him I have a nightly reading ritual.

"Good night then, Commander."

"Good night, Princess. I hope you find what you're searching for."

Then he's gone. I remain in my chair until my heart beat slows to normal again before I stand and announce to my ladies that I'm going to bed. They call a response I barely hear before I shut myself in my bedroom.

Alone in my bed, I clutch the cloak to me, disappointed it no longer smells like him. It's been freshly laundered and smells of lavender soap. I listen for a long moment, until I'm satisfied everyone else is asleep. Then, carefully, I unwrap the fabric to reveal a small book, about the size of my hand. It's leather-bound, but crudely so, like many of the journals I've seen merchants keep to record their earnings.

I cross the room to the window, and hold the book to the moonlight. The cloudless sky gives me a decent view of the weathered pages beneath the cover, but I have to squint to read the cramped handwriting.

This is love: when we could not love God, He became a sacrifice to atone for our iniquities. By his wounds, our souls are healed.

I read it twice, three times, and let the words wash over me. The warmth I sometimes associate with prayer fills me up in a way I haven't been in a long time. As if there was any doubt, my body's reaction confirms this as the Aletheia- the words given to the people by my God. Though I know I'm alone, I still glance over my shoulder to see if someone watches me.

Did Felix know this was here? I flip through the pages and find line after line of words. It's too much to take in, but I skim them all, looking for mentions of God. He's everywhere, and I know this gift wasn't an accident. The Commander has given me something more precious than I can comprehend.

Worrying about Felix's motives fades into the night as I pull a chair to the window and begin to read. A few of the lines are familiar to me as I can recall Levi speaking them to me in the night, but most are new. All are powerful. They fill in pieces of the puzzle I didn't even know I was missing.

I knew about the God who became man and sacrificed himself, but I never thought to imagine the extent of his power, his grace. And, strangely enough, I had never thought of him as a king. But I see it written before me now. The Most High King. And because I have believed in him, he has called me his daughter.

For the first time in my life, I think I understand what it means to be a princess.

A feigned headache gives me an excuse to keep to my room much of the next day. I give my ladies the day off except for Hannah who brings me tea and offers to braid my hair. When I'm sure we're alone, I show her the book, and she weeps over the pages with such reverence that it brings tears to my own eyes.

She doesn't ask me where I got it, though I'm certain she knows. Perhaps she knew when Felix arrived at the door last night and that's why she seemed nervous about his visit. Possessing something like this would be punishable by death, but only after the Emperor had tortured you to extract any information he could about the Insurgo camps.

So why does Felix have it? What more does he know? Why would he think me trustworthy of such a precious book? All these questions ricochet in my head as I ready for dinner until the headache I've pretended is real. I'd hoped he visit me today, that we could talk in private, but Hannah overheard the kitchen staff talking about Emperor Cyrus inspecting the troops today as they were put through their paces.

I imagine Felix leading his men, those who trust him with their own lives but have no idea he sympathizes with the very people they're taught to hate. At least I think he does. It's the only explanation I can come up with.

I arrive at dinner before the other eight girls in hopes I might catch the Commander's eye and have a word. But he's not there. Everyone files in and takes their seat as the servants bring the covered dishes to the table. Unlike every other night, the place at the end of the table receives a plate as well, though the large chair remains unoccupied. A sort of hush falls over our group.

From my place at the far end of the table, I would have to lean far forward to watch the Emperor enter the dining room to grace us with his presence for a meal for the first time since we've been here. But I don't look because I'm distracted by the placement of an equally large chair at my end of the table. And while everyone is rising for Cyrus to make his grand entrance, I stand and come face to face with his son.

Breath rushes from my chest as his startling blue eyes pin me beneath his gaze. A meaningful look, not unlike the one he gave me outside the stables though Cassia held his arm.

We all take our seats once more, everyone silent as we consider what it must mean to have the Emperor dine with us for the first time. Nothing good, I'm sure. At least from my position at the far end of the table, I don't bear the full weight of his glare.

Course after course is served, and conversation slowly begins again. Though Ronan sits to my left, it's the conversations from my other side that catch my attention. The other girls twitter softly with excitement as they share details of their time spent with him, but I silently sip my tea. Cordelia speaks of his gentle nature, Cassia of his strong arms, and Gloriana—why couldn't it be anyone but her—gloats about his soft kiss.

Envy burns within me as I clutch my tea cup so tightly my knuckles turn white. Why doesn't he speak to me? His note said he'd have to be discreet, but his absence feels more like avoidance than discretion. All the girls have spent time alone with him, some more than once.

"Ladies." Emperor Cyrus rises, and everyone falls silent. He pauses, reveling I'm sure, in our rapt attention. Our entire empire is just a plaything in the palm of his hand, and he's feeding his ego from the perceived reverence of nine girls who only want to marry his son. "Ten days from today, Prince Ronan will celebrate his twentieth birthday and be officially ordained as the rightful heir to Aurora and the Atlas Empire."

Everyone claps, which Ronan acknowledges with a nod of his dark head. He is, of course, already the heir to the throne, but at twenty, he would be allowed to rule without a regent should something happen to his father. The age of adulthood is slightly different in every country, with Austrina being the youngest at sixteen and most of the others at eighteen. It's something I've not thought of often. If this hadn't happened, would my father have called me home in two months for my eighteenth birthday to crown me as his proper heir?

"There will, of course, be a grand celebration," Cyrus continues. "And we must make it interesting. So each of you will be given a chance to receive the guests beside my son. The guests will then vote, and the three of you receiving the lowest tallies will be sent home the following morning."

A collective gasp sounds from the mouths of the others, but I'm too paralyzed to join in. Three at once? Based only on the opinions of the guests? Madness.

Beneath the table, warm fingers curl around mine, and I have to steel myself not to jump in response. Ronan keeps his eyes straight ahead even has his hand squeezes mine, and it's a small measure of comfort in the midst of the uncertainty.

It's gone as quickly as he offered it. The Emperor has taken the decision out of Ronan's hands, and he means it to be the end of my time here. But surely the rescue of the Insurgos can't rest on my ability to make strangers like me. That's not my strong suit.

Slow building panic gnaws in my chest until I'm nearly shaking. Never before have I worried so intensely about being sent home because Ronan did the choosing. I need a plan—something to prolong my time or to get the information I need about the Insurgos before I leave. If there's any truth to their planned rebellion, the evidence of that history should be in the library. Felix will kill me if I...

I'd nearly forgotten Felix and his gift. There must be something in there that will help me. My hands relax as the memory of the book calms me. I look around the room at each of the guards until I find the Commander, and my heart leaps.

His dark eyes, which had been obviously trained on me—too obvious considering the rumors circulating about us—shift toward the floor when he catches me looking back. My heart sinks again. It's exhausting, trying to balance Felix and Ronan as well as the court politics and gossip. For a fleeting moment, I think I wouldn't be sad to leave this place.

Then Ronan brushes my hand once again under the table as he stands to leave. It's only then I notice that most of the plates have been cleared and the Emperor is absent as well. Thoughts of following Ronan, making him speak to me, are quelled when Cassia and Gloriana nearly knock each other down to get to his side.

So I simply watch him leave.

A flutter of knocks pulls me from my light sleep, and I feel sure I only fell asleep moments ago while reading Felix's book. I quickly stuff it under my mattress and glide soundlessly to the door. I take a brief moment and compose myself, smooth my hair, until I realize I'm hoping for Felix on the other side of the door. My hands fall to my sides.

Caution prevents me from jerking the door open. Instead, I crack it to reveal a disheveled Ronan who alternates quick glances between the door and the hallway behind him.

"Let me in," he whispers with wide blue eyes that nearly glow in the dark.

He darts through the door before I shut it gently behind him. When I turn around, he stands near the foot of my bed, a mischievous smile curling his lips.

"Are you crazy?" I can't help echoing his smile. It's the first time I've really spoken to him in days, and I hadn't realized how much I've craved his presence. So sure and confident in the midst of uncertainty.

"Absolutely." The child-like brightness in his eyes fans the embers of something I hadn't known existed in me. "But I had to see you."

Before I can register his movement, he takes my hand and pulls me to him. We're only inches apart as I look up into his handsome face. Only our hands touch, but I feel closer to him than I ever have. However, when I blink my eyes closed, I see all the other girls as if they stand between us. Reluctantly, I take a step back.

"Emilia?" Hurt laces his voice, but it's not enough to bring me close again. I'm not above sacrificing some of his pain to protect myself. It's a lesson the military teaches well.

"Why now?" I ask. Trust is not something I take lightly, and though this is the moment I've been wishing for, doubt shadows me. Above all, it may not matter.

"My father has forbidden me to see you, for us to be alone. He's had a guard outside my room every night."

"But Felix wouldn't—"

"It wasn't Felix. Father knows better than to station my friend as my captor."

"Then how did you get away?"

"It doesn't matter." His hand cups my jaw and his thumb rests just a breath away from my lips. There's something new and exciting in his touch, unlike the first night at the masquerade where he admired me but didn't know me. "I tried to appease him for as long as I could, but I can't quiet this restlessness in my heart. It's only still when I'm with you."

The urge to kiss him, to still his lips as well as his heart, rises like a tidal wave in me, but I stand motionless until it ebbs. My kisses are not what he needs.

"Will you sit with me?" Though I'm not sure what to do with him, I'm not ready to let him go. "Maybe we can stir up the fire in the sitting room."

"I'd love to."

We enter the sitting room, and I grab a poker to stir the embers in my fireplace. After some prodding, a small fire springs to life with a gentle crackle. Ronan has pulled a blanket from the back of one of the chairs and spread it in front of the fireplace. He sits on it and beckons me to join him.

"I wasn't sure I'd see you again before I was sent home." I maintain my distance, though he's still close enough to make out the flecks of gray in his eyes.

"You're not going home, Emilia. My father has his ideas about who I should marry, but after my birthday, the choice will be officially mine."

That doesn't guarantee my place here—for obvious and not so obvious reasons—but I don't tell him that. Men are fickle creatures, especially those that wear the crown. So instead I say, "I was afraid our last conversation about the Insurgos made you think differently of me."

"It did, but that's not a bad thing. When I am king, I want a queen who will help me consider all the options. Our talk made me consider things I haven't before, or that I haven't been willing to voice anyway."

Hope warms me. "And what is that?"

"That either my father is wrong about the gate, or there may be a God I know nothing about."

"Perhaps both." Words pass my lips before common sense stops them. Caution was never my strong suit. Though Ronan appears to care for me, it may be nothing more than curiosity. And my experience with royals is that they will always choose their old ways over their loves. Their tradition over truth. My father certainly did.

"You speak bluntly." His tone has changed, hardened to the formal one I've heard him use in court. Not the gentle one he spoke with moments ago. "I don't mind it now that we're alone, but you'll force my hand if you say such things in front of the others. Keep your head down, Emilia. The foreboding unrest in the court has everyone on edge."

Hushed words I overheard near the stables and the library come to mind. Everyone seems on edge, waiting for something without knowing what. The unknown is far more worrisome than facing an enemy head-on, but we don't have that luxury here. Ronan speaks of the competition, but something more beckons to all of us.

An answer to his instructions seems unnecessary, so I let the silence linger. This is the lesson of queens—one I never wished to learn. My mother often gave council to my father in private, but she never opposed him in public. Not even when he ordered her death. It's the nature of queens to make their king look strong, even if she is the strong one.

I never wanted that, and I'm not sure I can do it. Those sorts of roles breed resentment, and from that sprouts the seeds of infidelity. Affairs with power are sometimes more dangerous than those with other people. And I never, ever want to be responsible for the deaths that inevitably come with the crown. Levi was too much.

"Are you angry with me?"

I'd like to forget all the pretenses and give Ronan complete honesty. Tell him I don't want to be his queen, not because I don't care for him, but because I'm terrified I might be the sort of queen the Emperor and my father would be proud of. Is that the sort of queen who would please Ronan, too?

I'm so certain of what I want, of what I need, until I'm with him. Then I question everything.

"Not angry. Just thinking." In the dimness of the room, I don't feel compelled to force a smile. The fire waves with tongues of heat and light, and memories threaten again.

"About what?" His shoulder nearly touches mine now, and his gaze is like the tiniest press of fingertips on my skin as I stare ahead. "No one knows anything about you. Even the other girls can't tell me anything about you."

If he's been asking the other girls what they know of me, it's no wonder they all hate me. If he asked me what I thought of Gloriana right now, I'd throw him out of my room. Prince or no prince. "Felix told you about me," I gently remind him.

"Only that you saved his life and that you would be observant enough to pick me out at the masquerade ball no matter what costume I chose. If he knows more, he won't say." A hesitant pause. "*Does* he know more?"

He's really asking if there's something between me and his commander. Rumors have made their way around the court, though Ronan has done his best to quell them. Now he asks for the truth for himself.

"He knows well that I can handle a short sword better than most of the guard." There must be more than that, but the realization strikes me that I know absolutely nothing about the Commander, and he likely knows very little about me.

"It's a shame queens don't ride into battle." Ronan's tone is a mysterious mix of teasing and…insecurity? "Surely he's privileged to more than that. You two are practically joined at the hip."

"At your command," I remind him. "It was his assurance that kept me sane since I last saw you."

"Then I'll thank him for that." His fingers twitch as he almost reaches for my hand then thinks better of it. "I've heard you excel at the defense training."

Despite myself, I roll my eyes. "Don't play coy. I know how the others talk of me. Surely you must have heard I fight like a man. That it makes me less of a lady in the eyes of your court."

"Is that what they're saying?" He rubs at the corner of his mouth and pull his eyes from me toward the fire. "I shall have to rectify that."

I don't ask how he plans to do that because I'm afraid of the answer. Though I'm sure Ronan's visit was meant to reassure me, all he's done is call to question my feelings about this entire journey.

I've been strong more times than I can count in my seventeen years, but with him I feel helpless, at his mercy. He's a good man, a great one maybe, but I'm not sure I like who I become around him.

Being saved by the Prince is not the sort of girl I want to be, and his words are reminders that my impropriety will only be sanctioned as far as he allows it. But Ronan is a powerful man, and his power will only grow. If I could sway him now, he would see my wishes carried out.

"Tell me more about your mother."

This request knocks the breath from me. *God, protect me from harm.* "You know her story," I say slowly though my heart pounds. "It's what you asked me at the picnic."

"No." He reaches for my hand, but I pull mine away. His frown deepens the crease between his brows. "Tell me about her. What was she like? How did your father know she sided with the Insurgos?"

"She was wonderful." Tears threaten again, and a knot forms in my gut. I don't want to give my memories to Ronan because I can't do so without revealing the truth about myself, and it feels too soon for that. But in the stillness of the room, with the heat of the fire loosening my reservations, I feel vulnerable. As if I already lay open before him and that he asks my story rather than reads it for himself is only because of his chivalry.

"As a child, I didn't understand what she did when she prayed, or who she talked to. But her words brought comfort to me, stirred something in me I'd never felt before."

"The spirits moved when she spoke. I've sometimes heard of priestesses being able to do that."

"Yes, but not the spirits we know. She spoke to this unknown God as one talks to a friend. No sacrifices made, no money tossed on an altar. Only her words." A few tears spill over, but I wipe them furiously. Such girlish weakness. This isn't me. "And then she died. Without a fight or a protest."

"Your father had her killed."

Why does he insist on voicing the painful details? With my hands in my lap, I don't hide the tears. And for a moment, I don't care if he sees me for exactly what I am, because instead of a princess, I'm a little girl missing the warmth of my mother's arms with a crown too large to stay upon her head.

It's Ronan's warmth I feel instead, and I don't fight it. His arms drape around me, and his hand guides my head to his shoulder.

"I'm sorry," he whispers with raw emotion that makes me reach for him as well. His muscles tense beneath my arms, as if he's not used to being hugged. I don't care. This isn't for him. "I can't imagine how you must have felt."

"She did nothing wrong." The fabric of his tunic muffles my words but the truth of them rings loud. I can tell him everything now and risk it all, or I can hide and wait and let him fall for a girl he'll never really know. "This God she served, the Insurgos' God... He's different than the gods we grew up with."

"Because of the Gate? Because he can inspire his people to revolution?"

The revolution is the last thing on my mind because I know nothing of it. And the Gate… Those are not the things I think of when I think of my God. "No. Because he cares." I lift my eyes to Ronan's. "I don't want to hide it anymore."

"You don't have to hide with me." His fingers drape my hair over my shoulder then graze my cheek, leaving teasing heat in their wake. "Emilia, you're the most genuine person here, and that is why I can't stay away from you. I'm so sick of all the pretending."

It's too much, so I force myself from his arms and stand. His eyes on me as I pace only increase my anxiety. "You don't understand. I'm not the real thing, but God is. He's the reason I'm here. Not for you and certainly not for me. There's more than what we learned as children."

"You want me to believe the gods who helped my father and my grandfather build this empire are part of someone's imagination?"

Though I stand over him, the subtle inflection of Ronan's voice is meant to remind me who I am speaking to. It's effective, but I've come too far to back down now. If he means me harm, I've given him more than enough cause.

"Yes." I shrug as tears break my voice.

"Emilia." That he doesn't stand somehow makes him seem in control. The lopsided smile he offers does calm me marginally. "I love that you are so passionate about this, and I won't lie that it intrigues me. But I have a responsibility to my country to uphold the principles of our gods. The Crown Prince can't go chasing every myth and legend that flits through here. Caelus will only bless my rule if I'm loyal to him."

"And I'll become a martyr like my mother."

"I hope not. Certainly not at my hand." When he finally stands, he doesn't touch me. "What your father did to your mother was cruel. I won't be that man. If you want to believe in this God, I won't stop you. That's all I can offer. Anything more would be treason."

"So you don't plan to send me home?"

"Emilia." The way he says my name as he strokes his fingers across my face is nearly enough for me to believe in him. The feelings he stirs inside me are unlike anything I've felt before, but it may not be enough. "You've bewitched my heart. I don't understand it, maybe because my father is so against it, but I don't want to think about your leaving. Even if I'm not what you came here for, can you promise me you'll stay?"

I don't answer because I'm praying for the words to say. He doesn't plan to kill me, so that's a start. But I'd hoped for something grander. How can I hope to worship freely with a future husband who still thinks my God might be a threat to our kingdom? Though marrying Ronan—if I can make that happen—might put me in a more powerful position, it's still rife with all the things I never wanted—the responsibility and theatrics of an arranged love between two people whose countries are more important than their hearts.

"I have nowhere else to go." It's the harsh truth I've tried to ignore. When Felix ripped me from my home, he took away my past and my future.

"Neither do I."

Nothing is said for a long time as we return to the blanket, both content to stare at the fire. I've never thought of Ronan as much of a mystery, but his handsome face is unreadable. To his credit, my confession hasn't put space between us, and I'd like to believe that's real. He won't be my only answer. If I can't sway him now, he'll never agree to allow me to worship freely or allow the Insurgos to become part of our society again. But his tolerance is a step forward, and if I could find out more about this revolution, perhaps I could make my own destiny apart from him and the weight of the crown.

Ronan and I lay on the blanket with our feet facing opposite directions, our faces side by side. My hair fans out behind me so that he barely has to raise his fingers to wrap my strands around them. The gentle tug on my hair and the rhythmic sound of his breathing lulls me into a heavy blanket of warmth. Only the dying fire makes a sound as we stare into space, his fingers still tangled in my hair, but each of us lost in our own thoughts.

15

In the weeks that Ronan ignored me, training with Felix became the highlight of my days. We saved our tamer sparring for the set lesson times when we knew everyone would be watching, but our unofficial meetings were ruthless and exhausting. I never complained, not even when I limped into dinner and endured more of the same whispers.

But since Ronan came to me last night, I don't know what to expect of the self-defense lessons today. He promised to rectify the not so subtle verbal abuse I've endured, but I don't want him to do so at the expense of my strength.

And of course there's Felix, who went out of his way to look the other way at dinner last night. So many unasked questions are stacked between us. Unfortunately, sparring surrounded by soldiers and my competitors isn't the place to talk.

"You seem distracted." Felix tosses me a wooden staff and removes his cape before picking up a staff of his own. Wind whistles as he twirls it deftly in his hands.

He's right, of course. My eyes are too busy scanning the training ground for any sight of the Prince. It's a disappointment.

I felt so sure he'd show up today, where he could watch me—and the others—without showing any favoritism.

"Highness, would you prefer to practice your running and hiding today?" Felix goads me with a mischievous smile, and his words have the desired effect. He's a better actor than I expected.

I whip my staff on either side of my body, getting a feel for the weight and balance of it. I've not fought with staffs before, but it can't be much different than long swords, can it?

Just how wrong I am becomes clear when I jab for Felix, he steps aside, then whacks me along my back with the back end of his staff. I catch myself just before I tumble face first to the ground.

He frowns as I turn to face him. "Too impulsive. Use your head, Princess."

Around me, the other girls are still learning to break choke holds or evade an attacker. No one else holds a weapon. But Felix doesn't commend me on that accomplishment, rather he criticizes my lack of skill. I'm in a class by myself as far as he's concerned, but it's a class I'm failing at the moment.

So I crouch low with one hand still on my staff, which I've pressed into the soft dirt. Then I beckon him toward me with a nod of my head.

He raises an eyebrow then cautiously crosses the dusty ground between us. I wait, fingers curling tighter around my staff, until he's within a body's length from me. As he raises his arm to strike me, I jump and throw all my weight to the side, using my hands to propel me around the staff. My feet strike his chest and throw him backward to the ground as I land on shaky legs with heart pounding.

Silence fills the air in the training area, and I sense without looking that everyone has stopped their activities to observe us. Felix props himself on his elbows and looks up at me from his back as the sound of solitary applause pulls everyone's attention away from us.

It's Ronan, dressed in royal regalia, walking toward the Commander and me with a wide grin. "Impressive," he calls, loud enough to be heard by all. And I realize this is his way of saving me from the stares and whispers. "Who knew Princess Emilia was such a natural at the art of self-defense?"

He did, of course, as did Felix. Ronan steps into our circle and offers a hand to Felix, who graciously accepts and is pulled to his feet. Together, the two of them look me over until I'm uncomfortable with the silent conversation they seem to be having about me. Finally, they exchange a whisper, and Ronan leaves the ring only to set himself atop the half-wall beside it.

"Please continue." He waves his hand at us as if we're only a slight amusement, but I know every action he takes has a purpose. This is no different.

I meet Felix in the middle of the ring, each of us slowly circling the other. A layer of dust covers half his face, giving his skin a bronzed look. I aim to make the other side match.

"What did he whisper to you?" I ask softly.

"He asked me to take it easy on you." Felix twirls the staff again until it hits his palm with a resounding smack. "I told him no."

Now that I've used up my element of surprise on him, our fight is grueling. He won't hit me hard enough to leave bruises—

at least not where they're visible—but he takes every avenue I leave open to land a blow or trip me to the ground.

By the time Ronan calls the match, I'm covered in a muddy combination of sweat and dust, and Felix doesn't look much better. Though he didn't intentionally hurt me, I know he's clearly better with the staff than I am. Hopefully the match looked fairly even to the untrained eye. And that's exactly who this display was for.

Now that I'm given a moment to rest, I see the crowd that assembled, including every one of the girls and their sparring partners. A mixture of shock and awe color the girls' faces while respect shines on all the guards'. They may still whisper about me, but they'll be careful what they say to my face now that they know I can hold my own with one of the best warriors in the realm.

"Commander Fidelis, see that the Princess is returned safely to her room where she can rest and prepare for dinner. She'll be joining me in my private chambers for the meal."

Ronan is past me before the shock of his order sets in. Jaws drop all around, including Cassia and Gloriana's.

"Majesty, perhaps you'd like to watch me spar next?" Cassia calls after him.

Ronan pauses, then turns slowly to her. "Can you guarantee me a fight like that one?"

We all wait because everyone knows she can't, nor should she be able to. Princesses don't fight as I do. It's unbecoming a lady, but Ronan has made it clear that it's highly valued by the Crown Prince.

"Perhaps next time," he calls, not waiting on her answer.

As everyone watches him go, Felix joins me with his side nearly pressed against mine. "Are you hurt, Highness?"

I know why he uses my title and not my name, but I still have to resist the urge to roll my eyes. I don't want to be treated like a fragile little girl from anyone, least of all him.

"Fine," I tell him as I wipe the dirt from my face. "Did you know he was coming today?"

"No. Ronan does what he wants."

Like coming to my room in the middle of the night because his father forbade him to see me. Believing that Felix knew nothing of his plans to attend the sparring isn't a stretch. "So would you have fought me the same way if he wasn't watching?"

He hesitates too long, and I know the truth. "Maybe not. But I value my head, and I don't want it chopped off for marring your beautiful face."

Beautiful face. Were those Ronan's words or his? "I want you to teach me, tomorrow, when there's no one to watch. And don't have a care for my face. It's the last thing I'll be worried about if I ever actually need to use these skills."

"We'll see. After you dine with Ronan tonight, you might have other plans for tomorrow."

I'd nearly forgotten the dinner invitation. It's unbelievable that my first official audience with Ronan is a private dinner in his chambers. From the looks the other girls gave me, I'm sure no one else has been to his rooms. Probably no one else has been to the royal wing, either, and suddenly I'm plotting a way to sneak into the library on the way back from dinner.

Felix reads my face. "Planning mischief?"

"Seeking truth," I respond. "I have read it can set you free."

Only a quick flash of something across his dark eyes indicates he knows what I mean. I'm proud I've committed those words to memory. That my God is truth and he can set me free. Free from what, I'm not sure, but it doesn't matter right now. It only matters that now Felix is fighting back a smile, and hope wells up in me.

He believes, too.

Soon I'll demand to hear his story, to let my heart gush in gratitude for his gift of the Aletheia, but now is not that time.

Still I find myself looking forward to it. Maybe even more than dinner with Ronan.

My ladies have dressed me in a rich red silk with considerably less volume than most of the dresses we're expected to wear to dinner. Something similar to the custom in Borealis where things are slightly more practical and less extravagant. Less is more in this case, and the cool fabric drapes over my curves with a subtlety that is somehow mesmerizing.

At least that's what I gather when Felix appears to escort me and silently gapes for a full ten seconds before he manages to pull it together and remember he should speak to me. "I...I've never seen you in something like this."

It's true. I haven't even seen myself in something like this. Instead of playing dress-up with similar gowns from my mother's closet, I bound myself and donned leather armor and scratchy trousers. Certainly not by my choice, but it happened just the same. Now I stand here in clothing from my country, the living God in my heart, and a loyal soldier at my side, and I feel more like a princess than I ever have. Only one thing is missing.

"Take me to Ronan?" I ask as I hold out my arm for Felix to take. For the first time, this feels possible. If I can forget about having to impress the guests at Ronan's party to make the next cut, I might allow myself to hope this could have a happy ending.

Felix leads me down a familiar path toward the royal quarters. I nearly ask him about the Aletheia, about his story, but this isn't a safe place for us so I resist. He seems to sense my hesitance.

"Something here worries you?" He still holds my arm, but it's a loose grip, as if he can't believe I've allowed it at all.

"Hmm?"

"You were fine when we left your room. In fact, I've never seen you more confident, but you're quiet now. The closer we get, the more I see you withdraw."

For a man of few words, he's eerily observant. And he's not wrong. There's an uneasiness in the pit of my stomach that grows harder to ignore with every step. Had he not said anything, I might have passed it off as nerves about dining with Ronan. But it's something more.

We pass a door, vaguely familiar, and something cold washes over me.

"Emilia?" Felix stops and releases my arm to step back and get a better look at me. "Are you cold?"

He reaches back as if to remove his cape—a new one, I've noticed, since his old one still sits beside my bed—but I shake my head.

"No, it's not that." With the excitement of the last few days, I'd nearly forgotten about the conversation I overheard outside this doorway. Perhaps I wanted to forget it, but it nags at me now, and the need to share it with someone is strong. But not here, at least not explicitly. "You've been busy," I say, "with the guards' training. There must be something big on the horizon."

Felix takes my arm again and directs me down the hall before he speaks. "I probably shouldn't tell you this, but in a few weeks, the Emperor will welcome some high profile guests, and his Imminence wishes for security to be at an unprecedented high."

I raise an inquisitive brow, but he only shakes his head in response. Either he doesn't know the guests, or he's been sworn to secrecy. The mysterious conversation I overheard takes on a darker tone. Could an attack be in the works for the Emperor's guests?

Before I can ask anything else, Ronan appears in the hall, dressed in a simple blue tunic and dark pants. A wide smile parts his lips as he leaves his doorway and moves to take my arm from Felix's.

"I thought you'd never get here." He's still beaming as he presses his lips to my temple in such an intimate gesture that heat tinges my cheeks. Then the Prince holds me at arm's length to peruse me. "Though you're certainly worth the wait. Absolutely stunning."

When we step inside his chambers, the savory scent of our food reminds me how hungry I am, but I'm nearly too distracted to acknowledge the rumble in my stomach. Instead, I'm admiring the soaring ceilings with gold fixtures, the thick red curtains lining the huge windows, and a bed larger than three of my military tents. Beneath the opulence, I find traces of the Prince—books spread haphazardly across a desk, weapons displayed proudly, and a painting of a ship tossed violently on the waves. What these say about him, I can't begin to guess.

"I hope you don't mind, but I've dismissed the servants tonight," Ronan's still at my side, probably inwardly laughing at my awe of his quarters. "I thought it would be nice for us to talk frankly."

"I'd like that." It's a kind gesture on his part, but I suspect he values his privacy more than being waited on.

"What of the guards I assigned here for tonight?"

I'd nearly forgotten Felix still stood behind us, lingering in the doorway. He doesn't sound happy with this arrangement.

"Dismissed." Ronan waves a hand at the Commander as he leads me toward what I can only assume is his dining room. The scent of food is stronger here. "You're the one I trust. If you think we need to be *watched*, then by all means, you can stay."

There must have been a conversation between them I wasn't privy to. It doesn't escape me that Ronan chose the word "watched" instead of guarded or protected. Of the two of us, who does Felix not trust? His face betrays nothing as he silently takes his post just inside the dining room.

I'm surprised by the simplicity of it when Ronan leads me inside. The room isn't much bigger than the one where I sometimes take tea—the same one where Ronan and I spoke just last night. A fire crackles in the fireplace, and a small table is set with two large plates. It's better than I could have hoped. A dinner with the Prince that doesn't involve a large audience or worthless pomp.

Ronan settles me into my chair before taking the one opposite me. His eyes alternate between me and the plate in front of him. He seems nervous, though I can't imagine why.

"I asked your ladies for a list of your favorite dishes. I hope everything's satisfactory."

An uncontrollable giggle bursts from my lips before I can quell it. Ronan frowns, which only makes me laugh harder. This is ridiculous, all of it. That I'm sitting here with the Prince, who's gone to special trouble for me and then seems completely at a loss for what to say.

Just as I'm sure he'll send me back to my rooms for having lost my mind, he laughs, too. Soon we're both in stitches while Felix looks on, bewildered, from the doorway.

Finally, Ronan stands and grabs my hand. I sober immediately as he directs me to the rug in front of the fire. He leaves my side and returns with both our plates. Without ceremony, he sits on the rug with the plate in front of him and gestures for me to do the same.

"Now. This is more us, don't you think?" His smile reminds me more of the man who visited me in such clandestine fashion last night rather than the stilted prince who sat before me moments before.

"Very much so," I agree. From behind us somewhere, I hear Felix sigh. "I was afraid after last night that you might have changed your mind. So when you showed up today—"

"Emilia, when are you going to realize I'm not going to change my mind about wanting you?" He pins me beneath his stare. "All of the things you think will put me off are the same things that make me want to know you that much more."

"It's ridiculous, isn't it? That we're talking marriage and we know almost nothing about each other." It's more than ridiculous. It scares me a little. Not only that he's my best chance, but that my feelings for him only grow stronger. Could be dangerous to care so much for a stranger.

"And if we'd been betrothed as children, it wouldn't be much different. You in Borealis, me in Aurora until our wedding day. Neither of us with a choice."

"Yes, I guess one of us having a choice is preferable." I smile as I take the first bite of my rapidly cooling food.

"One of us? Haven't you also chosen me?" He looks hurt, as if it's never crossed his mind that any of us might be here against our will.

I choose my next words carefully, though emboldened that he seems to enjoy when I speak plainly. "It would be unwise to fully commit to a course of action without all the information. Escape plans are…necessary."

"Spoken like a true soldier. I sometimes forget where you learned all you know about fighting, about war."

He might forget, but I never will. My metaphor wasn't for show. It seems foolish to tell him how much I might care when there are still several other girls who might be Empress in my place. Perhaps the best lesson I learned as a soldier is that once you've embraced an idea, there's no putting it back in the box. Precisely why soldiers who believe they can win are twice as dangerous as the realistic ones.

"I can show you," he says softly. The distance between us vanishes as he scoots close to press his side against mine. Long fingers trail down my jaw, and his bright eyes find mine. "We might have to keep playing the game for a bit longer, but I can show you that you're my choice."

"You don't really know that. You can't."

"Why? Because I don't know a few trivial things about you? I know your mother was a traitor to the empire, and you've spent the majority of your life paying for it. I know you fight as well or better than most of my soldiers, and you enjoy it. That you gave up your one symbol of royalty to save a servant girl in the marketplace. And that you sympathize with the very people who would like nothing more than to have my father's head on a platter." He kisses my cheek, and the warm press of his lips warms the cooling tears I hadn't realized were falling. My life summed up in so few words. Is that who I am? "And I know that I've never felt like a king until I met you."

He shifts slightly and everything changes as our lips meet for the first time. I'm unskilled, and I try not to think about all the practice he's had, but Ronan doesn't seem to mind. Something inside me wakes up, and I understand what he meant when he said I made him feel like a king.

His lips leave a phantom tingle on mine when he moves away, ducking his head slightly as though he's suddenly shy. It's a side of him I've never seen and only reinforces how little I know. I wipe away the remainder of my tears and reach for his hand.

"What would it take?" he asks as his eyes drift to me again while his fingers twine around mine. "To show you I'm serious about you. Ask me for anything in my power and it's yours."

Behind us, Felix clears his throat, and I jump at the sound. I'd forgotten we weren't alone. But the weight of Ronan's question pulls the veil around us again, and it's only me and him and the thing I want most. Anything in his power. Granting clemency to the Insurgos isn't within his power and won't be while his father lives. Strange how the longevity of this plan hits me only now. While Ronan may have power to temper his father's belligerent heart and the raids on the villages and camps, he cannot give me what I desire until he's Emperor. At best, the Insurgos will wait twenty years to be reinstated as citizens of Atlas.

It's not enough, but Ronan still waits on an answer. Faith. I want to ask him to have faith in God, but it's not something I can beg him for. He'll have to experience it, and the only way for that to happen is if he knows the truth about the crusades, about his father, and about the gate the Emperor seeks. Now I know what to ask for.

"The library." My words are small but strong even if they seem to confuse Ronan.

Dark brows drawn down, lips pursed as if ready to speak, but no words to say. That's how my prince looks at me in the silence of the small room. Finally, "you always surprise me. Just when I think I have you figured out, you go and ask for a library. Not jewels, not favors, but a room full of dusty books."

"Knowledge is power. Charms and baubles are wonderful, but they won't help you in a war...which, if rumors are to be believed, is coming soon."

"What have you heard of war?" His stiffened posture reminds me not to be too comfortable. Though I want to believe him, Ronan is as unpredictable as a storm.

I don't want to tell him the details of the conversations I've heard. Maybe it's foolish to withhold my trust even as my feelings grow, but my gut tells me it's a good idea. "The tension in court is apparent to everyone, and the Commander spends all his spare time away from my training with the guards. Aurora has an army, so why would your father need to train his personal guard if not in preparation for some sort of battle?"

With a quick glance over my shoulder, I see the frown forming on Felix's face. If he were allowed to speak freely, he'd probably tell me I'm too observant for my own good. The darkness mirrored in Ronan's eyes tells me the Commander may be right about that.

"Officially, it's simply a training exercise." Ronan looks away, though his hand still wraps around mine. At least that's something. "Father's been talking of a huge state dinner in the coming weeks with some very important guests. He intends to put the guards through maneuvers to impress the guests. That's all I know."

"Do you believe him?"

"Emilia." Felix can't stop himself from speaking up this time, and Ronan and I both look in his direction. He pauses, inhales as if to speak prepared words, then exhales with a shake of his head. "You can't just say things like that. To question the Emperor…"

"Unwise at best," Ronan finishes for him. "But then my father always did like to call me a fool. It's all right, Felix. She can speak freely with us."

An apology's on the tip of my tongue, and then I realize I'm not sorry. Maybe no one has ever asked Ronan these sorts of questions, but if there's hope for him to be a better ruler than his father, it's time he thought about them.

"I'm not sure what to believe anymore," the Prince confesses with a half-hearted smile. "You're much of the reason for that, which explains my father's dislike of you. But he's the king and I'm not, so what I believe doesn't matter. His word is law."

But it does matter, so very much. That's what I want to tell him, but I don't. There will be another time and place for that conversation. I subtly shift the topic. "Well, he certainly wants rid of me. The idea to have guests at your party vote who to keep and who to send home is aimed directly at me. There's no way for me to out-charm the other girls."

"Perhaps lessons then." A genuine smile finds its way to his lips. "I know the guests well and what each of them would like to hear. I could teach you."

"That will be difficult when you're not supposed to be seen with me." Even as I say it, I can tell he's warming to the idea of a challenge. If I'm honest, it excites me, too.

"Then I think we just found another use for that library."

"Now, how would you handle this one?"

I lean back against a bookshelf, Ronan opposite me, and smile as he assumes the air of yet another of his future party guests. We've been at this game every day in the week since we shared dinner in his rooms. Sometimes for only a few stolen moments, others until the wee hours of the morning when both of us are too punch drunk to focus.

"Good evening, your Highness." Ronan pitches his voice high and shrill as he stands and mocks a curtsy in my direction. "I'm so glad I have a chance to speak with you. I've sent several letters to the palace, but received no response. Perhaps you can help me."

"I will try," I say through a laugh as Ronan launches into a long tale about his assumed character's neighbor and how the older and less beautiful woman is sabotaging him/her by replacing her creams and herbs with ones that cause her face to break out in a terrible rash.

I miss most of the details because I can't help but admire him like this. Each day he seems more at ease with me, more relaxed, and I feel for the first time that I'm seeing a glimpse of who he really is. Who he would be if he didn't carry the burden of the crown.

"So you see, this is really an outrage against you, Highness, because she's cheapened the beauty of this kingdom." He finishes with wild gestures and a wink, which sends a heady lightness surging through me.

"Yes, well, this does seem to be a serious problem." I take his hand and pat it gently, reassuring the imaginary guest. "Perhaps you should stop using these herbs and creams. A natural beauty such as yourself needs no enhancement. You already outshine everyone in this room."

"Perfect," Ronan says in his normal voice before pressing a smiling kiss to my lips.

Though we've shared a few quick kisses in the last few days, my response to them is as strong as the first time. So when he pulls his mouth away but keeps his forehead pressed to mine, I inhale a shaky breath.

"Hi," he whispers with a reverent intimacy as his eyes search my face. It's moments like these I can see my future so clearly. With a husband who loves me and who will learn to love my God.

"Hi," I whisper back as I brush his black hair from his forehead. "Aren't you tired?" The sun has long since vanished behind the horizon, and the only light in the library comes from the torches Ronan lit along this row and the small lantern to my left, which puts out enough light to cast shadows across the lines of his face.

"Not when I'm with you. I've never felt more awake, more alive."

"You've got a long day tomorrow," I remind him. As if either of us could forget. His birthday festivities have been all anyone's talked about since the Emperor announced it more than a week ago.

"Yes, it'll be such hard work having someone put a ring on my finger and letting people adore me." I can still see the grin on his face, when he moves out of the light to sit beside me against the bookcase. He holds up his right hand until it just catches the light, and we both stare at his long fingers, imagining what it will look like once he bares the signet ring his father will present to him in the morning. It's a great symbol of power, second only to the crown.

I try not to think about how the ceremony will require him to make an oath to Caelus. To swear to uphold all the tenants of the gods, to allow them to govern his rule. Instead I smile as if I'm blissfully happy for him because that's what he expects me to be.

"There's a priestess travelling from Borealis to preside over the ceremony," he tells me. "Do you think your father might come as well?"

My body stiffens with an involuntary shudder I hope Ronan can't see in the relative darkness. My father won't come. "It's a religious matter, so his presence would only overshadow that of the priestess. Besides, without the other kings being invited, he has no reason to be here."

"To see his only child?"

It's a question because Ronan doesn't quite believe it either. What should be a reasonable suggestion seems ridiculous where my father is concerned.

"He hasn't seen me since he sent me to the outposts. Can't imagine why he'd want to start now. Perhaps if I'm chosen to be your bride, he might see that's worth a visit." Bitterness edges out the apathy I tried so hard for.

"You *are* chosen to be my bride." Ronan presses his lips to my temple and reaches for my hand. There in the deserted library, I can almost allow myself to take comfort in his declaration.

"Well, he doesn't know that, does he?"

Ronan pulls back as if I've jabbed him. "So long as you know it. And if you would give me something, *anything*, then after tonight, everyone would know it."

He asks for too much. If it were him and only him, I might be willing to tell him how he makes me warm inside, that I look forward to our moments in the library as much as sparring with Felix, and when he reaches for my hand, I feel steady in a way I never have before. But Ronan is never just Ronan. There's the crown to consider. The same thing I've both grasped for and pushed away. If I take him, I take the crown, and my path is set. And how many more Insurgos will die before I can convince him that there's a better choice than the one his father made?

His sigh breaks the silence—a sound both discouraged and resolute. He expects more from me, but he won't give up on me yet. I grab hold of that with both hands.

16

Sunlight breaks through my window far too early. It seems I've only just left Ronan in the library for the comfort of my bed. Despite waiting patiently for him to fall asleep so I could slip *The Unholy Crusade* beneath my skirts and retreat to my room, my eyes grew heavy long before his did.

He's distracted me from my real purpose behind gaining access to the library. I'm ashamed I've thought mostly of my own feelings these past few days and little of my ill-formed plan to learn the Insurgos whereabouts. As if I needed more evidence of my selfishness.

Today will be more of the same. I'll sit through a ceremony where Ronan pledges his life and the future of our empire to false gods instead of learning what I can about the true one. But my time here hasn't been in vain. Without a trip to the palace, I would never have met Hannah or Felix, and I wouldn't have learned the Aletheia they know. And of course the Gate and the Ancient. Hard to believe that a month ago, I'd never heard of either even if I know nothing more than a name for each of them.

I dress in a somber gown with the help of Hannah and Cecily. A dark blue suitable for the signet ring ceremony we're required to attend. Arriving just before the ceremony begins allows me to take my seat at the back of the temple. I stand when instructed to do so, bow when appropriate, and mouth the words to a blessing I do not know.

So much pretending is exhausting. Though the other girls linger afterward to show Ronan their support, I slide out the back door and wander down to the stables for a few stolen moments with Athena. Even she can't reassure me. She's on edge as well—more than usual—so I leave her for the confines of my room.

Not until I begin to ready for Ronan's celebration that evening do I let my mind drift to my most immediate worry. My tiara…or lack thereof.

It seems silly to worry about such a thing with all that surrounds me, but it's not unfounded. Tonight I'll wear the finest dress I've ever seen and have my hair pulled and tugged until the style is the pinnacle of beauty and fashion. Then I'll make my way to the ballroom to take my turn greeting the guests and spewing words I don't mean.

And none of it will mean anything if I don't have my crown.

My eyes find Hannah as she busies herself with some last minute hemming on my white dress—a conscious choice on the part of my ladies because it looks dreadfully like a wedding gown—and hums softly to herself. I would give my crown for her all over again, even if it means my ridicule and possible exile tonight. She's worth a thousand crowns, but knowing I've done the right thing doesn't completely comfort me.

They dress me in the rivers of white fabric, silky smooth against my dark skin. In a culture that values the pale skin of those who don't have to lower themselves to outdoor work, I've been the odd one out. But tonight, with the glittering white draped over me, I look dark and lovely. Once again, my ladies have managed to highlight my differences rather than attempt to mask them. I love them for it.

No one mentions my lack of diadem, and Cecily tries to make up for it by weaving diamond-like jewels through my black hair. I have to admit it's a dazzling effect when I move and they catch the light, but it's still nothing compared to even my small tiara I brought from home.

The knock on the door barely registers as Cecily leaves my side to answer it and one of the other ladies takes her position with my hair. When I catch Cecily's wide eyes in the mirror upon her return, I raise my hand and everyone around me stops. Slowly my maid approaches me until she reaches my side, and I look down at the wooden box and note she carries.

"From the Empress," she reverently whispers and raises the box to me.

I take it from her with steady hands and flip the latch on the box before raising the lid. A gasp catches in my throat at the dazzling display before me. Rows of diamonds and sapphires arranged intricately on a gold frame send prisms of light scattering around my room.

A tiara. She's sent me a tiara.

My mouth gapes as I lift the crown from its bed of velvet within the box. It's far grander than the one I gave away, though much less impressive than the one that usually adorns the Empress's head.

"And the note." Cecily's voice shakes as she takes the box from me and hands me the folded parchment.

This time my hands tremble as I hold the crown in one hand and unfold the letter with the other. The writing is smooth and elegant, though I can't possibly know if the Empress wrote it herself, but she did sign the bottom.

Emilia,

I thought you might need something to wear tonight. This was the crown I received upon my engagement to the Emperor. May it bring you as much happiness tonight as it has brought me.

The carriage ride I took with her and how she'd known about Hannah flashes through my mind. Why was she helping me when her husband hated me so much? Certainly for Ronan's benefit then. Had he confided his feelings in her?

"Let me, Highness." Hannah gently takes the crown from me with a tender smile. She raises it high before placing it gently on my head.

I close my eyes as she fusses with my hair, arranging it in the combs to make certain the crown will stay put. When she finishes, I open my eyes to take in my appearance in the mirror. Even after having grown used to some degree of finery, I scarcely recognize myself. Along with the tiara, my eyes sparkle with both awe and happiness. I look like a queen, or at least as close as I ever have to one.

When Antony arrives to escort me to the dinner, his eyes go wide before he can replace the stoic mask of a guard. I remember him telling me the day we rode into the city that I looked beautiful in my crown. What would he say about me now if he felt he could speak freely?

I don't ask because those are words I want to hear from Ronan. For as much time as I've spent with him in the last week, I still want to dazzle him, to make him reveal our connection in front of everyone. Tonight is the first time that's even been a possibility.

The ballroom is already full when I arrive, more people milling around than even the night of the masquerade ball. This time no one wears a mask, but we all play a part.

I spot Ronan immediately with Gloriana on his arm, and daggers of jealousy jab me in the ribs. The pain dulls as I remind myself this is expected. We'll all take a turn on his arm and give our platitudes to the guests and hope it's enough to impress them.

From the looks of things, Gloriana seems to be faring well with the male guests, but the women look at her with thinly veiled contempt. Not surprising. Even on her worst day, Gloriana has always been able to make everyone girl around her feel like they were beneath her.

Forcing myself to mingle with the guests is difficult, but people seem pleased I've sought them out even without the Prince by my side. I spot Felix perched atop the stairs, and he gives me an encouraging nod, so I smile and go on.

By the time Ronan finds me and quietly slips his hand in mine, my smile is genuine. I've heard so many stories from those on the fringes of the crowd. They're my people, the ones who are here because their birth gave them noble standing but their heart never embraced the expectations.

"I haven't been able to stop looking at you," Ronan whispers in my ear. For the breadth of a second, it feels like we're the only ones in the room. "Neither has anyone else for that matter."

"The other girls must love me then." I half smile when I look at him, but it's not as funny as it might be. Just as Felix warned me, I've painted a target on myself.

"Not as much as I do." He kisses my temple, and the people around us sigh at the gesture. It's the most direct he's ever been about what he feels, but it means little to me by comparison. Royals rarely have the luxury of love, and this soft affection I feel for him may be as close as we'll ever get.

Ronan speaks to those nearest us before taking me on a turn around the room. To everyone else, I'm sure it looks as if we're wandering aimlessly, but I know he's looking for just the perfect people to introduce me to, the same ones he prepared me for. I remember his training well, smiling and laughing and deflecting attention away from myself whenever possible.

The latter is no easy task as this crown is impossible to look away from, and as a result, people gape at me before managing an awe-inspired greeting. By the time Ronan releases my arm, my cheeks hurt from the wide smile I've kept plastered on my face.

"You did beautifully," he says as he kisses my cheek. In the undercurrent of his words, I hear the promise of something I'm not ready to believe. That I am safe. That tomorrow will be the start of something real for us.

He leaves me without another word to attach himself to one of the other girls. I don't dwell on it long enough to see who.

Though I no longer have the Prince on my arm, several people still approach me, and I lose track of time talking with each of them. It might be minutes or hours before Felix pushes his way through the small gathering and rescues me.

Once he's extricated us, I exhale deeply and allow my shoulders to relax. Before I can ask what's going on, he shoves a plate of food into my hands.

"Eat," he instructs with little emotion in his tone. But I recognize that restraint. It's not indicative of indifference, but rather of holding something back.

"Thank you." I take those precious moments to turn my back on the crowd and shovel the finger foods into my mouth. Thank goodness Felix realized how long it had been since I'd eaten because I'm famished.

I look up at him as I finish chewing and think I see the corner of his mouth pulled up in a lopsided smile. It's difficult to tell though because I can only see his profile while he's got his vigilant eyes trained on the crowd.

I've just swallowed the last bite of food when the Emperor stands and the room falls silent. He exudes an air of authority just by breathing, and no one dares move until he says so.

"Thank you all for attending this momentous occasion in the history of our great country. Your future stands before you in the form of my son." Cheers erupt all around the room as Cyrus claps a hand on Ronan's shoulder. The Prince bears the weight of it stoically, but I know I haven't imagined the flinch he quickly masks at the contact. "He is the face of our empire, and today he becomes a man. In four short weeks, he will choose his bride who will stand beside him as the future Empress of Atlas."

I had almost forgotten the competition wasn't scheduled to end until Natalis Solis, the annual celebration of Caelus. The thought of Ronan being able to end it early is a nice one, but, as I suspected, not accurate. Cyrus is still the Emperor, and now more than ever, he will attempt to assert his authority. And I will still have to endure to the end.

The crowd around me begins to disperse, and I look to Felix for clarification on all that I've missed while my mind wandered. He shakes his head, and his smile is gone. My lack of awareness disappoints him as well it should.

"He's dismissed everyone. The guests are casting their votes for which of you to send home, then everyone's gathering in the Arena for the evening festivities." Felix nearly spits the last word, and I swallow hard.

I think about claiming to be ill, and it wouldn't be far from the truth, but out of everyone here, I should be the most accustomed to the Arena's activities—or at least the brutality of battle and war. But this isn't battle. It's senseless killing of Atlas's most unfortunate souls. It would be suspicious to retire now, and, I suspect, it would be exactly what Cyrus wants. So I throw my shoulders back and join the rest of the girls.

Surrounded by guards, we're ushered from the ballroom and out of the palace. My companions titter beside me about the details of the ball and how Ronan introduced them to everyone as the most beautiful woman in the room. Those things barely register to me as we are marched across the dusty path toward the grand circular structure I've tried to ignore since I arrived in Aurora. Though I raise my skirts, dirt stains the bottom of them, turning the bright white a dingy brown.

The Arena carries a dark aura. Even as a child, I knew this though I was never allowed to attend. Had I grown up in Borealis, I would have been expected to make regular appearances once I was older, maybe even bless the killings before they happened. Such is the life of the priestess and princess. But it wasn't my life.

Death itself is troubling for me. I have watched those I love die and taken my share of lives. Both leave marks I can never erase. But there's something inherently wrong about watching people die for sport. Which is what Emperor Cyrus expects us to do.

We file into the seats in the center of the Arena. Though it was built to hold a crowd, it's only ever full on special celebrations like this one. Ronan's birthday celebration has brought all sorts of people from Aurora to the games, even those who weren't invited to the dinner we just left. They bow reverently then cheer loudly as we settle into our box, surrounded by guards.

Ronan and his father arrive, and somehow I get sandwiched between Ronan and Cassia while Gloriana sits on his other side. As if I wasn't miserable enough.

Our silk dresses and glittering crows look gaudy against the stone and dirt backdrop, and Gloriana's bright laughter deepens in contrast to the somberness that settles over me. Do they not know what comes next? Men—traditionally criminals against the empire—will march onto this dusty stage to die. Their blood will stain the ground red, and everyone will cheer. Then the winner's reward will be to survive to fight another opponent.

I know this even though I've never attended these games. Some of the men in my company of soldiers used to reminisce about their trips to watch the spectacle. I didn't understand it then, and I certainly don't understand it now.

Emperor Cyrus must have made some gesture, because the gates at either end of the Arena floor open, and a man emerges from each one to raucous cheers from the audience. A cold sweat breaks on my neck.

One of the men is old enough to be my grandfather, with a bowed back and graying hair that I can see quite clearly from our seats. He doesn't strike me as a marauder or a bandit. His physical handicaps wouldn't allow it. That can only mean his crime is much worse. An Insurgo.

The man he'll face is closer to my age and looks as though he's seen his share of hard times. Maybe an Insurgo or perhaps just the wrong place at the wrong time. Whatever the reason, both these men have drawn the short straw today. Their crimes—or lack thereof—don't matter. Cyrus has found them guilty, and one or both of them will die today because of it.

The game master drops his hand, the signal to begin, and the men are shoved toward each other. The crowd roars in anticipation with each movement, many of them rising to their feet. If I'd been sitting anywhere but the royal boxes, people in front of me might have blocked my view. But because I've been given the best seat in the Arena, nothing obstructs the violence of kicks and punches and moans of pain.

I feel every sickening blow as if it were a punch to my own stomach. Before long, I'm not even watching the fight anymore because I'm doubled up, staring at my feet and trying to block out the cheers all around me. How can anyone enjoy this? Monsters, all of them.

The older man falls to his knees, bloodied and nearly broken. It won't take long for the younger man to finish him. Even from some distance away, I see the older man's lips move in what can only be prayer, and tears pool in my eyes before I wipe them furiously.

I have to leave now or I'll be sick. My hands shake as I push myself from my seat and sway slightly. Ronan grips my arm as I'm trying to walk away, but I manage to slip from his grasp. I'm sure Cassia makes a snide remark, but I'm too far gone to hear it.

My feet find steady ground outside the Arena before Felix catches up to me.

"Are you ill, Highness?" He maintains a careful distance as I stumble forward, always close enough that he could catch me, but never near enough to make contact.

I collapse onto the nearest bench, my hands and face clammy both from cold sweat and the tears I've tried to hide.

"How can they enjoy that?" These are obviously people who have never seen battle, felt the slice of a sword parting flesh or the sting of a well-placed, incapacitating blow. Otherwise they would never cheer to watch people die. "Death is sport to them."

"Entertainment and executions." It's a measured response from the Commander, one I can't interpret. "A tradition started after the Great Crusade when Insurgo prisoners overran the prisons. Some were sacrificed in front of the temple and others for sport."

The Unholy Crusade. I almost voice the title I read in the library, but I stop myself before I do. Still, "I don't need a history lesson."

If he's put off by my short response, he doesn't show it. In fact, he's as stoic as ever. That's one thing the military never did for me—train all the emotion out of me. The childish part of me wonders what I would have to do to break Felix's cool demeanor, to make him break character. It's the sort of thing I used to do to my father's guards when I was small.

"Would you like an escort back to your room?"

If I take his offered arm, it means I'll miss out on an evening of celebrating Ronan's birthday. But it also means I won't have to watch people being beaten to a pulp and cheer as if I support it. To pretend to be as my father was—unscrupulous in my political advances. It's not really a hard decision.

We walk in silence to my room. Though Felix often catches his breath as if he means to say something to me, he doesn't. It's just as well because I have nothing to say in response. Him thinking me weak is bad enough without my helping it along.

He opens my door to a quiet stillness and enters first. My ladies are at the festivities since I felt their hard word deserved a night off. Once Felix seems satisfied no one lurks behind the curtains or under the bed, he motions me inside. I'm too distraught to comment on his paranoia.

I expect him to ask his leave of me and return to the games, but he stands just inside the door I closed behind me with his hands clasped in front of him. "Is there anything I can get for you, Highness?"

Out of here, I want to say, but I'm not sure it's entirely the truth. "I think I'd just like some company, unless you have to get back to the party."

"Ronan asked me to keep an eye on you tonight. If you want me to stay a while, I can do that." His words are innocuous enough, but he sounds uncertain.

"What do you know about the Crusades, Felix?" This might be my only chance to ask him in private, and I don't intend to squander it. "What of the Insurgos?"

He doesn't relax exactly, but there's a shift in his face from soldier to young man, and it's the closest to vulnerable I've ever seen him.

"The Crusades were masterminded by Cyrus's father after his advisors brought him reports of strange Insurgo communications." He walks to the window and looks out, resting his large hands on the sill. "Their writings spoke of wars and the 'King of Kings', and it didn't take much to convince the Emperor the Insurgos were planning to overthrow the government. So he wiped them out with the help of the other kings."

"My grandfather ordered several raids," I say softly. "But it was before I was born."

"Me, too." Felix turns back to me now, and I sink to sit on the bed under the weight of the sadness in his dark eyes. "But the stories are horrible enough. Not unlike the stories supposedly told in the Aletheia about God himself when he became human and was killed. Worship of their God was declared the highest form of treason, and thousands were put to death—some with merciful swiftness, but most in the arena for sport."

"And then Cyrus realized they might still have something he wanted," I supply. "So he raided any suspected Insurgo villages for information. For the Aletheia."

"*I* raided," he corrects me. "I gave as much warning as I could, but I still burned villages to the ground in the name of Caelus." Venom laces every syllable of the false god's name as Felix's voice shakes with anger.

"But you gave me the Aletheia."

It's not a question, but I hope he'll answer me anyway. My eyes follow him as he deliberately crosses the room and sits on the bed with me, though much too far away for us to touch.

"Sometimes, I think we are the same." His lips twitch in a sad smile.

"We are," I insist, "in every way that matters."

"I haven't been as brave as you." Strange words coming from the Commander of the guards. "If I was, I wouldn't have let you think you were alone in this."

I start to correct him, to mention Hannah, and then realize it's not my secret to tell. "But you were alone, before me I mean. How did you keep it secret while living in the capital? While carrying out the raids?"

"I was a coward, Emilia," he hisses with pain in his eyes. "I've told no one, not even Ronan, who you spoke to so easily. Fear kept me silent, and I'm not proud of it. But I've always hoped for a day when I could leave here and join them."

Hope leaps in my chest. Clarifying the "them" is unnecessary. "You know where they are? Why haven't you joined them?"

"I can't yet. The reason I'm here… Guilt is a heavy weight."

Penance. I can't imagine something he could have done that would require years of penance in the most dangerous place for an Insurgo. "Le—" I choke on Levi's name, "my friend taught me that God frees you from your transgressions because he already paid for them. You don't have to pay for it, too."

For a moment, I think he might cry, but he doesn't and I'm grateful. I don't know what I would do with such a strong man reduced to tears. "People are not as forgiving as God."

"But who can argue the pardon of a king?" I don't ask out of a sense of righteousness, but because I don't understand it completely either. After all, I sometimes still feel Levi's blood on my hands. There's so much a don't know. Even the details of my God's sacrifice are a mystery to me. But Felix said he became a man and was killed. Certainly they must be one and the same.

"God commands my destiny," he says in a stronger voice, more like the one I've come to know. "When it's time for me to leave here, he will make it clear."

With all the worrying I've done about being sent away from the palace—which may still happen as Cyrus could easily rig the voting, especially after my display in the Arena—it's never occurred to me that God commands my destiny. I've known he has a plan—or at least hoped so—but this feels different, and I like it.

It's on my tongue to ask him to come with me if I leave—as reckless and ill-advised as that request would be—when he rises and adjusts the sword on his belt. Our conversation is over, and I don't argue with him. I've gotten the confirmation I wanted about him, but there's so much to process that I don't know what to ask next.

Felix excuses himself without another word, and I watch him go. Alone in my room, I distract myself by removing the tiara and placing it back into its box. Then I untwine the jewels from my hair until it falls in waves down my back. I'm considering changing out of my gown when I hear a soft knock at the door.

I'm not surprised to find Ronan stands on the other side, and I invite him in with nothing more than a nod. Once I shut the door, we stand, facing each other in a silent stalemate.

Reading him is impossible at the moment, though not because of an absence of emotion like Felix. Rather Ronan's emotions are everywhere at once. His mouth is set in a firm line, and the line between his brows suggests anger, but there's a tenderness in his blue eyes that gives away his concern.

"Are you okay?" He's measuring his words, trying to keep his voice even, but it's a wasted trick on me.

"I'm fine now. Watching those men try to kill each other though, I can't do it."

Finally his façade cracks, and he throws his hands up in exasperation. "You're a solider, Emilia. You're supposed to be used to that sort of thing. How am I supposed to stand up to my father for you if you keep pulling stunts like that?"

"No one should be used to that," I snap before I remember who I'm talking to. A short pause gives me a moment to regain my composure before I speak again. "War is not a game. Neither is death. Especially the death of men who weren't given a choice to fight."

"They chose it when they became criminals." His tone carries the warning that I always hate—cautionary and superior.

Maybe he's really as clueless as he seems. I hope so, because I don't want to believe he knows that at least one of those men was innocent of everything except being an Insurgo. That man had no choice.

"Emilia?" The sudden softness in his voice pulls my eyes up to meet his. "You can't feel so deeply for every criminal that's punished. Not everyone is worth saving. And don't we choose our own fate?"

I'm not sure I agree, but it's a wonderful thought. To be in control of my destiny instead of waiting for things to happen. Then I think of Felix and his assertion that God commands his destiny, and it rings true in a way Ronan's words don't.

A choice between the Commander and the Prince, but my heart knows immediately which one is right. It gives me a boldness I've lacked until this point.

"Should I pack my things then?"

"No," he says, voice full of pity as he pulls me into his arms. I don't relax against him. "Three of the girls went home tonight. You, Cordelia, Gloriana, Cassia, Juliana, and Octavia are left."

Only six. More than half of our original number are gone, and though that should reassure me, the uneasiness remains. I don't ask Ronan if he still plans to declare to everyone that he's chosen me because I know he won't, at least not yet.

He kisses my forehead—chaste compared with the other kisses he's given me—and lets me go. The frustration is plain on his face, but despite that, some warmth remains in his eyes.

When he tells me goodnight and leaves me alone, I'm more confused than ever.

17.

Despite our decreased numbers, the room where we gather to await the Empress the next day seems uncomfortably small. Each of us carries our own baggage, I suppose, and it's finally impossible to ignore each other.

Of my five competitors, three are a mystery to me, and two I don't trust. It makes for a lonely breakfast as I nibble my pastry perched on the arm of the sofa.

Though this opportunity was supposed to be a new start, I realize I've approached it much the same way I approached my military life. No one here really knows me. I've kept to myself, harbored my own agenda, and made no real effort to make friends. I should feel safer for it, but right now I just feel alone.

I wish Felix or Ronan were here, but they're both with the guards. Putting them through their paces or something. It's for the best since both of them made my head spin last night for very similar reasons.

My pity party comes to a merciful end when the door opens and the Empress strides in with her head held high. We all scramble to our feet only to offer a deep curtsy as she takes the chair near the window and flicks her fingers in a signal for us to rise.

"Please be seated," she instructs in the high, clear voice I associate with authority.

We all obey without question as has been ingrained in us since we were born. Even as royals, we don't ask questions, we follow orders. Until we're queens at least. Then we give the orders.

"You ladies are about to be given a wonderful opportunity." The Empress takes a quick sip of tea, then rests the cup on the table next to her. "It's not every day you have the opportunity to show off your hospitality in such a grand way."

All around me, the others are nodding as if they know something I don't. Either I missed an announcement after I excused myself from the Arena, or this is some rite of passage they expected but I don't know about.

"In a week's time, we will host a state dinner and welcome the Council to open discussions about the problem of the Insurgos. Of course, an elaborate state dinner must be coordinated for the visiting royalty."

I don't hear anything else she says for several minutes. My heart pounds in my ears, and a cool sweat lathers the back of my neck. It took a moment for the implications to hit me, but I understand now.

My father is coming.

The Council is nothing more than a fancy name for the gathering of all the kings of the empire. For security reasons, they almost never meet. The last time the kings of each country gathered with the Emperor was just before the Crusade. Nothing good will come of such a meeting.

I force myself to rejoin the conversation, which has skimmed over the politics of the meeting and seems to focus solely on the décor and the music. The Empress is mostly silent now as the other girls toss out ideas.

"What do you think, Emilia?" Cordelia is once again trying to include me even after all those times I've brushed her off at dinner. "Should there be lots of color or just white and gold?"

"White and gold," I say with no hesitation. "The white will provide a neutral backdrop for each country's colors, and the gold will emphasize the brilliance of Aurora."

"Yes." Gloriana looks surprised that I've apparently agreed with her. Not nearly as surprised as I feel. "Lots of gold in the fashion of the sun for our Sun King."

"And we'll each wear a white dress in the fashion of our home country," Cassia suggests.

It would be a good idea if it were an original one, but I saw the way she and Gloriana envied my white dress from last night. They must be dying to look as bridal as possible.

"The party should be your first concern," the Empress reminds. "When you are queen, you arrange everything else first and leave your own wardrobe to your ladies. That's why it's so important to have quality servants."

By the time we've discussed every possible nuance of the banquet and assigned each other tasks, my head spins with the information. That's not including the feelings I've repressed about seeing my father again.

Those hit me square in the chest as soon as I'm far enough away from the other girls to breathe again. They're probably still discussing lace and diamonds, but when I close my eyes, all I see are flames and ash. It's like my father's hand still rests heavy on my shoulder, preventing me from reaching my mother in time.

I was powerless then. I will not be powerless now.

This is what royals do. We seize power when necessary. We march into places we have no business being and take what we want.

I've never been that person, but I'm about to become her. Because I can't possibly go back to my room without confronting either Felix or Ronan about this. Did they know my father was among the rumored guests? Perhaps more important, do either of them know the details to be discussed about the Insurgos?

Losing sight of my purpose would be easy. Between my father and planning the state dinner, my mind is crowded with frivolous things.

"Emilia!"

I cringe as Cordelia's voice echoes down the long hallway. The heels of her shoes click against the tile floor as she races to catch up with me. For a split second, I consider rushing around the corner and pretending I didn't hear her, but I hesitated too long for her to ever believe that.

"I didn't realize you'd already left the drawing room." She pants in a very unladylike manner as she reaches me. "The Empress suggested you and I work together to arrange the food for the party. I thought we could discuss it while we took a stroll through the gardens?"

It sounds like a lovely idea if only I weren't so determined to extract information from the Prince and his Commander. "Perhaps later? I was on my way down to the training areas to watch the soldiers."

"Well, I certainly can't blame you." She offers a blushing smile as she ducks her chin. "They are quite handsome, aren't they? Especially Commander Fidelis. All the girls were so jealous when Ronan partnered you with him for the self-defense lessons."

"They were?" I'm not surprised they think Felix is handsome, but I'm a little baffled that anyone even noticed with Ronan nearby. To hear them all talk, I thought they were all unfailingly loyal to the Prince. My surprise must be evident on my face because Cordelia immediately tries to amend her statement.

"Of course, we were only thinking of whichever poor girl didn't win Ronan's hand. Though I guess that's silly. Can you imagine one of us marrying a guard?" She laughs a little harder than necessary until I realize she's no longer laughing but crying.

"Are you okay?" I look up and down the hall for help with the crying girl in front of me, but we're still alone. "Whatever it is, I'm sure it's fine."

"I'm sorry." She sniffs and wipes her tears. "It's just that I haven't told anyone except Livia. Since she's been gone, I've held it all in, and I'm about to burst."

I'm not good at this, but my heart breaks at her tears. Never had I considered that someone else here was as miserable or lonely as me. "You can tell me," I say as I loop my arm through hers.

"I don't love him," Cordelia whispers as she bows her head and lets me lead her. "I never wanted to be here."

The door to the garden is just ahead, and I wait until we've exited through it before I answer her. Even then, I keep my voice low. "It doesn't seem fair. None of us were given a choice."

"Yes, but not all of us are in love with someone else."

The stillness of the garden cocoons us, but I still feel too exposed to be having this conversation. But poor Cordelia... She loves someone other than Ronan? For a heart stopping moment, I'm afraid it's Felix, but why would that matter?

"Tell me about him," I say as I lead her through the lush wall of green. If we wind our way through the garden, we can still arrive at the training grounds in time for me to speak to Felix or Ronan.

"His name is Samson, and he's a captain in my father's guard."

Oh. That makes sense. What doesn't make sense is the way the tension seeps from my muscles when I realize she isn't going to say Felix's name.

"We've known each other since we were children. My heart has never belonged to anyone else."

My heart has never belonged to anyone at all. After seeing the mess it makes, I'm not sure I want it to. "Can't you ask Ronan to send you home?"

I'm privy to information about Ronan's heart the other's don't know. He would understand Cordelia's predicament. I'm sure of it.

"My father would kill me. Now that Livia's been sent home, I'm the only chance our country has."

For as much as I despise and fear my father, perhaps I should be grateful he hasn't applied any direct political pressure. Maybe he knew he wouldn't need to. Or maybe he had such little hope of me winning Ronan's hand that he didn't think me worth his time. Some things never change.

Cordelia and I emerge from the gardens on a stone path, which leads to a short balcony overlooking the training ring. She doesn't question me as I direct our steps in that direction. We both lean against the short stone wall, towering ten feet or so above the heads of the soldiers in the rings below.

I spot Felix immediately and find him looking right back. He has almost a sixth sense where I'm concerned, which is both flattering and frustrating. Next to him, Ronan stands in profile, barking orders at the soldiers closest to them.

"If Ronan sent you home." I say to her, "and your father didn't know you'd asked to be sent home, would that change things?"

"No." She sighed and leaned her cheek on her hand. "He would still be disappointed, and he would never let me marry Samson. A guard and a princess don't belong together."

Felix is still studying me. It's a strange feeling to be scrutinized from such a distance. Even stranger to be able to communicate my displeasure to him with a slight shake of my head. He nods once in response. He'll find me when he's released from training. Then I'll have my answers.

"Thank you for listening to me." Cordelia takes my hand and gives it a gentle squeeze. "I knew if anyone would understand, it would be you."

"Why me?" I ask, even though I think I know.

"You and the Commander... Everyone thinks there's something there."

With a heavy sigh, I pull myself upright from my position against the wall. Cordelia deserves some semblance of my truth. "The Commander was assigned to me at Ronan's request because my own father couldn't be bothered to send me with any guards or protection. I would have been alone if it weren't for Felix. He's been a dear friend to me but nothing more."

The pity I look for on Cordelia's face never comes. Instead, her pretty features curve into a soft smile. "Then I hope you win. You deserve the crown and the prince, and I'll do whatever I can to help you get them."

This is different than my short-lived friendship with Davina. Cordelia is an ally, one I ignored for far too long. And if she's willing to throw her support behind me, the least I can do is help her out with the banquet like she asked.

"You said we were in charge of food, right?"

She raises fair brows at my change of subject. "Yes."

"Then let's visit the kitchens on the way back. Only the very best for our kings. I hope you're hungry."

She laughs as she takes my arm again, and we leave Felix and Ronan behind.

With a full stomach and a lighter heart, I return to my rooms only long enough to retrieve the Aletheia and then venture back to the garden. Because I hope Felix will come looking for me, I let Hannah know where I've gone. But once I've stepped out amid the lush green trees and colorful flowers, thoughts of anyone else fade.

I could forget the rest of the world in here, and that's exactly what I plan to do. Just me and my book and my God.

Hushed voices break through my reverie, but I'm already on top of the men before I can think to hide myself. The two of them sit on the bench Davina and I occupied what feels like ages ago, sheets of paper spread out between them.

"Highness," one of them acknowledges me, and they both stand then bow slightly. Even from their stooped positions, they exchanged worried looks.

"I'm so sorry," I say, choosing my words carefully. I've interrupted something important, something devious, and my mind darts back to the other conversations I've overheard just by wandering around the palace. "I didn't realize the garden was occupied. Then again, I've had my head in the clouds these days."

My flighty response seems to ease some of their worry as they rise slowly and offer me condescending smiles. Good. They think I'm a harmless girl who's too in love to notice anything around her.

"We'll just be going, Highness." One of the men—a voice I'm certain I recognize from my earlier forays into eavesdropping—begins shoveling the papers from the bench into a bag. I try not to let my eyes linger on the single sheet that falls to the ground behind them unnoticed.

"That's not necessary," I protest weakly. "I can find another spot."

Except the three of us know they must give up the spot to me because I want it and I am royal. That sort of privilege makes no sense to me, but I won't argue it this time because there's something they don't want me to see, and I *will* see it.

"Of course not, Highness," the other man says as he glances at his companion, then back to me. "We were just leaving."

They make a series of stumbling, awkward bows, then disappear through the trees. I wait several minutes to make sure they're gone before I let myself breathe deeply. Then, keeping my head up to watch my surroundings, I lean backward to blindly reach for the paper they left behind the bench.

Once I've snagged it, I stuff it inside my small book and tuck the whole thing under my arm. It isn't safe to read here today. Probably not the smartest idea I've ever had, but it's only a symptom of the fleeting security I feel in my position with Felix and with Ronan. In reality, I'm still a traitor to the crown, and I'm in no position to flaunt that.

I leave the garden behind, looking over my shoulder as I navigate the hallways to make certain I'm not being followed. Letting my guard down like that could have gotten me in trouble. Instead, I'm hoping it gained me some information. My fingers itch to pull that paper from between the pages of my book and read the information there.

As I round the corner just past the kitchen, momentarily distracted by the delicious smells though I'm not a bit hungry, I slam into a solid form. The jolt sends me backward until Ronan's hands grasp my arms and pull me upright again. With wide blue eyes, he looks just as startled to see me as I am to see him.

"Are you all right?" He's looking me up and down, presumably for injuries, but his eyes linger a little too long at the package under my arm.

"I'm fine, thank you." The way we left things last night leaves me unsure how to relate to him. Something large divides us, though I'm sure we'd both like to pretend it doesn't exist.

"Hannah told me you'd be in the garden." He lowers his gaze to study his shiny shoes. "I thought, perhaps, you'd like to have dinner with me in my room tonight."

"I'm not hungry." It's petty, but it's a small measure of control I can exert over him. Even that is an illusion. He could order me to join him if he wanted.

"The library then?" When his eyes find mine again, they're full of hope and the hint of a smile. This is his peace offering. I want to accept it, but I don't want him to think this is over.

"The library," I finally agree.

The slight curl of his lips widens into a boyish grin, and a warmth grows inside me with the knowledge that I caused that smile.

"I'll have Felix escort you after everyone has gone to bed."

I don't ask if the late hour is because our meetings are still forbidden, or if he simply likes the thrill of it. Likely a combination of the two.

"I'll be waiting," I say, in my best attempt at flirting. The other girls make it look so easy. Then I think of poor Cordelia and her predicament, and I sober up. For once, I'm grateful I don't have anyone waiting at home, and this entire game seems silly once again.

No one else greets me in the halls as I return to my room. If Hannah is surprised I've returned so quickly, she says nothing. She busies herself with changing the sheets on my bed and humming softly. I wish I had her peaceful spirit, but my heart craves revolution and change, not softness and obedience.

In my other rooms, my ladies are cleaning on their hands and knees, but they too seem happy. Both guilt and frustration grip me as I study them. They are content with far less than I have. What room do I have to complain? But their complacency frustrates me to no end. Can't they see things have to change?

"Can I help you with something?" Hannah makes a small curtsy at my side, though I've told her several times the gesture isn't necessary.

"I need a minute alone." Though the paper I stuffed in my book may be nothing of importance, I don't want to take the chance of anyone else seeing it. If my instincts are right, I don't want someone else to have to bear this secret. "Can you distract the others?"

Hannah's face falls a little, but this isn't the rejection she thinks it is. Rather, it's a show of my faith and trust in her. Though she knows something's amiss, she'll never let on to anyone else.

Once she's left my bedroom, closing the door behind her and saying something to the others about my headache, I sink to my half made bed. The sheets are still warm from drying in the sun, and I'm tempted to take a nap, especially if I'm going to meet Ronan late tonight.

But I won't be able to sleep until I've satisfied my curiosity. With slow, purposeful movements, I open the book on my bed and remove the folded paper from it. At first it seems like nothing more than a list of names, but then I recognize one or two of them from years spent in my father's court.

This is a list of guards and dignitaries accompanying each king on their journey to Aurora for the Council meeting. I might have thought nothing of it if I wasn't certain I recognized the voice of at least one of the men in the garden. It's the same voice I heard near the stables and the library. The same man who talked of war and Insurgos and dispatching kings.

My blood runs cold despite the warmth of the room. Why would they have a list like this? I don't like what it all adds up to. When I flip over the paper, I like it even less.

I only know what this list is because I see my own name on it. Under the name of each king, which is crossed out with a single dark line, are the names of their heirs.

I stare at the paper, attempting to reason with myself. Have I made this into something it was never intended to be? Maybe years as a royal and then a soldier have made me paranoid. But what if I'm right?

Felix. He's the only one I can trust with this. Ronan's out of the question because, if I'm right, his father is the mastermind of it all. The Prince might claim to prefer me, love me even, but this is one thing he will never believe from me.

"Hannah," I call, loud enough to be heard through the closed door. She's at my side nearly before I can hide the paper.

"Yes?" Her eyes dart around the room, looking for my obvious request.

"Bring Commander Fidelis to me, please. Tell him it's urgent, and the utmost discretion is required." I'd like to write him a note conveying the urgency, but today is a reminder of how easily paper can fall into the wrong hands. Besides, I have confidence that Felix will come no matter what.

"Yes, ma'am." Hannah curtsies, then rushes out the door.

"Cecily." I rise from the bed and move toward the other room where I can see my ladies are still cleaning. Cecily rises from her knees and curtsies to me.

"I'd like for all of you to take the afternoon off," I tell her. Behind Cecily, the others stop their work to look at me with wide eyes.

"B-but, ma'am, we're not through with the cleaning."

"The place looks spotless." My smile is meant to assure them, and it seems to be working. "I want to reward you. Take the afternoon and walk in the garden or visit the markets. I'll need a new dress for the state dinner in a week. Perhaps you can look at the fabrics, maybe pick out something for yourselves as well."

"Emilia, I—"

"It's not up for discussion." I try to keep my voice light, but I'm desperate for them to leave. Felix and I need to speak alone, and though I trust my ladies, I can't chance them overhearing. Best for them to just be gone when he arrives.

"Very well," Cecily replies in a somber tone.

Though when she and the other three emerge from their quarters a few minutes later dressed in clothes for the market, I see bright smiles on all their faces. They say their quick goodbyes, and I am left alone.

Felix doesn't come immediately. By the time he arrives, his knock on the door wakes me from a nap. I stumble to the door and pull it open as my memories began to coalesce. I blink up at him under heavy eyelids until I remember why I've called him here. Then everything narrows to sharp focus, and I fist my hand in his shirt and pull him in the door before anyone can catch him standing in front of my door.

He's breathless and covered in dirt nearly the same light brown as his eyes, which are currently very wide as he stares me down. I'm half expecting some cutting remark, but I don't have time to wait for it.

"I need to show you something."

"Wait. You're okay?"

I look up from digging the book out from under the mattress to see his eyes are still wide and his chest still heaves with exertion. He must have run all the way here.

"Yes, I'm okay," I say from my position on my knees.

Felix lets out a disbelieving laugh that sounds more like a gasp and joins me on the floor. His back rests against my bed as he wipes the dirt from his face. When he looks to me again, two streaks of his dark skin are visible beyond the grime...

"Hannah said it was urgent. She wouldn't take no for an answer. Haven't I asked you not to scare me like that?"

"Your concern has merit," I assure him. "It's just misplaced."

My fingers brush the cover of the book, and I pull it from beneath the mattress. Felix immediately sobers when he sees it. I sit next to him, our shoulders nearly brushing as I hand him the page I retrieved from the garden.

Something heavy hangs in the small space between us, and I struggle to give it a name. Can you really trust someone you don't know? I supposed it's no different than soldiers in battle. I can only hope Felix understands the weight of the trust I've placed in him.

His face remains a blank mask as he scans the writing. It's what I've come to expect from him, but I scrutinize his features for any sign of comprehension. If I could will him to understand, to come to the same conclusion I did, I'd feel better about my own thoughts. But he is missing some of the pieces I've gathered, and it's time I told him all of it.

"Your name," he says softly, his thumb brushing over the messy script of my name on the paper. "This is a list of the heirs of Atlas except for Ronan, but I don't recognize what's on the other side of this."

He turns the paper over to examine the other list again.

"I think it's the names of those traveling with the kings to the Council." My eyes don't leave his face as I speak, and I'm not disappointed. His dark brows, looking faded with dirt, turn down in a fleeting frown. He quickly schools his features into his usual stoic façade. Not jumping to conclusions. Not surprising.

"There's something else." Felix places the paper in his lap and turns his gaze solely on me. "You wouldn't call me if there weren't something else."

My mouth is dry as I try to swallow, to prepare to speak. I don't want Felix to think me a fool, but I don't really want to be right about this either. "I've heard things in the palace. Things I wasn't meant to hear."

"Out with it, Emilia."

"I think, at the state dinner, there's going to be an attempt to assassinate our kings."

There. I said it. But Felix doesn't react as I expected. He doesn't react at all.

"Twice I've overheard men talking," I continue, "and each time they've mentioned Insurgos and war and dispatching kings. Today I met one of those men in the garden. In his hurry to get away from me, he dropped this."

"Repeat their words to me," he instructs. "Exactly as you heard them."

So I do. I tell him about diving into a pile of hay in the stables to listen and stopping outside a doorway on my way to the library one night. I even tell him about the Emperor's suspected involvement. When I've finished, he slumps back against the bed and rubs his chin, eyes fixed on the floor in front of him.

"You should have told me sooner."

"Would you have believed me without something like this?" I wave the paper in front of his face. "It's just my words against someone else...someone the Emperor apparently favors."

"Of course I would believe you. You've given me no reason to doubt your word."

"What do we do?"

"What *can* we do? I assume you don't know who this man is—the one you saw in the garden. Even if you did, as you've pointed out, he seems to be acting on the Emperor's instructions. This isn't an assassination. It's an execution."

He doesn't have the answers. I don't realize how much I was counting on him to until I feel the burden fall to me. I buckle under its weight. But as my shoulders slump, his hand tentatively rests on my back.

"I'm sorry." He's close enough I feel his breath on my cheek as he speaks, and I smell the musk of the dirt on him. "We'll do what we can. *Everything* we can."

"And what if it's not enough? We don't know who's involved. We can't trust anyone."

"We can trust each other." He removes his hand from my shoulder but doesn't put space between us. "And that's enough."

18

In the week preceding the state dinner, I think often on the Empress's words to me during our first outing. She'd told me it was a queen's job to appear ignorant of threats to security while noticing everything that went on around her. I manage to fail at both.

At the daily meeting with Cordelia and the other girls to discuss the details of the party, my mind is conspicuously elsewhere. When I'm not occupied with those meetings, I wander the palace halls, taking note of everything I see. Still, when the day of the dinner arrives, I've gathered no new information about the assassination attempts.

The only positive to come from this is that it's distracted me from my father's arrival. The very thing I was so upset about a few days ago now seems almost trivial in comparison to saving at least four lives. If only Felix and I had been able to let others in on the secret. We do trust each other, but contrary to his words, I'm not sure it's enough.

I'd hoped to arrive late to the dinner tonight, but as a hostess, I'm expected to greet the guests beside the other girls. The room is already filling with the lesser nobles and guards, but the six of us stand at the head table, waiting to greet the visiting kings. All around me, people titter with excitement, but I'm trying to keep a tight lid on all emotion. I think of Felix and how he always seems so solid and steady. That's what I need to be.

All hope of that vanishes as the trumpets blow and herald the entrance of the four kings. Zephyros, Austrina, Euros, and Borealis. My attempt to focus on the other kings because I've never seen them before is in vain. In a betrayal I should have known was coming, my eyes can't look away from my father.

He looks much as I remember him from this distance. Not as tall as Ronan or Felix, but still taller than most men in the room and his posture still as regal as ever.

I don't realize I'm shaking until Cordelia grabs my hand and pulls me slightly behind her. Hiding isn't an option, at least not yet, but I'm grateful for her feeble offer of protection.

"Look straight ahead," she whispers out the side of her mouth. "Don't focus on him."

I've underestimated her from the very beginning, and I'm sorry for it. She knows nothing about my father, and I've given her little reason to like me, but she's still doing what she can to comfort me. I only hope one day I'll be in the position to return the favor.

Her advice has merit, because when I focus my eyes straight ahead, I look past my father and see Ronan instead. How fitting. My past and my future in one room.

Somewhere in the background, Emperor Cyrus is greeting the kings. I don't hear him introduce us, but Cordelia nudges me as we collectively curtsy in the monarchs' general direction.

As we rise, the crowd disperses, and I'm jostled apart from Cordelia. Instead, Cassia stands beside me, looking as surprised as I feel. Her wide eyes quickly narrow as she takes in my gold dress and the tiara the Empress loaned me once again. The perfect shape of her lips morphs into an ugly sneer.

"You always have to show everyone up, don't you?" Despite the swelling music and laughter all around us, her low, harsh tone cuts through it all.

"I never agreed to wear white." At least I don't think I did, but it was probably decided in one of the meetings I didn't pay attention to. The other girls are dressed in varying styles of white silk, and Cassia has even gone so far as to have her ladies fashion some lace in her hair that looks suspiciously like a veil.

Rather than standing out, the gold dress actually allows me to blend in. Around us, men and women wear a rainbow of colors, though almost everyone from Aurora has donned some sort of gold accent. It is the country's signature color. Even dressed in all glittering gold, my dress doesn't provide the sharp contrast the bright white of Cassia's does.

She looks at the group of people around us and seem to come to the same conclusion. "Look at you. You look like nothing more than commoner among the rabble. But that's exactly what you are, isn't it?"

"I have as much right to be here as you do." My voice betrays me with a little quiver. My father's presence still has me rattled, and I can recover quick enough to block Cassia's arrows.

"Well, we both know that's not true. Your father can't even look at you. His disgusting, tainted daughter who he sent away to die." She walks a slow circle around me, and her gaze brings a hot flame to my cheeks. "It would have been better for everyone if you had."

Her words sting as if I've been slapped, and all I can do is stare with mouth agape.

"Emilia, will you walk with me?" Ronan appears from nowhere to rescue me from an answer with an oblivious smile. "Oh, I'm sorry, Cassia. Have I interrupted something?"

Her eyes don't leave me, and she doesn't bother with a fake smile. "Not at all, Your Majesty."

"Isn't this a glorious evening?" Ronan has subtly positioned himself between me and my accuser. "We haven't had such a spectacular gathering in all my years. I commend you ladies on such a fine job."

"Of course, Ma—"

"Come with me, Emilia." Ronan interrupts what I'm sure would've been a magnanimous response from Cassia. The hatred in her eyes as she peers over the Prince's shoulder sends a shiver up my spine. Fortunately, he pulls me away before I can wither under the power of it.

Away from Cassia and the venom she spewed, I take a heaving breath as Ronan gently pushes me up against a marble pillar. He closes in, and I instinctively place my hands against his chest to push him away. I need space. The wide open spaces of my country's borders seem a lifetime away.

"Don't move and don't push me away." He pulls my hands from him and clasps them loosely in his own. His tall figure hems me in, cutting off my view of the room. For that moment, I see only him. "You're shaking. Just calm down They can see your weakness. They're vultures, the whole lot of them."

"But they've figured out that I don't have my father's protection. I certainly don't have your father's." I try to look past him, but he catches my chin between his thumb and forefinger and doesn't let go until I meet his eyes.

"And you will stay by my side tonight because you have mine."

It sounds good, but I have my doubts anyone will believe it. I don't believe it. "But they'll know it's not real. They all know you don't take your time with me as you do with them because I've kept it our secret."

"Then we must make them believe." He steps back, still holding one of my hands. It's the most affection and preference he's shown me in public. "Can you do this?"

"Can you? There's a reason we've kept our liaisons secret. And what about Cassia or Gloriana? They look beautiful, Ronan, obviously the most beautiful girls in the room. If you snub them in front of their short-tempered father, you're likely to start a war."

"Yes, yes, they're lovely. But I've seen you, and I can't look away. How could I ever be happy with the moon when I've already looked upon the sun? You're radiant, Emilia."

Heat crawls up my neck where he cups his hand at the juncture of my shoulder. The whole room looks at us, and the murmurs hiss just below the music. Ronan doesn't seem to hear them.

Accepting his offer seems the only logical course of action. No one will dare speak words against me while I'm on the arm of the Prince.

We take a turn around the room, and I listen as Ronan makes talk with each of the kings and their ambassadors. But when he steps toward my father, I let go of his hand. Ronan's eyes question me, but I have no answers. All I know is that I can't face this man, not here with so many eyes on us.

"I'm thirsty." It sounds like a convincing lie because my mouth is suddenly dry and my voice hoarse. "Excuse me while I get some refreshments."

Though waiting for him to dismiss me would be the proper thing to do, I turn on my heels and move toward the drinks. Behind me, Ronan speaks Felix's name, so I'm not at all surprised to have the Commander join me at the table.

"Are you all right, Highness?" Felix reaches past me and offers me a cup of sparkling gold liquid, the same color as my dress.

I accept and tip it back, letting the cold substance slide down my throat. It's sickly sweet. "I can't even look at him."

He doesn't need me to specify who I mean. We both look on as Ronan chats warmly with my father, their laughs loud and genuine. Disappointment leaves a bitter taste in my mouth that my drink cannot mask. After all I've told Ronan about my father, I'd hoped he would be a little colder toward him. More like Felix who stands at attention at my side, as if he would deflect any attack from the king of Borealis.

But not even his company can deflect the stares from my father. Just a quick glance my way then back to Ronan, but it's enough that I can't hide the shaking anymore.

"Perhaps you are ill and should return to your room," Felix suggests as he takes the glass from my trembling hand and returns it to the table before I can send it crashing to the floor. "You look very pale."

He doesn't mean it as a slight, and I'm sure it's the truth. Time has aged my father, but not bowed him. If I close my eyes, I can still feel his iron grip on my shoulder as he kept me from running toward the flames of my mother's sacrifice. No, murder. He murdered her, and the kingdom cheered him for it.

It's not that different than what will happen if Emperor Cyrus succeeds in his plans. I've seen no signs of assassins here tonight, but the distractions and my anger may have clouded my vision. The gathering of kings is far too good an opportunity to pass up.

"I can't leave," I tell Felix, though I desperately want to. My bed calls my name, and I long to bury myself under mounds of covers and sleep for ages. But I would never forgive myself if I missed the opportunity to thwart Cyrus's plan. My father's blood won't be on my hands because that would make me no better than him.

"I'll look after him for you."

His offer pulls my eyes away from my father and Ronan, and I examine the guard before me. After all I have told him of my childhood, I know he feels no warmth for the man who wears the Borealis crown. But Felix understands in a way I never could have hoped someone would. If I were to leave this in his hands, I trust him to act for me. But for my own peace of mind, I want to be the one to see it through.

"I believe you would." I'm sure there's wonder in my eyes because I hear it even in my own voice. Felix is a good man, the rare sort that defies all expectations. It's a shame he's a guard because he would have made an excellent king. "But this is my burden, not yours. You have enough to watch out for tonight. It's unfair to ask you to watch one man when you should have your eye on at least three others."

He won't argue with me on that point because this makes the most military sense. The more eyes you have on the targets the better. And because he doesn't have to devote time to my father so long as I'm there to watch, he's free to scrutinize the other three kings. The guards, of course, are doing their part, but Felix is like me, and if anything happens tonight, he'll shoulder the blame himself whether it belongs to him or not.

With a confidence I don't feel, I throw my shoulders back and force my feet toward Ronan. The Empress's crown shifts slightly on my slick hair, but I adjust it with a small shake of my head. Chin lifted and back straight, I adopt the regal air the rest of the girls have shown since the first day.

"Ahh, Emilia." Ronan welcomes me back by raising his arm and ushering me against his side. "Your father and I were just discussing our horses. I told him about that wild thing you insist on taming."

Up close, my father looks much older than I remember. Lines crease his mouth and eyes, and streaks of gray line his beard. There's something else, a softness in his eyes as he looks me over, that I have never seen before.

"Emilia always loved wild things," he concedes with a weak attempt at a smile.

Can he guess how I feel about him? Has he wondered about me once in the years since he sent me away?

"Hello, father." I bow slightly to him. Not the deep curtsy that my position once demanded, but the acknowledgment that we are equals in my eyes. If anything, my favor with the Crown Prince places me above him.

"My daughter." He clasps his hands on my shoulders, pulling me away from Ronan long enough to press kisses to either side of my face as is the custom in our country. I hold my breath while he does so. "You are more beautiful than I could have imagined."

"Isn't she though?" Ronan seems more than happy to keep the conversation going, and I let him. "And full of so many surprises."

He knows more of my secrets than most people. How odd that a man I've known for so little time knows me better than my father.

"I don't doubt that. She has her mother's spirit."

My knees buckle a little, but Ronan pulls me tighter to him to hold me up. How dare my father mention my mother? Is it a ploy to get a reaction from me? I can't give him the satisfaction.

"And your gift for rule," Ronan adds.

That's what breaks me. Not Cassia's words or my father's presence, but the innocuous words uttered by my prince. I feel the blood drain from my face as I put distance between myself and Ronan.

Two sets of eyes study me with an intensity that prickles my skin as I look around the room. It's like I'm seeing it all for the first time. The abundance of food, the opulent décor, the frivolous conversation. This isn't why I'm here. Yet, I've somehow managed to convince Ronan I will be a ruler like my father.

It's the exact opposite of what I wanted. This can't be what Levi meant. What God meant. Cassia is right. I shouldn't be here. Levi died to get me those words, and I've obviously misjudged the path they were supposed to lead me on.

"Emilia?" Ronan reaches for my hand, and I allow him to take it. Maybe because I feel lost. Probably because I'm drowning in this, and I'm reaching for the first life raft that comes along. "Are you all right?"

His bright blue eyes ask questions he can't give voice to, but there's also a reprimand buried in there. A warning for me to pull myself together. As he so callously reminded me after my show at the Arena, he can't campaign for me with the Emperor if I don't act like a princess.

And that's all it is. A campaign. A political move. It leaves a bitter taste in my mouth.

"I'm fine." The words are forced, and I'm sure Ronan can tell. "But it's rude of me to monopolize your time when I'm sure the two of you have important matters to discuss."

With a curt nod of my head, I leave Ronan and my father to figure out exactly what matters I'm insinuating.

I don't leave the ballroom right away because as I start for the door, I catch sight of Felix and remember I'm supposed to be surveying the crown for assassins. An hour ticks by before I concede defeat. If there's anyone here with dark motives, they're much too stealthy for me to detect.

The heaviness on my shoulders doesn't get any lighter when I leave the ballroom. Tears threaten to spill down my face, but I'm determined not to let them until I've left everyone behind. My feet know the way back to my room even though my mind is engaged in other matters.

I can't stay here anymore—not at the party, not in the palace, not in Aurora. But there's nowhere to go. *Please, God, give me clarity. How am I helping your people while I'm here?*

The scent of leather and spice reaches me, and I don't have to look to know Felix stands behind me. It's a comfort I don't want. If he's watching me, who is watching my father and the others?

"Are you all right?" No hint of emotion or concern colors his tone, and I'm grateful for it. If he's stoic then I must be as well.

"Yes, I'm fine." But my hands shake as I open the door to my chambers and motion for him to follow me. The room feels smaller as my emotions and Felix's presence fill it up. "Did you see anything tonight?"

"Nothing." He sighs as if disappointed. Or maybe, like me, he wonders if he's failed to notice something that might change the course of our history. Sometimes I think we might be cut from the same cloth.

Was I wrong about this? But I know what I heard, and I thought I understood the strategy of it. All the kings of the realm in one place and not even a whisper of trouble.

"I'll keep watching until they leave. There may still be trouble." He's sheathed his sword, but his dark eyes are ready and alert. Always at the ready. Does Ronan know how fortunate he is to have Felix as his protector?

"Thank you for believing me."

His lips part, but he hesitates over the words. Then, "I don't just believe you. I believe *in* you."

"Don't." I don't like where this is going. The weight of unrealistic expectations hangs between us, and I know he's getting ready to pin them on me. "I'm just a girl who happened to be born to a king. Everyone knows I'm not queen material, even Ronan, though he won't admit it."

"I have to believe the sum of my existence is not to serve this king who will not acknowledge my God. I believe in you because the signature of the divine is all over you." The back of his hand brushes my cheek, and I find the treacherous hope in his eyes. He pulls his hand away quickly, as if he can't believe the uncharacteristic gesture belongs to him. He's never touched me like that. "There's freedom in your eyes."

"I can't be this person you think I am." Not an hour earlier, I was terrified to look my father in the eyes. How can anyone think I'm born to rule? "And if you truly want what you say you want—

the same thing I want—then you know I'll never be able to sit on a throne and obtain it."

"And will you abandon Ronan then, or let him crown you as his queen? He loves you, Highness—"

"The Prince knows as much about love as I do. No one born into the palace expects to marry for love. Political advantage is fed to us nearly before we can walk. That he might pick me from the girls he's allowed to choose from doesn't mean he loves me." I don't know where this venom comes from except that seeing my father helped me realize what a charade this whole thing has been. I'm merely a pawn in a game, and I'm tired of playing.

"But he would honor you above everyone." Why Felix argues for the Prince, I don't know. It's a reminder of how little I know about him or what he really wants.

"I don't doubt that. But I do not want a man who honors me as his queen if he doesn't love me as a woman." These are the sort of choices I hadn't expected to make, at least not for a long while. If my father had named me his heir, I would have eventually been pressured to marry but not for many years.

Tonight convinced me of many things, and I will never be comfortable suffering through state dinners that fill our stomachs while Insurgos and others starve in their huts and caves because people like me have persecuted them for the truth they hold dear. For a few hours tonight, there was no difference between me and my father, and I won't let that be said of me again.

"There is no one but you to save us." He pleads softly, a reminder that though we appear to be alone, our conversation is still traitorous. "However you choose to do it, I'm on your side."

Bold words from the man who commands the Emperor's guard. Foolish, too. Because even if people choose to follow me, I'm not sure where to lead them.

"You think Ronan is the key to this? That if I marry him, he'll come to believe as we do?"

"It's the path of least resistance. Though he may be skeptical, he won't punish you for your belief. No matter what you think, I believe he loves you the best he knows how."

"And I thought my father loved my mother."

"I did."

Felix and I freeze as those two words send icy daggers into my chest. My father stands in the doorway, barely more than a shadow against the hallway lighting.

Felix whirls to face him, pushing me behind him with his hand on his sword before I can register the movement. But I don't fear immediate harm from my father. Still, what has he overheard? Though he appears to be alone now, he could easily call for the guards to arrest me. Would the Commander protect me then?

"I'd like to speak to my daughter alone." My father doesn't ask. He simply commands, but Felix isn't his subject, so the Commander looks to me for answers. "What? She has no control over you. I am the King of Borealis. If I command you leave—"

"You are not *my* king." Felix's voice has taken on a growl, menacing but eerily calm. "She is the future Empress of Aurora and Atlas, and I will do as she commands."

I'm too shocked to immediately respond. I can't recall anyone ever speaking to my father this way. It could cost Felix his head no matter how right he may be.

"So you're that confident of her winning, are you?" My father straightens his shoulders and lifts his chin so that I think the crown he still wears may slide off his head. "You're both young and foolish, as is the Prince. Cyrus will choose who he chooses, and it won't be you, my daughter."

Those words are similar enough to Ronan's to make me believe there's some truth there. Now that Ronan's of age, he's supposed to be allowed to make his choice, but a part of me never believed that he'd be allowed to. Apparently he won't.

"Why won't it be me?" It takes considerable effort to keep my voice neutral. I've invited my enemy to wage war on my confidence.

My father takes a step forward, and Felix shifts toward him. I stop him with a hand on his arm and feel the tension in his muscles. Ready to pounce if anyone threatens me, though he knows what I'm capable of even without a weapon. Perhaps he thinks I won't be able to fight my father. That was once true. Not anymore.

"I did not want to execute your mother."

Those sudden words pull a gasp from me even as Felix subtly places a steadying hand on my back.

"I had my suspicions about what she was, the God she served, but I was willing to overlook it because it seemed harmless. I continued to believe that until the moment Cyrus insisted she was anything but harmless. His words became truth. Because he threatened to take it all away if I did not make an example of her."

"But you still chose the kingdom over her," I say softly as bitter bile burns my throat.

"Of course I did. If I hadn't, you would have been penniless on the streets, exiled—"

"Don't talk to me about exile!" My hand wraps around something smooth and hard, and I realize I've somehow extracted one of Felix's daggers from his belt without being stopped. Perhaps he didn't want to stop me. With the way we're both seething, we may fight to see who gets the first shot at my father. "And don't pretend you did it for anyone but yourself."

"I loved you both—you and your mother—but you'll see if Cyrus allows you to marry Ronan. Your first duty is to your country. It's your life or the lives of your thousands of subjects. So I chose the death of one over the death of many. Those are the choices you'll have to make when you're queen."

My hands begin to shake, and Felix takes the dagger from my hand. Just as well since I'm not sure I could hit anything with it at the moment.

"Why did you come here?" I can't argue the thread of truth in my father's words. How they underscore my greatest fears about ruling. But I don't believe he sought me out, without the protection of his guard, to tell me this.

"To tell you I'm proud of the woman you've become. And that I saw the way the Emperor looked at you. If you can make it out of here alive, Emilia, you're free to come home. Back to the palace to sit as my heir."

It's enough to take the wind out of my sails, and I turn my back on him before he can see the emotion on my face. Felix is right beside me as I walk the few steps to my bed, and with a subtle shake of my head, he knows what to do.

"You're dismissed," he tells my father.

I expect an argument, but none comes. Maybe he plans to talk more with me when I've returned to Borealis. Or maybe he simply doesn't care. After all, he could produce another heir. Perhaps he cared a shred for my mother after all, and I am a reminder of her.

"I leave in two days," my father says, presumably to Felix but for my benefit.

And then he's gone, and I have a mountain of decisions to make. The heels of my hands press against my eyes until I see spots.

"Not tonight," Felix says once he's sure we're alone again. "Don't think anything of it tonight. Rest."

I'd love to, but that's easier said than done. "He's not wrong," I say as I began pulling the pins that held my hair in place. It falls around my shoulders as if it can shelter me from the world.

"No, he's not." Felix surprises me by agreeing. I look up to find him by my side again, looking down at me with a fierceness in his frown that leaves me feeling both protected and afraid of his fire. "He's absolutely right to be proud of you."

"If I've made my father proud, I've done something very wrong." But something deep in me feels—satisfied? That's not the right word, but I don't know how else to describe it. His motives may be ambiguous, but his invitation to come home was real. So why don't I feel happier about it? "All those things he said about the throne are true. And they'll be true no matter if I reign in Borealis or Aurora."

"It may be the truth of those pagan men who sit on their thrones, but you are not them. Our God is truth. Follow him, and he will not steer you wrong."

"Tell me that passage from the Aletheia again." My mind fails me, but I know his will not.

"'Fear not, for I am with you. Be not dismayed for I am your God. I will strengthen you, help you, and uphold you with my righteous right hand'."

I'm about to thank him for the words that bring me much needed comfort when he continues.

"'All who rage against you will be put to shame and confounded. Those who strive against you shall be as nothing and shall perish.'"

Something strong beats inside me in response to his words. "Where did you get that last part?"

"It's from the Aletheia. A part I thought I'd forgotten, but the words just came to me."

The promise those words offer awakens something in me. What would I do if I knew I could not fail? Certainly not stay here and wait for an offer of marriage that would only make me feel like a prisoner even if Ronan did love me. But to be free, to worship as I choose… I'd assemble every Insurgo I could find to reconstruct the Aletheia. Felix has given me a good start, and Hannah has added. What else could we learn if there were more of us?

This is why Cyrus thinks we're dangerous. Because he is our enemy, and God has promised that those who come against us shall be made nothing. Or has he? Maybe this promise isn't meant for me. It certainly doesn't seem to be coming true yet. Perhaps it has to do with this gate everyone keeps talking about.

"There is more to it, I think."

"Yes," Felix agrees with a defeated sigh and looks away from me for the first time since my father left the room. "I wish I could remember more. If I had known I wouldn't always be able to read the Aletheia, I would have tried harder to memorize it."

His words floor me, and I sink down on the bed with a hand pressed to my breathless chest. "You... you read them?" This never occurred to me. Even when he gave me the book with his cramped handwriting, I assumed he'd simply had a stronger oral tradition, more time to hear the words, than I had. But he's actually seen them. Held them in his hands. I have to know more.

He seems to realize he's said too much, but I don't understand why. There should be no secrets between us where this is concerned. "When I was a child, copies were plentiful. I read them daily."

There's something else undercutting his words. He said if he'd known he wouldn't be able to read the Aletheia... not if he'd known it would all be destroyed. There's a subtle difference there, one I might be exaggerating, but it gives me a renewed hope. If there were copies as recently as his childhood, might there still be one left?

"What happened to those copies?"

"I don't know."

It's hardly the answer I'm expecting, and I don't think it's all he has to say. "Felix, this is important. The Emperor wants it to learn about the Gate of Life. Why shouldn't we learn about it as well?"

"It's not a real gate, Emilia."

Nothing he could have said would have stunned me more. "What do you mean it's not real? Cyrus has burned villages and killed people for years all for something that doesn't exist?"

"The gate is only part of his quest. He wants the gate so he can live forever. Only then will he feel he can take on the Insurgos and the Ancient of Days."

"And you knew the truth... all this time?"

"Who was I supposed to tell? Until you arrived, no one here believed in God. Was I just supposed to ride off into the sunset and rally the Insurgos to fight back?"

"Why not?" It's exactly what I would have done if I had the information to do so. That he's done nothing with it burns me.

"Because it was always going to be you." The mounting tension between us crests like a wave, then crashes down with these words.

I'm wrung out and depleted. Once again, someone presumes to have my destiny figured out when it's as blurry as ever to me. "So the gate doesn't actually give life, but that won't stop Cyrus from destroying everything until he sees that for himself. What about this Ancient? Are you going to tell me that he doesn't exist either?"

"I know nothing about the Ancient. Maybe he's their leader, or maybe he's misunderstood as well."

I'm tired of pulling everything out of him. So I do the one thing I hoped I'd never have to. Command him. "Tell me everything you know."

So he does. How the Gate of Life is actually the path to God in the Aletheia, and the immortality is the eternal life we received through God's sacrifice, though the details of that are vague. He paraphrases the Aletheia I've never read that speaks of a narrow way and a broad way. How his copy of the Aletheia was called the New Covenant, and though that must mean there was an Old Covenant, he was never able to read it. And if there is a gathering place, he doesn't have a clue where it might be.

"When I was a child, there were still pockets of believers. I grew up in a community where we didn't worship Caelus or the other gods. For us there was only one. Believe me when I say I want nothing more than to fight back, but we can't stand alone, Emilia. We need someone to lead us."

"Did you hope to convince Ronan? Is that why you ended up in the palace? The Crown Prince is the perfect person to lead your revolution." I watch him shut down before my eyes, but I keep pushing. "Why are you here, Felix?"

"That's enough about me for tonight." He's across the room before I can react. "Sleep well, Princess."

19

I avoid court for two days while the Council of Kings meets and presumably discusses waging war on my people. I've come to think of them that way now. My people. When I decided I didn't belong here, I meant it. I just don't know how to leave. But after my conversation with Felix, I'm determined to do it.

The Commander himself is a source of frustration for me. He knows more than he's telling me about the Insurgos—maybe about their hiding place, but definitely about the Aletheia. I don't know why he's so vague about his history, not when the truth could help so many people.

"Are you going to say goodbye to your father?" Cordelia sits opposite me on my bed, Hannah and Cecily behind us braiding our hair.

That's the question that's been on my mind since my father left my room two days ago. "I don't know. He did offer for me to come home after this, but that hardly fixes the problems between us."

"It's a start," Cordelia suggests.

After the dinner, I told her my story, leaving out the Insurgos of course. There was no use in hiding it if Cassia knew as much as she did. By the next morning, rumors whispered among the palace staff suggested I wasn't even royalty because my father had disowned me and my mother was a traitor. Therefore, they reasoned I had no place here. The least I could do was tell Cordelia the truth of it all.

"It is." But it might be too late. If my father had reached out to me before I came to Aurora, I would have returned home without question. Now I'm not certain I belong on a throne or in a line of succession. I belong with the Insurgos, wherever that may be.

"My father says the caravans begin leaving around dusk. I wish they wouldn't travel at night, especially not with those bandits prowling the hills outside the city. Weren't you attacked before you arrived in the city?"

It seems so long ago now that Felix and I were fighting off bandits and burying our fallen soldier. "Yes, we were. Several men snuck into our camp at night."

"How terrifying." Cordelia shivers, then pats her braid Cecily has just finished. "How are you so brave, Emilia? I wish I could be more like you."

Those aren't words I ever expected to hear. My entire time at the palace has been characterized by awkwardness and roughness. That I lack the innate grace and demure countenance of the other girls is obvious. That anyone—especially gentle Cordelia—would ever want to be like me is unfathomable.

I say as much to Hannah a few hours later after Cordelia leaves to bid her father farewell.

"Oh, Emilia, it's God's light in you." There's such wisdom in my maid's eyes that for a moment, I feel like I'm sitting at my mother's feet again, listening to her talk to God. "People don't always recognize it for what it is, but it's irresistible."

Maybe she's right. There was something about my mother, about Levi, that entranced me before I understood it. The same way I'm drawn to Hannah and to Felix.

"But I'm not what I should be," I argue. From my window, I can see the dozens of horses and carriages in the courtyard as yet another delegation prepares to leave. "I've gone about everything backwards and managed to make a mess of it all. I should be more like Cordelia, more like Davina was, but I don't know how to be that girl."

"Then just be you." Hannah grasps my hand much the way Cordelia did the night of the dinner. "God made you exactly who he wanted you to be. There's a reason you're different. Embrace it."

I embrace her instead. What would I have done if I hadn't met her in the market that day? If I'd kept looking forward instead of sliding off my horse? I don't think I would have survived here as long as I have without her. She's been a confidant, a skilled servant, and a friend.

"Maybe you should see your father before he leaves," she says after a moment. "Our God makes all things new. Even broken hearts."

I nod slowly and look out the window once again. Since the sun has just dipped below the mountain horizon, it's impossible to make out any details of the people milling around below my window. Is it my father or one of the other kings? Only one way to find out.

I don't bother with the usual finery it's appropriate to wear when greeting a king. My plain blue gown will do just fine. Besides, I'm not greeting him as a king but as my father, though that doesn't register in my heart. Forgiving him is not something that will come easy to me.

The back stairway leads from my hall to an opening near the stables. I leave Hannah behind and take that route to avoid any onlookers or questions.

It's the first time I've left my room since the ball. Now that Cassia and Gloriana know I'm vulnerable and I don't have the protection of my father, there's nothing to keep them from removing me as they did Livia and Davina. Until I have a guard to keep me company, I'll have to move with stealth.

I arrive in the courtyard just as the last caravan is pulling out, and my heart sinks. Through the darkness, I squint to make out the flag flying in front of the carriage. Euros. So it wasn't my father anyway. Maybe I was foolish for coming. He didn't make a second attempt to see me before he left.

Cordelia spots me and joins me near the stables. Without a word, she squeezes my hand and sniffs. That's my only clue that this time, she's not offering comfort but asking for it. So I squeeze her hand as well.

"Seeing him makes me miss home," she says after a moment. Several people, a few guards and stable hands, still mill around us, but no one gives us a second look.

"And Samson," I add.

"And Samson," she agrees. "I-I had hoped he might accompany my father on this trip, but now I'm grateful he didn't."

"Why?" I would think she would welcome any chance to see him, even if she couldn't openly reveal her affections.

"There's something foreboding in the air," she whispers ominously. "Look how the clouds cover the moon. Hardly any stars. It's a dangerous night for travel."

She's right. Dark clouds drift past the sliver of moon, making the night seem impossibly darker. Were is not for the torches lit around the grounds, I wouldn't even be able to make out who was standing next to me. Exactly the same sort of night my caravan was attacked on.

Oh.

Now I understand. I need to find Felix. We've let our guard down too soon.

"I'm sorry, Cordelia, but I need to find someone. I'll see you in the morning?"

"Yes, for tea in the drawing room."

I squeeze her hand once more before darting amongst the stable boys and guards. It's difficult to find a familiar face in the dark, so I'm grateful when I literally stumble into Antony.

"Princess." He steps back with a hurried and subtle bow. "What are you doing down here? It isn't safe."

No doubt Felix has informed him of the increased threat against me, or rather the decrease in the defenses around me. Either way, I'm sure Antony has orders to report me to the Commander whenever he finds me somewhere I'm not supposed to be. Which is exactly what I want.

"Where's Felix?" No use going through the charades. I need to find him now. I've kept a handle on the fear that threatens as my suspicions grow, but some of it leaks out in my voice, and it's impossible to shove it all back down. This isn't the eerie calmness of battle, but the dread of helplessness. I may be too late.

Antony doesn't answer me, but he does grab my arm and pull me away from everyone else. I'm about to ask what he's doing when I realize he's directing me toward a figure leaning against a horse pen.

The thread of proper posturing I'm hanging by frays, and I break from Antony to run toward Felix. He must hear my panting, because he looks up with a smile while I'm still several feet away. As I near him, the smile fades, and the apple he's been holding out for Athena falls from his hand. He meets me halfway in the space between us.

"What's wrong?" He doesn't look me over for injuries as he has every other time he's asked this question. It's much more serious than that.

"We…were…wrong." The words come in short gasps as I catch my breath. "The plot was never for the party. How could it be with all the extra security?"

"Emilia, slow down." Felix's large hands rest on my shoulders as he stoops slightly to look me directly in the eyes. "Tell me."

"It's tonight," I say, voice breaking. "He wanted to hire desperate men, bandits, to do this. They'd never be allowed in the palace, but they own the hills around us. The caravans are vulnerable in the dark."

The understanding dawns on his face followed by the hopelessness of defeat. "It's too late," he whispers. "They're all gone."

I can't accept that. There has to be something we can do. But I can't leave. Even if Felix would let me, which I know he won't, my absence will be noticed. The Emperor doesn't need another excuse to have me exiled… or worse.

"Please." I hate that I sound so weak when I beg. And I can't believe I'm about to beg for one man's life while several others hang in the balance. "I know I have no right to ask this of you, but I have to try to save him. If something happens… I'd go if I could, but—"

"Emilia." He grabs my arm, his hand completely encircling my forearm. "You only had to ask me once. If you want me to go, I'll go."

That he would blindly obey this request, knowing how I despise my father, rattles me. Then I understand. He would do anything for me. Somehow, I command the Commander.

"Go," I whisper. But he doesn't move. Wind whips around us as we stand in the shadows, trying to see each other in the thick velvet of night. It hits me then that I'm sending him on what might be a suicide mission. Because he would give his life for my father's if that's what it takes, though I'm not sure how I know this. I might not see him again.

So ill-advised as it is, I throw my arms around him for the briefest moments. "Be safe," I whisper into the cape wrapped around him and inhale leather and warmth. And then I let him go.

I'll miss this time with him. But that isn't the right word. People miss their pet when it runs away or the way the sun feels on a winter day. Felix deserves a stronger word, but I'm not strong enough to give it to him. Because it would mean laying myself bare for a man who can't care for me and probably wouldn't even if he could. Of course, I can't care for him either, though I might have if we'd both been different people. Different lives, different responsibilities. In that life, I wouldn't walk away from him.

But I do because I must.

20

I take the back stairway to return to my rooms, but there's no way I can go to bed after what I've just done. *God, did I do the right thing? What if I'm wrong? What if he never comes back?*

Even I'm not sure which "he" I mean. Saving my father was the point of this, but I don't want to think about the danger I've put Felix in. Even if he takes Antony and a few others with him, there's no guarantee this will have a positive outcome.

Though it's getting late, I still pass several people as I absently walk the halls. Most pay me no mind, but a few whispers break through the fog surrounding me. Yes, I want to scream, I am the tainted princess with the broken crown and the broken heart. Nothing to see here. Just move along.

The number of people I see dwindles to almost none as I enter the royal quarters. Just a few servants finishing up their evening chores. A maid dusting the window sills as I pass the Ronan's room gives me a timid smile. I return it the best I can.

I continue toward the library, the destination I've finally fixed my mind on, and pass two more men who look down at the floor as I pass them. One even makes a fist, a thinly veiled threat at best.

I should be used to this reaction and the disrespect, but something about this feels like a punch to the gut. Even the servants don't—

Wait a minute. I stop and close my eyes, recounting everything I can remember about the men I just passed. One is a bit of a fuzzy memory, but the other I recall with astonishing detail. Hardened dark eyes, a crooked nose, skin too dark for a palace worker. And when he'd made a fist, was it really a threat or an attempt to hide something else? Something like a tremor?

I've seen that man before. At the gate outside the city when I visited the children. Why is he in the palace? Better yet, what business does he have in the royal wing?

Unless… No. I whirl around and find the men have disappeared. Where could they have gone? Into one of the rooms?

The library. My heart gallops in my chest. I've missed something very important. The list in my room of all the heirs of Atlas was missing one name. Glaringly obvious now. Ronan.

Cyrus is going to sacrifice his own son to sell the massacre as an Insurgo attack. And I've sent away the one soldier who might believe the madness swirling in my brain.

It's late. Ronan's likely in bed. He'll never see them coming if they use the passages from the library to enter his room.

Every second I stand here is a second closer they move to the Prince. Without another moment of deliberation, I run away from the library and toward Ronan's room. I try the knob first, but it's locked of course.

The maid outside the room is gone now, and I abandon all attempts at propriety. "Ronan!" I shout as I bang on the door. "Please, open up."

My hands throb in protest as I keep knocking, and panic's vine claws up my throat, nearly cutting off my air. I can't be too late. If I try to go through the passages in the library now, I will *definitely* be too late.

The door gives way under my hand, and I almost collapse into the Prince in relief. But it's short lived as I look over his shoulder and see the two men have just entered the room from the back entrance.

"Down!" I yell as I shove Ronan to the floor before a dagger sticks into the door where he just stood. But protecting him isn't enough. I have to fight back.

It's surprisingly easy once I wrench the dagger from the door and launch myself at the men. I deliver a sharp blow under the chin of the shorter man, and he crumples to the floor. The second man, the one I recognized, attempts to fight back, even succeeding in getting his arm around my neck.

Then I remember my lesson with Felix, and slide my foot behind my attacker's so I can jab his ribs and use his lack of balance to overthrow him. The whole thing's a blur, but seconds later, when I stop seeing red, I'm pressing my knee in the man's chest with the dagger pressed to his throat. Despite the fluttery feeling in my stomach, my hands don't shake at all.

Everything around me remains out of focus until a hand on my arm pulls me off the man, and guards swarm around the two attackers. The dagger clatters to the floor, and I look up expecting to see Ronan at my side.

Antony faces me instead and all the bravado I've displayed crashes down around me. I dissolve into tears and bury my face in his shoulder.

Then I'm pulled from the guard into another set of arms, a familiar set. Ronan wraps me up and presses kiss after kiss to the top of my head. Where my cheek rests against his chest, I can feel the pounding of his heart, and my tears fall faster. Tears of happiness that he's alive, and tears of despair the Felix has not taken provisions like I hoped. If Antony is here, Felix is alone.

"I don't care right now, but someday I want to know how you knew." Ronan ducks his head so his lips are near my ear. "How can I repay you? Anything you want is yours."

But he's wrong. The thing I want most has never been his to give.

Hannah bursts into my room as the sun is rising the next morning. Her entrance sends the door bouncing against the wall, and I jerk from my sleep with a start. She doesn't need to speak, because I've asked her only to disturb me when Felix returns.

I stumble from my sheets and allow her to wrap a robe around my shoulders before she escorts me from the room. She must have seen him coming from way off, because Felix is still at the stables when Hannah and I step out of the palace tunnel and into the crisp morning air.

He pulls the saddle from Ares and pats his horse on the haunches. The animal gives a gentle wicker. Then, though I'm silent, something draws his attention in my direction, and his gaze finds me. I'm walking toward him then, and he mirrors me. An unexplained hope bubbles in my gut until I'm close enough to see the defeat on his face.

It feels surreal, and I notice all the little details before I allow myself to process what they mean. The drops of faded crimson across his leather armor. The sag of his shoulders. The dejection in his eyes.

My father is dead.

I wait for the tears, but they don't come. Maybe I used them all last night. Or, maybe the dark part of me thinks it's justice being served for what he did to my mother, even if it's not what I wanted to happen.

"Emilia."

The million ways he says my name always astonish me. How can a man who's so solemn convey so much in a single word?

"T-thank you," I say. "For trying, I mean."

His head falls, and I think for a moment he might sink to his knees to beg my forgiveness. I'm not sure I could take that. Instead he clenches bloody fists and breathes deeply.

"There were five of them. I reached the caravan just as the fighting started. We could have beaten the bandits, but some of your father's guard betrayed him. By the time I realized this, it was too late. Your father's Commander and I took care of the traitors. We did manage to find out that someone had paid them a large sum of money to switch sides in the middle of the fight."

That "someone" isn't a mystery to me. Cyrus. He's succeeded in killing my father and who knows how many of the other kings. Our empire could easily plunge into chaos from that alone. If he insists on starting a war to avenge the killings, I don't want to think about how many more lives will be lost.

I clasp a hand around Felix's arm and will him to look at me. He does, and I'm reminded of the tenderness in his eyes last night as he told me all I had to do was ask. I want to say thank you, but it doesn't seem like enough. The request was selfish on my part and nearly disastrous for Ronan.

I'd nearly forgotten Ronan and last night until just now. But perhaps Felix sees it on my face much as I read my father's death on his.

"What happened here?" he asks. The worry in his tone is real, shadowed only by the regret of his own failure.

I drop my hand from his arm. "The assassins weren't only after the kings of Atlas."

"Are you all right?" His hands grip my shoulders as he frantically looks me over for injuries. There's a desperation in his search that hasn't existed before, but then, the stakes are much higher. "If anything had happened to you, I—"

Something about the look on my face silences him. He releases me and takes a daunted step back. "Ronan?" he asks with more emotion in his voice than I'm used to hearing when he speaks of the Prince.

"Yes, but—" I don't get to finish because Felix bypasses me and heads for the tunnel that leads into the palace.

Hannah and I follow after him. I worry about slowing my pace to match hers, but she waves me on, so I sprint down the tunnel, knowing exactly where Felix will be headed. I catch him just as he's raising his hand to Ronan's door. But he doesn't intend to knock. Instead, he barges inside, and I'm crazy enough to follow him.

By the time I enter behind Felix, Ronan sits straight up in bed with a dagger in his hand and a flash in his eyes. When his eyes adjust to the darkness enough to recognize the two of us, he sighs and tosses the dagger to the bedside table with a clatter.

"What in Caelus's name are the two of you doing here this early?"

Felix is too stunned to answer. I know he thought the worst, but there was no time to tell him otherwise. If our roles were reversed, I might have acted the same way. As it is, I don't have the luxury of a last glimpse of my father's body.

"Well," Ronan persists. "Someone answer me." Sitting up in bed, he doesn't look as shaken as he did last night, though his wrinkled sleep shirt and tousled hair suggest he tossed and turned away the few hours of sleep he might have gotten.

Felix finally recovers. "I needed to see that you are well. There was... an incident last night?"

I hear the guilt in his tone—that he wasn't here, that he couldn't protect his friend—but I bear the brunt of it. If I hadn't asked him to ride after my father, he would have been here for Ronan. For me.

"Yes," Ronan says slowly as he looks past Felix to me. His eyes question me—why haven't I told him? "Two men attempted to enter my room with the stated intent of killing me. I still don't know how she knew, but Emilia was able to intercept them and incapacitate them long enough for Antony and a few of the real guards to take them into custody."

"You did what?" Felix demands as he whirls on me. He doesn't dare say more, but I can read it all in his eyes. The realization of my involvement dawns on him. I faced down two assassins by myself, and I could have been killed. He wouldn't have forgiven himself for that either.

But he can't always protect me, and if not for me, he would have been here. I'll tell him that eventually, but not in front of Ronan, who eyes the two of us curiously.

"You?" Felix finally asks. "Why didn't you... Antony was here..." He stops himself each time he's mounting an assault on my choices. Because they are *my* choices, and though he thinks he knows better, I am still a princess, and to question me in front of Ronan would be in poor taste.

"Nothing I couldn't handle. The men were inexperienced, and..." I didn't think of this last night when everything seemed like a blur. No way were those men trained assassins. They didn't even fight as well as the bandits that attacked Felix and I outside the city. Perhaps it shouldn't bother me so much, but I can't swallow the lump in my throat.

"You're not invincible," Felix whispers so low I'm not sure Ronan hears him.

"She's a hero," the Prince insists. "And I'll see that she's recognized as one."

"No, please." That's the last thing I need. Cyrus may have heard I'm the one who foiled his plot, but he might be willing to let it slide if Ronan doesn't draw attention to it. "It's what anyone would have done. And I couldn't bear to think of losing you."

He's out of bed and across the room, wrapping his arms around me, before I have time to step away. I manage to peek over Ronan's shoulder and meet Felix's cool stare. I hug Ronan tighter. Right now, he's the only thing standing between me and a verbal lashing from the Commander. The Prince grips my chin lightly between his thumb and forefinger, and tilts it up until my lips meet his. It's a gentle kiss, but there's a shred of truth in it that hasn't been there before, and it's over nearly before it began.

And I don't look at either of them when I excuse myself and slip out the door into the quiet hallway.

21

The face of the assassin I recognized haunts me as I try to go about my normal routine. Of course, the palace today is anything but normal. Everyone is talking about the attempt on Ronan's life and the mysterious person who saved him. All activities have been cancelled.

The burden Felix and I bear only grows heavier because no one else seems to know about the death of at least one of the kings. I'm almost incapacitated with the thoughts jumbled in my brain. Felix and Ronan. My father. Cordelia's father. Am I now the queen of Borealis? Who's ruling the country until I return?

Mid-day the mood in the palace shifts from something solemn to downright dreadful. The rest of the girls and I are corralled in the Empress's drawing room, then marched into the great hall, which looks strikingly bare save for a row of six chairs and the line of guards that stand shoulder to shoulder around the large room.

The other girls exchange nervous whispers, but I keep my eyes straight ahead. I know what's coming, but I must remember to act surprised. I have no doubt Cyrus will be watching for my reaction to the horrible news he's getting ready to deliver.

"Do you think they're sending one of us home?" Cordelia whispers as we all take our seats.

I shrug in response. It's a good question, but not for the reasons she thinks. There's a war brewing. Will Cyrus opt to keep us here for "protection" or send us all home to our families? Well, send the others home to their families. I've no one left. I recall the Empress saying I'm the only girl here who stands to inherit her own throne. Maybe Cyrus will use that excuse to finally get rid of me. Honestly, at this point, I welcome it.

The Emperor breezes into the room without so much as a glance in our direction until he's positioned himself in his elevated throne. His handsome face is grave and dark, and I might believe his concern except he bears none of the hallmarks that Felix and I—or even Ronan—show. I've no doubt Cyrus slept just fine last night.

"Ladies," he says coolly. "I'm afraid I have grave news. As you know, caravans from each country departed our palace last night to make their journeys home."

He pauses, likely for dramatic effect, and makes eye contact with each of us. I look away almost immediately to study my hands in my lap.

"None of the caravans reached their destinations."

I gasp along with the rest of the girls and allow Cordelia to dig her nails into my arm. The sharp bite of pain keeps me focused. Cyrus continues as if we hadn't reacted at all.

"Riders returned to the palace early this morning from each country. There's been a coordinated attack against our kings. Our worst fears have come true. The Insurgo rebellion has begun, and they've struck at the heart of each country. While you were sleeping, there were assassins even here. They made an attempt on my son's life. Praise be to Caelus he was not harmed."

To my right and left, the others openly sob. I'm too angry at the audacity of the Emperor to cry, but I bury my head in my hands and pretend anyway.

"Each of you will remain here indefinitely until we can determine it's safe for you to travel home. For now, each of you should return to your rooms, and do not leave under any circumstances. Dinner will be served to you in your chambers. Tomorrow morning, you'll be required to attend the trial of the assassins who attacked Prince Ronan. That is all."

No one moves even after Cyrus exits the room as fast as he entered it. One by one, a guard from the perimeter of the room approaches the other girls and escorts them from the room. It's not easy feat since most of them are so distraught they can hardly stand. Gloriana has to literally be carried from the room.

Antony bows to Cordelia and offers his arm, and Felix is right behind him to do the same for me. I keep my head bowed as I accept, afraid someone will notice my tears aren't real. Once Felix and I are alone though, the hall emptied by the Emperor's command, I release his arm and tip my chin up.

"That was a good show. You were very convincing." He's studying my face now, presumably making sure my tears *weren't* real. If I made him doubt, then certainly everyone else will believe my reaction was genuine.

"Good," I say. "Then everyone will have no problem assuming I'm in my room mourning instead of the dungeons."

Felix clenches his jaw hard enough that I see it pop, then breathes deeply through his nose, steeling himself for an argument. Which won't do him any good because I've already made up my mind.

"Why do you want to go to the dungeons?"

It's the sort of patronizing tone I've heard parents use with their children, and I don't appreciate it. "I need to speak to Ronan's attackers. There's something I need to say."

What exactly I need to say hasn't come to me yet, but I feel the nudging to go anyway. This is something I've debated all morning, but after Cyrus's speech about the Insurgos, I'm certain it must be done.

"You're under orders to go to your room and stay there," he reminds me, though I can't imagine why he thought I'd obey those orders.

"We both know there's something bigger going on here. These men are going to trial tomorrow, and after that we'll have no chance to speak with them. Don't you want to know more about this plot? To see if they know what's coming next?"

My argument isn't all that dissimilar to the one I used on Milo to allow me to speak to Levi alone. My motives aren't either. Unlike my former commander, Felix seems skeptical, which I don't blame him for. But ultimately, I think he wants the same thing I do, which is to find the Insurgos and prevent their annihilation.

"You have to make this quick." He relents with a sigh. "And you can't go down there looking like that. You'll be recognized by everyone we pass."

"And what do you suggest I wear?" A woman venturing to the dungeon, even with an escort, is a rare occurrence. To go unnoticed, I would have to dress like a man.

"I've got something," he almost groans. "And don't make me regret this."

Felix's quarters looked exactly like I'd imagined them. Sparse and neat with almost nothing personal lying about. I tried not to snoop while he gathered some of his clothes for me to wear, but my eyes took in everything I could from my place just inside the door.

Now, as I stumble down the hall after him in ill-fitting clothes and shoes, I wonder if he's always been that way. Where did he come from and why is there nothing that speaks of home in his room?

He's been strangely quiet since he agreed to my plan. Or, more accurately, he decided there was no point in opposing it. Something's on his mind, and despite all the questions that rattle around in my own, I want to know what it is.

After he speaks a few low words to the guards standing watch at the gated entrance, they push the bars aside, and Felix and I step into the damp, dark prison. Light comes only from a few sparse torches and a slender window, too high for anyone to actually look out.

The dim lighting makes it hard to determine just how many prisoners there are, but it seems no one has a cell to themselves. Bodies huddle together in the corners for warmth, and the odor is almost enough to knock me down. I don't belong here, that much is clear.

Still I follow Felix forward until he stops in front of a cell near the end of the row. It holds just two prisoners, but until I kneel to their level, I can't begin to make out faces. The men I met in the hall last night stare back at me with cold eyes and hard faces. I swallow down my fear.

"Keep your distance," Felix growls above me. I'm not sure if he's talking to me or these men, but I know from their sneered reaction that they won't speak freely with me while the Commander stands over my shoulder.

"Leave us," I tell him with a calmness I don't feel.

"No." It might be the first time he's outright refused me. "You can't be alone with them. That's a condition of you being here at all."

"Then some space, please." I'd bat my eyelashes if I thought it would help, but Felix doesn't respond to that sort of thing.

He moves as far away as the next cell and stands at attention with his hand on his sword hanging from his belt. Marginally satisfied, I turn my attention back to the prisoners and lower the hood of my cloak.

"You." The man I recognized last night hisses the word. "Why are you here? Have you come to torture us?"

"Nothing like that," I promise. "I only want information."

"Why should we give it to you?" The other man sneers. "If not for you, we'd be living like kings right now."

An appropriate choice of words. "Is that what they promised you? Money? Titles?"

The men exchange looks before the familiar one answers me. "They promised us freedom. Instead we are given chains. Tomorrow they'll take our heads."

"Freedom is life's great lie," the second man utters.

I start to argue, but realize it's useless. Words not my own come to mind as I speak.

"It is true that we were all made to be ruled," I begin, choosing my words carefully. "But that doesn't mean you can't know freedom. But freedom is not choosing your own way. We need the rules and the structure. The freedom you crave can only come from one source—the God of the Insurgos. He can free you from the condemnation of your sins and wrongdoings. That's the freedom you crave."

Tears prick my eyes as I think of my father. How I wish I had said these words to him. And now I'll never have a chance. I chose my safety over his eternity, and I understand now what Felix meant by being unable to forgive himself.

"You forget that I live in the hills with the Insurgos. Their God has done nothing to save them from raids and starvation or to punish the wicked men who inflict the hardships." The man's eyes turn pointedly to Felix, and I feel rather than see the Commander recoil. With the guilt he already carries, those words would pierce even the strongest armor.

"The reckoning will come," I tell him, though I'm not as sure as I'd like to be. He's asking the questions that mirror my own, but I trust my God to do what is right. "Tell me who hired you, and perhaps I can hasten it along."

"You already know. Who else has the power to take all that we love unless we do his bidding?"

My heart cracks a little more. These men are only guilty of trying to protect their families. If—no, *when*—they are found guilty tomorrow, who will protect their families then?

"Can the Insurgo God change that?" the other man asks. Animosity has faded from his voice. He's genuinely curious now. "Can he save our lives?"

"He can save your lives…but I don't know if it will be in this life or the next." There's no point in lying to them. They deserve the truth from me. "But you can be with him in paradise in the next life."

"That's the lesson they teach the children in the camps. Do you really believe that?" The man grips the prison bars with his trembling hand.

"I do," I whisper. "You only have to believe."

Commotion stirs at the other end of the dungeon, and Felix steps forward to place a hand on my back. "Time's up," he tells me with a hard edge to his tone.

This is it then. There's nothing else I can say. I start to rise when the man grabs my hand through the bars. Felix pushes forward, ready to slice his hand clean off, but I stop him with a look. With wide, dark eyes, the man looks up at me and utters two simple words.

"Thank you."

⁂

Felix and I don't speak of what happened in the dungeon. He returns me to my rooms and waits as I change out of his clothes. Then I'm left alone with my ladies who are almost smothering as they offer their condolences on the loss of my father.

They also have questions. Ones I can't answer. Am I Queen of Borealis? Will I be returning home? Can they come with me? It takes patience I don't have not to snap at them to leave me alone. But they've done nothing wrong, and there's no reason to take out my frustration on them.

The next morning, they bring me a hearty breakfast, then dress me in a somber black gown. I'd forgotten mourning was more a ritual than a feeling in royal court. There's very little of the usual cheeriness as I'm getting ready.

As instructed, I assemble in the drawing room with the other girls. We're all dressed in dark colors, and even makeup cannot hide their bloodshot, tired eyes. I'm quite certain I look tired enough even if I didn't spend the night crying.

The same as yesterday, we're marched as a group from the drawing room to our next location. But I'm surprised to find that location isn't the ballroom or the other throne room. Those are the places trials are usually held.

Instead, the anxiety in the pit of my stomach grows as we exit the palace and are directed toward the Arena. If anyone else is surprised, they keep silent. No one looks at anyone else. The guards keep their eyes straight ahead, and each of the girls studies the ground in front of her. Am I the only one who knows what's going to happen? More likely, I'm the only one who cares.

We are positioned in different seats than we occupied for Ronan's birthday. When the Arena was full of patrons, it made sense for us to sit in the royal box. Because we are the only ones who will witness today's spectacle, we're given front row seats with only a short wall separating us from the dust of the Arena.

Cyrus, Empress Valentina, and Ronan enter after us, and take the seats directly behind us. We all turn to look at them. The Emperor's eyes meet mine, and I don't think I imagine the cold smile turning up his lips.

He means to execute these prisoners while we all watch. As if he dares anyone to stand against him. But someone must, and I know with a sinking feeling, there is only me. Felix is the only other person with the knowledge to do so, but I am the only one with the position.

It eats away at me as they parade the men in front of us, stripped naked and shamed. Though there is a great distance between us, I can almost feel their pleading eyes on me, but I know I've imagined it. I might have given them hope for the next life, but the idea of pardon, of sparing this life, would not have entered their minds. It should not have entered mine.

The force that pushes me to my feet is unseen, but I feel it as sure as someone jerked me up by my arm. And I am standing in the presence of the Emperor with no choice but to speak my mind or look a fool.

"You have something to say, Princess Emilia?" The cool, detached tone sends a shiver through me. Cyrus's blue eyes look me over with the sort of indifference a predator might feel toward its prey.

"Imminence, I would ask that you reconsider the lives of these two men." I can't look at Ronan, or I'm sure I'll falter. Unskilled though they may be, these men would have killed him if they'd had the chance. If I think about that, I'll never continue. "They are merely hired hands. The real crime is the one who paid them to assassinate the Prince. Perhaps if we question them, we might learn more about the real enemy."

This tactic failed me once before, when I asked to interrogate Levi to stall his execution. But all eyes turn to Cyrus now, waiting his response to my request, but he continues to stare me down. Does he know I know the truth of who hired these men? Even if not, now that I've raised the possibility, he must look like he'll put every effort into finding the true person behind the attack on his son. The kingdom will not rest easy until he does.

"Ah, I see you have a soft heart for the criminals. Not a redeeming quality in a princess." He rubs his beard as he pretends to consider my suggestion. "They've committed treason of the highest order. Not only that, they are the day's entertainment. If I return them to the prison, who will entertain us?"

Bile rises in my throat, and I struggle to swallow it down. Treason and entertainment. Cyrus has played everyone like a puppet-master and fooled them into enjoying it.

"You would entertain us at the expense of letting the Prince's true attacker go free?" Now I've done it. I've backed him into a corner he can't get out of, and like a caged lion, he comes out fighting.

"Perhaps you would like to entertain us." He spreads a wide palm toward the arena.

"Father, no." Ronan finally speaks, his dark brows upturned in desperation. "You can't let her fight to the death."

"Who said anything about death?" The way his lips curl around the words tell me that's exactly what he had in mind, but Ronan's right. "We only need a show equal to the one we would have gotten if I let these two assassins fight. But this might be better all around. It's not every day you see a princess in the arena."

There's a reason for that. Perhaps he's not heard the extent of my training, but my skills far exceed every other girl here. I know how to defend myself, and I have killed before. So if he plans to put me up against one of his gladiators, I'll fight to my last breath against any faceless warrior.

"I will fight if you'll spare them." I have to make sure the terms are absolutely clear.

"If I am sufficiently entertained by your show, I will spare them."

He wants me to kill whoever he pits me against or die trying, though it goes against what he promised Ronan. It's the only show he'll be happy with.

I don't waste anymore words. Instead, I hop the fence, and my feet find purchase on the dirt. Felix is by my side immediately, making great show of handing me his sword as he leans in to whisper.

"What are you doing?" The look in his eyes nearly breaks me. I've never seen him afraid before this moment. "You can't do this."

"I have to." I don't expect him to understand, though he's the only one who might. "I won't let him kill men whose only crime is wanting to feed their families."

He looks at me for a long moment. "Then remember what I've taught you. Keep your feet light."

"Father," Ronan's voice is clear over everyone's murmuring, "please release her from this bargain. She doesn't need to fight—"

"She chose it. Now I will choose her opponent." Prickles of his gaze crawl over my skin as I wonder who he might choose for me.

There's been talk of a new fighter—a giant from Zephyros— but his size will be to my advantage because I'm quick and light. Or the renowned swordsman from Austrina, who would present a challenge, but would be helpless if I could manage to disarm him. Or any number of brawlers, who might beat me down, but would surely tire before me. All in all, I'm feeling pretty good about my chances of coming out of this unscathed. Until Cyrus speaks.

"Commander Fidelis. You will face the Princess in combat."

Instinctively, Felix and I jump apart so fast I nearly tumble to the ground. It feels like someone has already punched me in the gut as the air rushes from my lungs. I find his face in the midst of my spinning world and see him similarly distressed. My anchor cut free, and I'm tossing in the chaos that's ensued.

"Imminence, I..." He's at a loss for words, though I'm surprised he spoke up at all.

"You are not to kill her, Commander. And spare her pretty face if you can." Cyrus's nonchalance ignites fire in my veins, but the only one I can take it out on is Felix. "Remember, Princess, impress me or they die."

I've fought Felix dozens of times, but always with the sort of restraint that leaves both of us only mildly bruised and a bit dusty from our spills on the ground. That's not what Cyrus is asking for here. And though I'm not afraid to do what I must to save these men, Felix will need some convincing. I truly believe he'll do everything to protect me, including throwing this fight. That can't happen.

"Don't hold back," I say as we both approach the rack to choose our weapons. I don't look at him, but I feel his eyes on me as I run my fingers over the smooth wood of the staff.

"Emilia, I'm not going to do this."

"It's an order," I snap with more force than I've ever used with him, and his surprise shows in his wide eyes. "You will fight me, and you will try to win."

His lips part as if he wants to argue with me, but he clamps them closed before the words can come out. I hate this taste of power, that I have reduced him to nothing more than a faceless crony to do my bidding. In trying to do something noble, I've still become one of the many things I hate about my position.

He follows my lead and grabs a staff. It's enough to do some damage, but not as deadly as a sword or a bow, which I would have chosen if I meant to do him harm. But I only need it to look that way and pray there's not too much collateral damage.

I delay the start as long as I can, hoping foolishly that Cyrus will change his mind. When I chance a glance at him, he's looking at me through narrowed eyes. I must do this.

Felix and I circle each other, and I have to force myself to imagine it's someone else standing in front of me. There's no good way out of this. No matter what I do, someone gets hurt...or worse.

When our staffs strike, the reverberation ripples into my palms, but I dance away before he can get in a body blow. But he's quicker than I gave him credit for, and his staff clips my side before I can escape his reach. The hurt on his face mirrors the pain in my ribs, and I hate that I take advantage of that.

My staff hits home on his shoulder, and he staggers back on his heels.

A lone cheer sounds from the stands followed by a laugh. At least Cyrus seems to be enjoying it. That only further fans the flame of my anger, and I lunge at Felix.

The sharp edge of his armor sends a white pain through my cheek, and I feel the skin split. The blood doesn't register until it's pouring down my face, into my mouth, and I spit it on the ground. To his credit, Felix doesn't waver as he lands a fist to my shoulder which knocks me to my back.

We go on this way until both of us are bloodied and bruised, and when I'm knocked to the ground, I'm no longer sure I can climb to my feet.

Finally, Cyrus speaks.

"Enough!"

The command sends me to my knees with my chest heaving. Felix lies only inches from me, but he raises his head then flops back, sending a small puff of dust into the air. I crawl toward him, but the Emperor's booming voice stops me.

"Well done, Princess. Guards, take her to her room."

Hands grip around my tender skin and hoist me to my feet. My feet drag lines in the dirt as I'm pulled away, none too gently, from Felix. The only thing that keeps me sane is the affirmation I received from the monster who is now parading out of the arena above me.

Ronan catches my eye as the guards escort me past his seat. His handsome face is drawn and solemn and nearly breaks my heart. I didn't consider what this might do to him when I made my decision. Yet another reason I cannot rule a country. I've acted for myself for so long, that I don't know how to consider someone else.

22

The insistent knock on my door barely registers through the fog of the trauma. I usually see clearly after a fight, but I never imagined a scenario like this one.

What did I do? Defied the Emperor, pardoned assassins, and nearly maimed my friend.

"Princess?"

It's not the voice of one of my ladies, who I sent away upon my return. Rather, the concern in the gravelly tone pulls the last bit of strength from me, and I stumble to my feet. My muscles ache as I pull the door open to reveal the man who risked everything to pull me up from drowning when I jumped in over my head.

At the sight of me, Felix's shoulders sag with relief, and he pushes his way past me, leaving me to shut the door. I do, and turn slowly because my head swims. He's right there, taking my hand and leading me to the bed to sit. The soft down sags under our weight, pulling me toward him.

"Felix." I don't know what to say, but his name feels right. All my gratitude seems inadequate. "Did I hurt you?"

My eyes scan for any injuries, and I note the dried blood that covers the area where I'm sure bruises will appear later. His lip is split, and he keeps his right arm close to his side. The hit I landed there was designed to inflict maximum damage, and it appears that it did. Not that he will ever admit it. Though he saved me, we are both too proud to say we are hurt.

"I was so worried about you. I came as soon as I could without arousing suspicions."

I don't say that I thought Ronan would beat him here—that I hoped he would. For his silence in the arena, I prayed the Prince would give me his support at least in private. That he might care enough to see if I was okay.

"I wanted to be alone."

"No, you didn't. But I'm sorry I'm not the person you were expecting."

His words chip at my walls, and it takes all the strength in my reserves not to lean on him. But now more than ever, I want to stand on my own. Though it was certainly ill-advised, my actions today make me feel stronger. I won't undermine it by falling on someone else or showing weakness.

Felix cups my face, thumb just below the corner of my mouth, and raises my chin until our gazes meet. Gentleness in his touch belies the fierce glint of his dark eyes. I wish I could read them. But he has always been a mystery to me, and though I feel laid bare beneath his stare, his stoic frown hides secrets I may never know.

My heart flutters against my chest in a way I've never felt before. I don't understand this, but for the brief moment, I feel as if I could do anything.

"You may have a scar. I am sorry, Highness." He trails a finger over the ragged edge of the cut on my cheek then releases his hold. Crimson flakes of dried blood fan across his hand. Mine or his, I'm not sure.

Something in the air changes. The gentle steadiness of his hands no longer calms me, but rather brings heat wherever he touches, waking part of me. The contact holds little innocence on my part, but I feel no guilt either. I live for the next touch and die when he takes it away.

"Emilia," I correct softly. In that moment, I want nothing more than for him to say my given name instead of the formality that stands between us. There are no prying eyes here to question our friendship or the gentle way he touches me.

"What were you thinking?" Felix's eyes harden as he stands and pulls himself to his full height. The tenderness is gone so quickly I tell myself I imagined it. He looks formidable in his rugged armor, stained with blood and dirt. "Those men, those assassins," he spits the word, "were not worth risking your life."

"My life is at no risk when it's in your hands." With great effort, I keep my tone even and expression blank. At least I hope I do. It has my desired effect as Felix's shoulders slump with resignation. This is a fight he will not win. To do so would be to concede that he can't protect me.

He doesn't try, and his eyes soften with a warmth that melts my frosty demeanor. "You did well today, Princess, even if it was a risk I wish you hadn't taken."

His words twist the dagger of my destiny a little deeper. "I wasn't very princess-like today, was I?"

"No." Dark eyes study me with the thinly veiled promise of something more. "You were a Queen."

Behind him, the door creaks open. Light from the hall silhouettes Ronan, who stands straight and tall in the doorway. He looks from me to Felix, and I'm glad we're no longer sitting on the bed together. Though he didn't come to my defense, I don't want to hurt the Prince.

Felix bows his head, first to me, then to Ronan, and exits without another word. I have no way to stop him, and I wouldn't even if I could. My place is here.

Ronan and I are alone now with nothing but the tangle of our thoughts, and his shoulders slump as he sighs. The slam of the door echoes through the room and in my head. I felt strong only minutes ago when Felix was my company. Now I clench my hands in my lap to keep them from shaking. Ronan will always hold a power over me, hold my life in his hands. And though I didn't consider his feelings before I acted today, I hope he won't view the fact that I saved his assassins as a commentary on how I value his life.

"Emilia."

I hear the truth in the way he says my name. The way his voice breaks, and as he approaches me, the way the blue of his eyes ripples like the ocean. There's no need to formulate a response because his arms around me silence everything.

Crushed against him, he holds my cracked facade together. And when he lets go so he can study my face, I nearly fall apart.

"Are you hurt?" His fingers graze my cheek, much the same way Felix's did, but then brush across my lips. There's a different sort of promise in his touch, one of intent and longing.

Before I can talk myself out of it, I grab his wrist to hold his hand in place and kiss the tips of his fingers. His breath catches in his throat, and I nearly falter in my resolve. But if I give up control here, there's no going back.

He takes it from me. With movements swift enough to rival my own, he pulls his hand from my lips and replaces it with his mouth. His kisses are gentle, caressing, though I don't have much to compare them to. Still, for a moment I forget the events of the past hours. Lips move from mine to press against my cheek, then my jaw, and finally my ear.

"I thought I might lose you today," he whispers, placing one final kiss against the tender skin below my ear. "What you did—"

"Was necessary," I insist. It's time he knew the truth. "Those men were forced into the plot to kill you. By your father."

"My...father? Em, did you hit your head? You should rest." He tries to coax me to lay down, but I slap his hands away.

"I don't need rest." I stand over him, looking at his swollen lips and flushed face. I did that to him, and it's a power I could get used to. "I overheard the plot. Your father sent assassins to the four kingdoms to kill each of the kings. He wanted it to look as if the Insurgo revolution had begun. He was willing to sacrifice you."

Ronan's face blanches, making his eyes stand out against the pale skin. "What would he have to gain by my death?"

"It would look suspicious if only Aurora didn't suffer a loss. He would use his grief to gather support for his quest to rid the realm of Insurgos."

He's silent for a while, weighing my words against the twisted truth his father told him. I've gambled much by asking him to believe me with so little evidence.

"The night you saved me, Felix rode after the delegation from Borealis…What happened to your father?"

The reminder is a dagger in my heart. Not as acute as my mother's death, but a wound that I suspect will remain open for some time. It's enough to finally pull the tears from my eyes. "Dead. I took too long to ask Felix to go after him."

Without a word, Ronan stands and opens his arms to me. When I don't go to him, he comes to me and wraps me up tight.

"You chose me over your father." He doesn't need an answer to confirm it. If he doesn't believe me, Felix will affirm it. "Now it's my turn to choose you."

It's as close to love as I've ever come. Short of God, I've never been chosen by anyone. Only passed around by those who viewed me as an inconvenience.

"I did what I had to do." Making him understand this is all I want. "Those men deserved a second chance to believe in God. I know they tried to kill you, but only because they believed there wasn't a choice. I had to give them one."

"Emilia." His body tenses against mine, and I know what he wants to say before he says it. "He killed them anyway."

And that's what finally breaks me.

I sink to the floor, pulling him with me as my tears soak his shirt. My sacrifice was worthless. Two men are still dead, and I can be sure the Emperor hates me more than ever. No wonder my mother didn't fight. It wouldn't have mattered anyway.

I don't know how long it takes for my tears to dry or the tremors running through me to subside. But I do know that when my body gives in to exhaustion and sleep slips over me, Ronan still holds me close.

23

A scream dies in my throat when I wake to a hand clamped hard over my mouth. I'm in my bed, and the room is dark, but when I inhale to try another scream, I catch a familiar scent.

Felix leans over me, his face barely visible once my eyes adjust to the darkness. I can still see the cut I made on his lip.

"We have to go," he whispers with his face nearly pressed against mine. "The Emperor convened a council late tonight. He's convinced them you're an Insurgo sympathizer. They want to arrest you on charges of treason."

I sit straight up in bed, nearly knocking heads with him. Instead of pulling away from me, he grabs my hand and drags me to my feet.

We haven't planned for this—though I'm not sure why not since in the back of my mind I've been afraid this would happen— but Felix and I move around the dark room in a coordinated dance. He strips a pillowcase from my bed and holds it out while I fill it with the few things I can think to grab. My small coin purse, food my ladies brought me yesterday while I was too distraught to eat, and finally the book of the Aletheia. Our eyes meet briefly when I place it inside the pillowcase, then he's knotting the ends and tossing it over his shoulder.

"Hannah," I whisper as he grabs my hand and pulls me toward the door.

Felix shakes his head. "There's no time. Once I get you to safety, I'll come back for her."

Something in his language reassures me, maybe because it sounds like he intends to come with me. I can face anything if I know I'm not alone.

We keep silent as we steal down the hallway toward the back staircase. I understand his plan. We'll exit the palace at the stables, mount the horses, and ride until we've left Aurora far behind. Maybe even to the Insurgo camps outside the city. Despite the overwhelming fear, that idea excites me.

But it's not to be.

I rush from the tunnel just ahead of Felix and run into a wall of guards. Screams tear from me as they seize my arms and legs. Amid my thrashing, I catch a glimpse of Felix looking on, mouth agape, just outside the tunnel.

It's over before it could even begin. My eyes plead with him to rescue me, to save me, but I don't fault him for not moving. He's done all he could. It simply wasn't enough.

And as they take me away, I catch his eyes once more. I'm not sure which one of us is more broken by that revelation.

✳

I didn't expect to revisit the dungeon this soon. In a bit of irony that I'm sure Cyrus arranged, I'm placed in the same cell Ronan's would-be assassins had occupied. For the rest of the night, I cry against the stone floor as catcalls from the other prisoners echo off the walls.

When daylight breaks through the high window, I steel myself for what I know is coming. I'll be led from the dungeon to confront the Emperor. I may or may not be given a trial. I certainly won't be given the chance to fight in the Arena. Not when there's a chance I might win.

I mark the passing of time with the meals that are brought to me. When I've received my meager dinner without so much as a hint of being let out, I begin to let my mind wander.

Is Ronan petitioning his father on my behalf? Perhaps Felix convinced him to speak up. Or was Felix arrested for helping me, and they've decided to have his trial first?

That brings a fresh wave of tears that continue each time I wake from my fitful sleep that night.

Shamefully, on the second day, I begin to pray.

God, I should have come to you first. What am I supposed to do? How can I save your people if I'm going to die?

Is this similar to what Levi prayed the night he visited me. He said he knew he would have to die to get me the message. At the time I hadn't understood what could be that important. Now I think I do. His death has pushed me forward from the beginning.

When I wanted to quit, I thought of Levi and his sacrifice. Is that God's calling for me as well? A martyr?

I pray off and on all morning and afternoon. For strength, for composure, for bravery, and for the words to say. Still, when an unfamiliar guard appears at my cell door, my heart jumps to my throat. I'm not ready to die.

He binds my hands behind my back, and three more guards join this one as we exit the dungeon. It seems someone finally took note of my skills as a fighter. I could defeat one guard, but four is impossible. Are any of them loyal to Felix?

I'd hoped to see the Commander one last time. I don't want my last memory of his face to be one of utter defeat. Most of all, I want him to forgive himself for this and whatever else he can't seem to let go of.

They lead me into what can only be the main throne room. I've never been here before, but I'm greeted with the site of the Emperor seated on his throne, and Ronan standing to his right. Cyrus stares me down, but Ronan will not meet my eyes.

Any hope I've held out begins to slip through my fingers as the guards position me directly in front of the thrones and push me to my knees. It's just as well, because I wouldn't have voluntarily bowed before my executioner. My eyes dart left and right in hopes of seeing a familiar face, but there are none. I thought the other girls might be here, forced to watch my sentencing if not my death, but it seems they've been spared that experience.

"Emilia Aurelius, you have been accused of heresy against our high god Caelus and his court. Additionally, you are accused of high treason against your country and your empire for your collusion with the Insurgo rebels." Cyrus's voice rings loud and clear through the great room, but his words are muddied with the memories of my mother's execution. My father said nearly the same thing as he pronounced her death sentence.

Silence follows his proclamation, and I refuse to give him the satisfaction of lifting my eyes.

"Will anyone speak for her?" The Emperor's voice booms out again.

This silence is louder than any I've heard before. Ronan will not speak for me. When I finally lift my head and my eyes find his, I know it with a certainty that belies my every feeling for him. He looks away. Whatever he once felt, whatever he once said, he won't choose me over his father and his own crown.

My fears have come true.

"How do you plead?" Emperor Cyrus asks. His voice booms through the hall.

In this moment, I understand my mother. Betrayed by the man who should have given his life to save hers, she chose to die for her faith rather than renounce it. How fitting that I now must do the same.

"Guilty," I say, my voice as strong as the Emperor's. My life won't be a sacrifice but an offering. I understand that now.

As I close my eyes, I picture the words written across Felix's pages. God's strength made perfect in my weakness, and I've certainly never been weaker. But if my faith impacts one person the way my mother's impacted me, then it will be worth it. And I don't have to wonder if I've found favor with Caelus and will be allowed to enter the afterlife. Thanks to Felix's Aletheia, I'm surer now than ever that I will see Heaven.

"Very well," Cyrus replies. "For these crimes you are sentenced to burn at the stake. May Caelus have mercy on you."

His words haven't even finished echoing in the room before the throne room's doors crash open and chaos erupts around me.

24

Dozens of guards pour through the open doors with weapons drawn and purpose in their eyes. For a moment, I think we're being invaded, and apparently Cyrus does, too. He shouts for guards to attack, but it's a mess of confusion as they're attacking their own kind.

Shouts and the clash of swords ring in my ears as I'm shoved to the floor by an unseen hand, unable to catch myself with my bound hands. And then I'm being lifted, the ropes that bind my hands sliced through with such precision that I only feel the wind off the blade. I know that swing as sure as I know my own name.

Felix stands before me, the steady ship in midst of chaos. But there's no time to say anything because he's shoving a sword in my hand and pulling me toward the door. My fingers curl around the pommel without thought. I was born to have a weapon in my hand. It is God who's trained my hands for war and my fingers for battle.

The Commander and I fight side by side, steel singing against the few guards who stand in our way. Emperor Cyrus shouts for our arrest, but the men are hesitant to attack their commander who they know they could best them even on his worst day. They circle us with weapons pointed toward the center of the circle.

No one moves, everyone hesitant of attacking first. I look to Felix for answers because I have none. We're trapped.

"I'll give you a boost, then run for the stables," he mutters, pressing his shoulder against mine.

I nod and step away from him. With a deep breath, I take a running start and just as I reach him, Felix drops his sword and cups his hands to cradle my foot and propel me several feet in the air.

The landing isn't my best as I stumble on the stairs, but I'm free of the crowd and sprinting down the hallways with a sword in my hand. At every turn, guards loyal to Felix—to me—direct me out of the palace. Instead of the main exit to the stables, Antony leads me down a short flight of stairs, which he says will empty in the rear of the tack room where two of my ladies—Hannah and Cecily—wait for me.

We pause in the damp tunnel when loud voices shout from in front of us.

"I'll check it out. Stay here," Antony whispers as he disappears into the darkness.

I'm left alone with only the sounds of my breathing and the steady drip of dampness against the stones. My heart still pounds against my chest, not so much with exertion as with adrenaline. This surge is familiar to me, but more powerful than any I've known before.

A crash sounds behind me, and I instinctively move forward, desperate to get away from those pursuing me. I may have been resigned to death, but Felix has reignited my passion to live.

Footsteps pound against the stone, closing in on me. I try to run, but I slip on the stones and bang my shoulder against the rock wall.

A hand closes around mine, impeding my forward progress and pulling me back toward the danger. But I look up into the shadows of Felix's face and feel the warm brace of safety despite the icy cold of the tunnel.

"Emilia," he whispers, close enough that his breath tickles my cheek. "This may be our last chance to speak."

"You're coming with me." Eyes wide, I search his face in the dark. The firm line of his lips betray my fears, which well up in me like water overtaking a dam. "Felix, you have to come."

He releases my hand and hooks me around the waist with a strong arm. My heart pounds again, now for a different reason, as I become aware of the warm press of each of his fingers into the small of my back. Chin slightly lifted, I meet his dark eyes. I wish there was more light to read them by, until I remember that he's never been an open book to me. All the light in the world wouldn't help me see what lies behind the soldier's facade.

"It's more important you get far from here without anyone following." He brushes the knuckles of his hand, the one holding the sword, against my cheek. Eyes search my face as if committing every detail to memory.

I want to do the same. It seems I've never really seen Felix before this moment, and he is about to be ripped from me. "You will follow me?"

He laughs lightly, humorlessly, and I feel the chill of it in my bones. "We need to work on your issuing of commands so they don't sound like a question. But yes, Princess, I would follow you anywhere."

His arm around me tightens, pulling me closer until nothing but heat and cold and desperation exist between us. His mouth presses to mine, pulling a slight gasp from my lips to his. Something inside me unfurls, like a sail finally catching the wind. All this time, Felix was under my nose, at my feet, by my side, but now he's in my heart.

And, when he pushes me away with the dismayed grimace of a man who can't believe what he's done, I want to scream. It's too soon, too new, to let him go. But I do, taking a step back when he releases me. I'm tired of walking away from him, and I promise myself this will be the last time I do it unless he asks me to.

I turn away because to see the regret on the Commander's face would be my undoing, and emotion isn't a luxury I can afford at the moment.

"Majesty?" Hannah's urgent whisper calls from the darkened tunnel. I'd forgotten she waited for me. But where's Antony? "Princess, are you coming?"

"Go," Felix urges in a hoarse whisper. "Ares is waiting at the post. Take him."

Felix' horse is the swiftest, most beautiful animal I've ever laid eyes on. "But how will you—"

"There are other horses. Take him and ride. Head for the Green Pass, and I will meet you on the other side. Don't stop for anyone."

His promise of a meeting, of seeing his face in light of that kiss, is the only thing that propels me forward.

We ride for what feels like hours, tearing out of the city and making hard toward the mountains. Tears sting my cheeks the whole way as the wind brushes past me. I knew Ares was fast, but I had no idea how fast. I force myself to slow him twice just so Hannah and Cecily and the five guards with us can keep up with him.

The rush of battle still sings in my veins, but it's tempered by worry for Felix and all those who fought on his side. While I'm running like a coward, they're fighting off those who would see me dead. I should be there, fighting beside them, but Felix would never allow that to happen, and for once I agree with him.

We reach Green Pass just as night is falling, and I pull Ares to a halt. Behind me, I hear the hoof beats of my companions slowing as well. Dismounting the white horse, my feet crunch against the icy ground. In this higher elevation, we're almost guaranteed to see snow.

When I look up, my five guards and Hannah and Cecily have dismounted as well, and they all look to me. Waiting on me to take charge. I don't know what to tell them. I didn't exactly have time to pack or formulate a plan. I'm hoping Felix accounted for that.

"We'll make camp here tonight," I say, adopting the tone I've heard my mother use when giving instructions. Gentle but authoritative. "Do we have any supplies from the palace?"

As it turns out, Felix *had* done a great deal of planning. The guards are equipped with tents and a few blankets as well as a small food supply. Even Hannah and Cecily have packed some food and extra blankets. We'll need them if snow falls tonight.

I direct the assembling of our tents the best I can because the guards refuse to let me help. I don't know these men, but they're loyal to Felix so I acquiesce. It's almost as if he were here.

Once our shelter is in place, I take a guard with me to begin scouting firewood. We each carry an arm-load back to our camp, and a few minutes later, we have the beginnings of a flame.

My eyes focus on the flames as I absently tear bits of jerky in half and manage to swallow a few. It's late. Surely Felix is making his way here by now. But what if something happened? Would we even know it?

The need to see him wells up in me like a geyser, and I'm on my feet before I remember standing. All eyes are on me, and two of the guards have reached for their swords. I like that they respond to my cues instead of solely what they observe for themselves.

"What is it?" Cecily asks.

I look at her for the first time since we left and wonder where my other three ladies are. Did they choose to stay behind? "We need to send a rider back toward Aurora and make connection with the rest of the guards." I stop myself from using Felix's name specifically, but I'm sure I'm still transparent.

"I'll go." The guard who helped me gather wood—Maximus—stands and adjusts his weapons belt. I'm relieved he volunteered so quickly.

"They're to meet us at this pass, but intercept them if you can." Despite desperately wanting to see the Commander again, it would be foolish to ask them to keep riding in their exhausted state. "Tell them to make camp further down the mountain and join with us in the morning."

Once Maximus leaves on horseback, I try to busy myself with organizing our few supplies or stoking our small fire. When I've nearly burned myself for the third time, Hannah takes my hand and leads me toward one of the tents—one I will share with her and Cecily tonight.

"Don't worry about him," she says softly while looking at my reddened palm. "He would do anything to get to you."

I don't ask how she knows of Felix's feelings for me. I remember his kiss in the tunnel and touch my fingers to my lips. He would take any risk to see me again. "That's what I'm afraid of."

"God has not given us a spirit of fear, but of power and love and a sound mind." She quotes the Aletheia, and in spite of myself, I smile.

The sound of a rider approaching sends my hand flying to the sword I've strapped to my side. Only when I see Maximus's face do I lower it to my side. Hannah brushes my hair back and stands shoulder to shoulder with me, preparing to support me no matter what news the guard brings.

"They are camped," Maximus announces breathlessly. I can see his breath in the air. "Only about a mile south of us. Felix wanted to press on, but once I arrived with your word, Antony convinced him to make camp."

At least he has Antony who will act as his rational judgment as Hannah has done for me. We are too much alike for our own good. That thought makes me smile as well.

"Thank you, Maximus. Please rest now. I've given Hector the first watch."

The guard gives me a slight bow, then retires to his tent.

"Perhaps we should all rest now," Hannah suggests, trying to hide a yawn with her fist. "You especially."

"There's something I must do first." Sleeping is out of the question if I can't see for myself that things are fine.

Hannah sighs. "I was afraid you'd say that." She shrugs off her own cloak and drapes it over my back. "Be careful, Emilia."

25

The snow will highlight my tracks through the dark woods, but I don't take the time to attempt to cover them. All I can think of is seeing Felix again. Until he's in front of me, I won't be satisfied with the simple message that says he's safe. Nor am I satisfied to wait until morning to lay eyes on him.

The hood of Hannah's cloak shields my face from the sharp wind and from any would-be onlookers. My stealth enables me to dart past the two guards that walk the perimeter of the small camp—though it's much larger than my own. I'll have to speak to Felix about that. If I can slip past them, someone else might be able to as well. Safety isn't something we can take for granted until we've crossed into Borealis, and maybe not even then.

"Highness." A familiar voice hisses my title, and I whirl around to find Antony motioning me from the shadows.

Relief that he made it out alive floods me. I have more care for this soldier than I thought. He's been as loyal to me as Felix, though I don't know where he stands on the issues of his faith. As soon as we are more stable, I'll make it my mission to find out.

"Antony." I follow his lead and keep my tone at a whisper. "Are you all alright? Did everyone make it out okay?"

"We're all accounted for, Highness. A few minor injuries, but with the guards who accompanied you and this small band, you have an army of nearly fifty at your disposal."

Fifty is hardly an army, but it's more than I would have had if Felix didn't command so much loyalty from his men. Until we get to Borealis, I'm not sure if my father's guards will be loyal to me or not.

"Very good. Where is the Commander?" I'm sure my eagerness shows, but the desire to clamp eyes on him is nearly breathtaking.

Antony's eyes fall, for only a split second, but it's enough to send my heart into my throat.

"Where is he?" My eyes scan the few tents illuminated by several fires. All the same tanned hide and nothing to tell me which one belongs to Felix.

"Come with me, Highness." He takes my hand, and we weave through the tents. Antony stops outside one, but holds me in place to keep me from running inside. "He took a blade in his side trying to fight his way out of that tunnel. Our healer says he will recover, but he needs his rest."

If he speaks more, the rest of his words are lost on me as I'm lifting the flap to Felix's tent and slipping inside. My movements are like the wind—gentle and silent—but they still when I see him in the dim light of flames from the fire that sits adjacent to his tent. Someone has left a lamp burning with a short wick—possibly the healer—and I move it closer to the cot so I can study his face.

His chest rises and falls with the shallow breaths of sleep, and I can't keep from running my fingertips across his cheekbones then his lips. I can still feel them pressed against mine in that tunnel. He stirs, and I shrink back into the shadows.

"Em…" He's never called me by such a pet name, but it warms my heart. It means much more coming from him than the times Ronan has let it slip from his mouth.

My fingers itch with the need to touch him again, and I crawl forward, the dirt soiling my dress, until I'm by his side. I shouldn't wake him, but I need to know he's not hurt badly. "Felix." I brush a strand of dark curls from his forehead. Slowly, his eyes flutter open under thick lashes.

"Highness." It's hoarser than a whisper, as if he doesn't have enough air in his lungs to speak.

"Don't. Say my name."

"Emilia… Is this a dream?" He's tired, I hear it in his words. The way his voice goes soft or how his eyes close at the end of the sentence. It unwinds me like a loose thread in a tapestry though I know he doesn't have his senses about him. It occurs to me that he still might regret that kiss.

"Not a dream," I say as I find his hand beneath the blanket and twine my fingers with his. "We're free, Felix."

He smiles as his eyes drift closed again. Seconds later, his breathing has evened out. I won't wake him again even though I want to ask about his injury.

Antony sticks his head in the tent. "Highness, shall I escort you back to your camp?"

"No. But send a message to my watchman, and tell him that I'm staying here. Our camps will join in the morning as planned."

He disappears but returns a short time later with a heavy fur blanket. "If you're staying here, you should be warm."

My thanks is superfluous since he's gone by the time I can situate myself under the warmth. The ground beneath me is hard and cold, but I've slept on worse. And though I'm running for my life, I can taste the freedom that the unknown offers. And Felix is beside me.

Sleep comes in small increments as I wake myself regularly to make sure he's still breathing. As always, he doesn't fail me. Sometime during my rest, my fingers have fallen from his, and as I lift his blanket to find his hand again, I catch a glimpse of the bandage against his bare side. It's a small wound if the size of the white cloth is a good indicator, but it's dotted with blood.

Maybe I should wake the healer, but I want to see for myself. My teeth sink into my lip as I hold my shaking fingers above the bandage. His muscles tense beneath my hand, and I look up to find his dark eyes boring holes into me.

"Sorry if I woke you." I rest my hand on the blanket next to him. "You're bleeding through the bandage. Someone needs to check it."

"It's fine." But he groans as he sits up and reaches for me. His fingers circle my wrist and his thumb brushes the back of my hand. "Are you hurt?"

"No. I'm just concerned about you. I was afraid you wouldn't get out."

"I told you I'd follow you."

I heard his words as he whispered them in the tunnel, but they sound different now, as if something weighs them down. Perhaps regret. The life he's grown used to, thrived in, is over all because he chose to follow me.

"You have to go back." It hurts to say those words because it's the last thing I want. "Tell them I threatened you, that you tried to hunt me down but couldn't. Anything that means you can get back to Ronan. You can't stay here."

"Is that an order from my queen?" He's gone still, rigid, as if he's holding something back.

"Of course not. It's a plea from your friend. I don't want to risk your life."

"Emilia, I'm a soldier. Risking my life is what I do." He cups my face, and his eyes flicker in the light. "Being a soldier is only as honorable as the thing you're fighting for. For the first time, I have something worth fighting for."

And he kisses me again, and though I'm more prepared for it this time, it still takes my breath away. But he's gone just as suddenly, before I ever have a moment to kiss him back.

"I-I'm sorry." He won't meet my eyes, so I do what I think I must. I grab his chin, though not harshly, and force him to look at me. It's probably just as well that it's too dark for me to see the depth of his eyes. "I shouldn't have done that. There are rules, you're the Queen…"

"Yes," I say. "I am the Queen. And I make the rules."

This time, I press my lips to his, and everything else disappears. Light and heat and all the things that aren't really there swell between us. My instincts drive my movements, but I still feel awkward as I reach for him to bring him closer. Unlike Ronan, Felix doesn't take charge, but he reacts to what I give him.

Until he pulls away harshly with a gasp between us. I'm not even sure which one of us utters it. But his eyes are as wild as I've ever seen them as we stare each other down with heavy breaths filling the space between my face and his. I'm about to reach for him, to calm the fevered look in his eyes, when he speaks.

"This can't happen."

I hold my breath, waiting for his reasons why, or a smile to indicate he's joking. But nothing comes, and I feel him slipping away. "Why not?"

"You are going to be the Queen of Borealis. At the very least, you're the princess. I'm a guard, not even that now that I've left the Emperor's service." He looks away, down to the blanket that still covers him. When his eyes flick up to mine, they're almost hollow. "You told me once that those born in the palace don't get to marry for love."

He's right, and I hate him for it. But now that Cyrus no doubt wants me to pay for humiliating him, it's more important than ever I make alliances. My happiness will have to become secondary to what I must do for my country and my God. It's so unfair that after all I've done, all I've lost, I'll lose Felix before I even have a chance to find out what it would be like to have him.

"And I'm here for Ronan as well as you."

Those words nearly knock me from the cot. "How dare you mention his name."

"It's not what you think." Even now, his voice is monotone, blank. As if he's following orders rather than giving them. "He made me promise to save you, to follow you. To keep you safe until he could come for you himself."

I do stand now, needing the distance I put between us. No matter how I want to forget the way the Prince looked at me as I bowed before him and his father, those bright blue eyes will probably be forever seared into my vision. "Ronan didn't say a word when his father was about to kill me. Why would he care if I live or die now?" Pretending he didn't hurt me doesn't ease the ache of betrayal.

"He wrote you a letter. It's in my sack."

My hands find the rolled parchment atop the meager supplies lining his pack. However long he was planning my jailbreak, it's clear he thought little of himself because there are very few personal items he's brought with him. But I don't for a minute believe he planned my escape spontaneously. Felix would have weighed the cost, and for some reason he thought me worth it all. But not, apparently, worth betraying Ronan's confidence in him, though I'm not sure Ronan's favor is worth keeping.

But I open the letter and the words scrawled across the page almost change my mind.

My dearest, Emilia. I trust my words find you well though I'm sure you're far from me now. You must hate me for my silence, and I don't blame you for your anger. But it was only what was necessary.

Had I spoken in your defense, nothing would be gained except I might die in the arms of a beautiful woman. My father certainly would not have spared either of us. While

your death might have given you martyrdom, mine would
have counted for nothing, and you've made me want to
change that.

I arranged for Felix to help you escape, and though it pains
me to be parted from the man who became as dear as a
brother to me, I've given him to you—to protect you, to
command as you will—until such a time I can come to you
and we can finish what we started.

There's more, but I don't read it. At least not now. This is already too much to absorb at once. I roll the parchment again and place it inside my dress where it scratches against my skin. No wonder Felix looked so tortured. He isn't free to love me, only to protect me for another man—a man he might have once thought of as his brother. I know nothing of the history between the two, but Felix was loyal to Ronan, and this sort of bond isn't easily broken, especially for a man who takes fealty as seriously as the Commander.

Then there's Ronan himself. Perhaps his decision was the right one, but the image of Felix running to my rescue while my prince remains still will be forever ingrained on my memory. But this is why Ronan will be a great king some day. Because he understands the pageantry that accompanies every action, that even the smallest word or movement might be construed as something it isn't.

"So you see," Felix says from behind me, "I am yours, but not in the way I'd like to be." A rustle of blankets precedes his exit from the tent, and I'm left alone with my thoughts and Ronan's words.

I don't go after him because there's nothing I can say to rectify this. We'll never be even. He said something like that to me once, and maybe he never meant it as I thought he did—in terms of owing and debts—but in position and status. If so, he's right about that. I am a princess, and I've chosen to become a queen. Felix is a guard—likely of low birth since I've never heard of his parents or their riches. We can never stand side by side. He'll always be below me.

So, I turn my thoughts to the point of all this. The Insurgos. All of this is bigger than me or even my country, and I can't let my confused heart get in the way of that. Even Ronan must be pushed aside for the moment. He may still be the best way to my goal, but I want to make my own path, narrow though it may be.

"However you choose to do it, I'm on your side."

I don't know why those words choose this moment to make a reappearance, but I can still picture Felix's face as he spoke them. Earnest and open in the secrecy of my room. Bold promises whispered in the dark, but he's remained true to them all. He believed in me before I believed in myself. It may be the greatest gift he could have given me. Certainly the only one I can accept.

I wait for what feels like hours before I concede that he's not coming back. Antony will see to his safety, and the healer can look after his wound, and when the sun comes up we'll all move forward. But for the first time, it won't be together in anything other than appearance. Compared to everything else I've endured, this pain is a slow ache, but it's there all the same.

The blankets still radiate with his feverish heat as I slip beneath them and tuck my chin to my chest. The thought of walking through the woods to my own tent is overwhelming, and I definitely need the rest. Tomorrow, everyone will look to me for answers that I don't have. The least I can do for myself is appear well-rested. And, I hate to admit, I want him nearby. At least here I can be assured he's only a short distance away.

I think of sticking my head out of the tent and commanding he return to me just because I can, but I don't. I wouldn't. If he feels even a fraction of the hurt and confusion I do, I wouldn't want to heap embarrassment upon it. He didn't say he didn't want me, and we both know it's his position that prevents it. To order him around would only magnify the disparity.

His scent still hangs all around me, and at first I almost choke on it, then I learn to control my breathing and the panic and take it in increments. The warm ruggedness I associate with him cocoons my body, but I still wish for his arms. Even though I know I shouldn't wish for that. I try to visualize Ronan instead, to associate him with this safe satisfaction I feel, but his image won't materialize.

And so I dream of battles. Of dark plains and armies and the banner of the Insurgos held aloft before me. Thousands of eyes on me, waiting for my next command. So real that when I wake, my hands shake as I push my hair from my face. And then I see him.

Felix lies on the hard ground beside my—his—cot, in much the same position as I assumed when I first entered the tent. He's put on a tunic, which just shows above the blanket he's draped over himself, and in sleep his face bears none of the hardness that marred it when he stormed out earlier.

I watch him sleep until the sun makes its appearance over the horizon. The gentleness I saw from him on rare occasions is more pronounced with his eyes closed and his mouth partially open. Dark lashes rest against pale skin, and I wonder how much blood he lost when he took a blade trying to get to me.

The significance isn't lost on me. Despite the events of last night, he's still at my feet, and I know his loyalty will not waver. He has so many choices when it comes to me—to save me, to let me live, to help me—but fate has denied him the one he wants most, so he won't waver on the others.

It won't be easy to travel this road with him at my side, because the ache is still there. Maybe I should be angry he acted on his feelings at all. If I'd never known there was a possibility, I wouldn't be feeling the loss of it now. But I don't regret it. If I only had myself to be concerned with, none of this would be an issue, but there is a nation to consider. And it's time I considered it.

Marrying Ronan isn't the key to liberating my people, even if Felix still believes it's necessary. I know in my heart there's another way, a better way. But it involves facing down the man who tried to have me killed. Because for as much as I don't know about Cyrus, I do know that he will stop at nothing to find the Gate of Life, even if it means wiping out the Insurgos to get there.

I'm expected to return to Borealis as its queen. People must already be looking for a ruler, and I wonder who has filled the crown in my father's stead. It may come down to a fight. But it's not a fight I'm prepared to win. Because I already know I'm not meant for the throne just yet. My place is elsewhere.

I will not wear this broken crown until I've found the Gate of Life.

The snow disintegrates into powder under my feet as I exit the tent. While I tossed in a fitful sleep, stared at Felix, plotted our next moves, the stark whiteness blanketed our surroundings. Beautiful though it is, it will make travel difficult. Those are the things I must think about now. Beauty is a luxury I left behind at the palace. My only concern must be getting my entourage through the mountains and into Borealis. From there, I'll have to decide how to enter the city and where to begin my search for the Gate. And there are no visible footprints for me to follow. I'll have to make my own way.

The wind swirls around me, whipping the white powder to obscure my vision. My makeshift fur cape isn't enough to keep the icy chill out, but I find a strange comfort in the storm. Because its changeable patterns, the rise and fall of the gusts, mirror the shifting moods of my heart.

Fear, apprehension. Relief, determination. I'm not sure which to feel first. If I could have kept my faith hidden, things might have been so much easier. Marry Ronan, worship as I wish, eventually change the tides of religion in the land. And I would have never known how Felix felt.

Snow stings my cheeks as I lift my face to the sky and close my eyes. My hands drift up from my sides, exposed to the elements as they slip past the relative warmth of my cape. A strange heat builds inside me as my lips move in prayer, openly for the first time.

Power courses through me as the heat expands, and I finally give voice to the words hanging on my lips. This is the life I've chosen now. So I let it go. All of it. The military camp, my brief stint in Aurora's court, the bitterness I felt toward my father.

I don't know how long Felix is standing behind me before he joins in my prayer and the heat fans into a flame burning inside me. It doesn't waver when we both fall silent or when he presses his side against mine. And when his fingers find mine beneath my cape, I hope he can feel it, too.

Acknowledgements

Writing Emilia's story has been an adventure itself. I'm so blessed to have had a wonderful support team.

Special thanks to:

My Darklighters partners Voni Harris, Amanda Holland, and Marcy Dyer.

The Christian Indie Authors (CIA) Facebook group for their collective wisdom and encouragement in this process.

My street team for their support and kind words in helping me make this book the best it could be.

My family, who supported me even when they didn't understand the craziness I rambled about.

And extra special thanks to Salem, my sister, who read my early work and believed I could do this anyway.

Join Emilia and Felix as their journey continues in

THE DESOLATE REIGN

COMING 2019

Turn the page for an excerpt from the first chapter

1

At the first sign of smoke, my gut tells me there are no survivors. The emptiness that has been slowly expanding in my soul opens into a cavernous hole.

My horse Athena prances nervously beneath me. Her wildness feeds off my apprehension.

"What's wrong?"

Constant as ever, Felix appears at my side. I don't look at him. My eyes remain fixed on the tendril of smoke behind the treetops in the valley below us.

"Smoke," I say. "They got here before we did."

"You don't know that."

But I do.

I know it as sure as I've known anything in my seventeen years. The Insurgo camp, one of the few we knew of, is gone. Weeks of cautiously winding our way from the mountains near Aurora to this settlement have cost us not only our only lead but also the lives of those Insurgos in the camp. I don't need to see it to feel the truth of it in my heart.

"What do you want to do?" Felix nudges his horse slightly in front of mine, and I'm forced to look at him.

Given that I've spent the time since we left Aurora trying not to look at him, I'm surprised to see he's grown his full beard back and looks much as he did the first time I saw him. Even the tenderness in his eyes has diminished. It only serves to intensify the sick feeling in my stomach.

"I want see it." I *need* to. "There may be survivors, and we owe it to them to do what we can."

"I'll round up a search party. I don't suppose you'd consider staying here."

"Not a chance."

My heart warms at the twitch of his lips. It's as close to our old banter as we've had in too long.

"Didn't think so."

I remain at my vigilant post as he rides off, hoping for signs of life in the valley below. A prayer rises in my heart, but even here in the freedom of the wilderness I don't let it pass my lips. God knows my heart, but I'm afraid it's too late. I should have been more decisive, less fearful. Instead of leading my caravan through the mountains to lose any Imperial troops who may have followed us, I should have come straight here. Once again, my fear has cost innocent lives. Just like with Davina...and my father.

"Princess?"

Felix calls me, and I nudge Athena back toward camp with my knees and a tug on the reigns.

ABOUT THE AUTHOR

A tomboy with southern belle roots, Amory Cannon was born and raised in Tennessee where she learned the importance of God, family, and college football. She's loved the written word from the time she was a child, convinced the squiggly lines on top of the Hostess cupcake really spelled out a secret message.

Amory is a proud momma to two adorable puppies–Luna and Argo–who provide lots of laughs and kisses. She is also an active member of the American Christian Fiction Writers (ACFW) and My Book Therapy (MBT) and answers writers' forensic questions at Jordyn Redwood's **Medical Edge** blog.

www.ingramcontent.com/pod-product-compliance
Lightning Source LLC
Chambersburg PA
CBHW030659120726
47905CB00001B/285